SATURDAY NIGHT AT DAISY'S

SATURDAY

NIGHT AT

DAISY'S

JEFFREY COHN

Harcourt Brace Jovanovich

New York and London

Printed in the United States of America

Library of Congress Cataloging in Publication Data

Cohn, Jeffrey
Saturday night at Daisy's.

I. Title.
PZ4.C6784Sat [PS3553.0435]   813'.5'4   77-92055
ISBN 0-15-179412-X

First edition

B C D E

To Phyl who always knew.
To Gerry whose faith often exceeded mine.
And to me . . . for the first time in my life
I finished something.

SATURDAY NIGHT AT DAISY'S

• •

I

• •

I took my foot off the accelerator, and the sparkling silver Mercedes ever so slowly inched forward on its own. I guided it carefully out of the slush and in through the clutter that collected in my garage. It was a treacherous course through garden-hose snakes, bicycles, and a host of bureaus patiently waiting to be antiqued by some nameless man—certainly not me.

When at last the vehicle was nestled comfortably amidst the rubble, I pressed the magic button and uttered a silent prayer that no shovel or hoe might obstruct the descent of the garage door, sending it and me into a flurry of incensed screaming.

When the door had completed a successful landing, I turned to Carol. "Well, we made it," I said.

I threw open the car door, smashing it forcefully into a large, rusty, snaillike creature which in earlier, healthier days might have watered my lawn.

In the few inches allotted to me in what was once a two-car garage, I stepped back and looked at the $18,000 extravagance that was supposed to give me pleasure. What a strange juxtaposition—*that* car in *this* garage, or as they say in Atherton, the fifth largest and second highest city in northeastern Pennsylvania, "it just don't fit."

While Carol was concluding her transactions with the baby-sitter, I sat at the kitchen table, poking at the evening paper, methodically turning pages, not grasping any of the contents. When the sitter had gone, Carol turned off lights, locked doors, and turned up thermostats in preparation for a typical shivering night in Atherton.

"It was a nice evening, wasn't it?" Carol asked as she entered the kitchen.

"Yeah, real nice." I didn't look up from the paper.

"It's fun having dinner with an old friend. Especially after so long."

"Yeah, lots of fun."

"What's wrong?" she asked.

"Oh, nothing," I said.

"What is it, Art?"

"It's those goddamn bicycles. Too many goddamn bicycles. There's no room for the—"

"Art, what is it really?"

I closed the paper, folded it, and looked at her. "You saw him. He wore a suit. The man wore a goddamn suit. And not a leisure suit either. A coat, a tie, a white shirt even. And he carried an attaché case. He could have been seventy. You were there, Carol. Didn't you notice? It wasn't good. It was boring!"

"I thought he was such a good friend."

"I thought so, too. When he called this afternoon, I looked forward to something special. I expected a lot more."

"It's a long time since graduation. You can't have dinner with someone once every fourteen years and just pick up where you left off."

"That's exactly what bothers me. I don't know *where* we left off! I don't know why I was friendly with him even then. We don't have anything in common. I guess we never did."

"Well, he thought you did. You didn't give him a chance,

Art. You were unconscious half the time. You didn't even listen to what he was saying."

"Didn't listen? Did you ever hear such crap? Oh, God! Did I remember the trip to Harrisburg? Did I *remember* the stag movie? The Spanish final? Did I *remember* this? Did I *remember* that? It was such a pain in the ass!"

"But that's *college*. What did you expect? A business meeting? A sales presentation?"

"He gave us plenty of that, too, didn't he? And it was just as bad. Worse even. How's business? How was last year? This year? Next year? Any fucking year? He's as bad as half the people in Atherton."

"Art," she said softly, "you didn't want to talk about *then*. You didn't want to talk about *now*. What did you want?"

"I don't know. Maybe some relief. A little joy. That's all." My voice cracked. I picked up the newspaper and walked into the living room.

Carol followed and sat next to me on the couch.

"He was just passing through on his way to Philly. He thought it would be nice to get together."

"Well, it wasn't."

"Okay, so it wasn't. So, let go of it. And fourteen years from now when he passes through, we'll meet him for dinner again. It's not the end of the world."

"Ah, but it is. Coming home I was thinking—doesn't it seem like we graduated only yesterday?"

"I have a feeling you're doing a number on yourself."

"Please answer the question."

"Honestly?"

"Of course, honestly."

"No, it doesn't really seem like yesterday."

"Okay, maybe not like yesterday. But certainly it doesn't seem like fourteen years."

"Okay, I'll play. Yes, the time went quickly. Is that what you want to hear?"

I nodded. "Now, here's the killer. If the next fourteen years go as quickly as the last fourteen years—I'll be—fifty. Just like that!" I snapped my fingers.

"I knew it. I really knew where you were heading all the time. You're really in a wallowing mood."

"I'm walking around being twenty-two and all of a sudden, I'm fifty. How did that happen?"

"Why do you do this to yourself? You're not fifty years old. My suggestion is that we make love right now and forget this." She got up and walked to the bedroom.

I was still sitting on the couch when she came charging through the hall. She wore only my tee shirt, her usual bedtime costume. Her arms were folded just beneath her breasts and she ran awkwardly. She was always cold and she rubbed her arms furiously, trying to eradicate the goose pimples. "I'm ready for you," she said, plowing into me, crumbling the paper and knocking it to the white shag carpet, which in spite of repeated attempts, never was quite clean.

We held each other, and in the general area of her lovely neck, I temporarily lost the black mood that had earlier captured my evening. But it didn't take me long to sink back. Soon I was again wearing my long face. "Carol, I just don't feel like it now. Let me come down a little."

She smiled. "Okay. If you change your mind, you know where I'll be." She bent down and kissed my forehead. Then she folded her arms, and shivering from the draft that penetrated the most expensive storm windows in Atherton, she ran off.

I flipped on the TV, and while it warmed up, I set my table for some late-evening activity. A bowl of pistachio nuts, a pack of Luckies, an ashtray, a bottle of Tab, and most important, a fresh deck of cards.

I had started my first round of solitaire when the TV came alive.

"Another big win for Keystone today," said the announcer. "The powerful Bears from Pennsylvania traveled to Syracuse and really poured it on with plays like this." A series of touch-downs were shown while the announcer explained the intricacies which I never quite understood.

What impressed me far more than any pass or punt was the Fight Song. So it was most appropriate that after each of the five K.S.U. touchdowns, the mighty Green Band struck up that famous song.

I began humming loudly and tapping my fingers in time to the beat. The music got louder. I drew a card, looked closely at it, and whistled shrilly against its edge. I thought of my evening, and held the card even tighter. Where had those fourteen years gone? My mind went racing through the past, and as the song reached a spine-tingling crescendo, I continued to clutch that card.

2

●●

"Throw the fuckin' card already!"

"What?"

"What word didn't you understand?"

"I'm really sorry, Mitch. I didn't hear you."

"Of course you didn't, y'asshole. You and shitfingers here
are making too much fuckin' noise."

Mitch is referring to Tom who has joined me in singing the
K.S.U. fight song, which blares out on a small portable radio.
I have also been whistling and drumming my fingers on the
old coffee table while I simulate a bass drum with my feet. We
all want to break the monotony of a six-hour gin game, but
my own preoccupation is to rattle Mitch. And I do.

"Now throw the fuckin' card!" Mitch shouts at me. "And
will you shut up! I can't concentrate with all your fuckin' noise.
And shut that fuckin' radio off! And you," he says to Tom,
"you're not even playing in this game. So get the fuck out of
here!"

Mitch is really beside himself. It's his senior year and he is
in danger of flunking out. He has been turned down by at
least twenty medical schools and has sent out feelers to the

dental schools. If these come back rejected, he will try optometry or podiatry or possibly, as a last resort, he will turn to chiropractic. His mission in life is to fuck up people's bodies.

Mitch spends much of his time now playing gin rummy with me, and most of the time he loses. He further punishes himself with vast quantities of potato chips. These he purchases in institutional-size cans. He has a catsup dispenser which looks like a large tomato and a mustard dispenser which looks like a large tomato, and he alternates. Tom is just a little guy and is afraid of pushing Mitch too far. He takes on a sad-ass expression and slinks into the bedroom to study for a political-science exam. He is really a good student—Dean's list since his freshman year. He will certainly get into law school, and he studies hard when he is not watching *Rocky and His Friends, The Three Stooges* or the young married couple in the apartment across from us.

Tom's father is a prominent attorney in Belvidere, New Jersey, and his uncle is the district attorney. His "people," as Tom calls them, are not millionaires. "We're not 'new money' folks, Art, but we are people of means." Once his "people" drove out to Keystone in a white Porsche and Mrs. Nelson told me that Tom Senior and she were quite proud of Tom Junior. "And you have every reason to be, ma'am," I answered politely, and I really meant it. But I never quite understood why this very Brahmin family would send their only son to a place like Keystone.

"You don't mind if I put the radio on in here, do you?" Tom hollers from the bedroom.

"Keep it low or I'll kick your fuckin' head in," Mitch replies.

Tom and I know that Mitchel Carpenter would never kick anyone's head in, but we usually defer to his power so as not to hurt his feelings. It's sort of like prodding a big bear and then running to the other side of the cage when the animal gets too close.

Tom gets his last licks in by softly whistling the K.S.U. fight song in the bedroom. He does it just below the threshold of Mitch's conscious level, which suits me fine. It tends to aggravate the big bear and disturb his concentration.

Of course, I have a big bowl of white pistachio nuts and spit a steady barrage of shells across the room into an open brown paper bag.

"You know, it's no fuckin' picnic playing cards with you!" Mitch says in an agitated voice as he depresses the handle of the mustard dispenser, shooting a big yellow gob onto a waiting chip. He is glaring at me.

"I don't understand, Mitch. What do you mean by that?" I answer in as concerned a tone as I can muster, and while never taking my eyes off my cards, I eject a shell, missing the paper bag by three feet.

"I mean, you're like a pig with those pistachio shells and you know exactly what I mean!" He pops the chip into his mouth and begins a vigorous flicking of the fingers.

"I didn't realize it bothered you that much," as I spit one shell, "but if it does, I'll stop," and I spit the second.

"Just play the fuckin' game!"

We play for one more hour, and as usual, Mitch is getting creamed. He is in to me for $83.00, and I have him going on a triple schneid. If the game should end this way, he will pay double.

Mitch is more agitated than ever and is now depositing catsup and mustard on the same chip. He draws a card, looks at it, looks at me and then at the card. He folds his cards and lays them down. He quickly eats three potato chips, flicks his fingers, and fans open his cards.

"Is it another queen?" I ask.

"None of your fuckin' business!"

"Okay, but I want to tell you that the queen I took is part of a spade run. I wouldn't even take that queen you're holding."

"Fuckin' liar," Mitch says, but in quite a moderate voice. He is looking for further assurances from me. He has picked another queen and would like nothing better than to dump it out.

"I'm not lying!" I reply in a hurt voice, and for emphasis I let go with a shell which banks off the wall and plops into the paper bag. "Did you see that shot?"

Mitch is either not impressed by my shot or is concentrating too hard on the queen. "Do you swear you're not saving queens?"

"Mitch, you're gonna rub the tits off that queen! C'mon, play!"

"I'll play if you swear to God you're not saving queens."

"Okay, I swear to God I'm not saving queens."

"Do you swear on Carol's honor?"

"I swear."

"Do you swear on your sister's honor?"

"Yes, I swear!"

"On your mother's honor?"

"Yes, dammit, I swear!"

"Do you swear on everything that's holy?" he asks and rapidly flicks his fingers, this time to free them not of potato-chip crumbs, but of heavy deposits he has discovered in his nose.

"For Christ's sake, yes, I swear! Now will you play the game or not?"

Mitch looks deep into my eyes and then deep into the queen's eyes. He slowly draws the card out of his hand and then, as if the card has become a red-hot potato, he lets go, flicking several times as the queen floats down onto the discard pile.

There's no need to rush now. I have all the time in the world. With the greatest deliberation, I eye the queen, Mitch, and the queen, in that order. I pop two pistachio nuts into my mouth. With a flourish, I gracefully pick up the queen and gently place the little lady next to her three sisters. "Mitch, my friend, I think that's gin!"

Tom is in the bedroom when Mitch splits the coffee table in two, and from a great deal of experience in these matters, he knows exactly what to do.

"You goddamn fuckin' son-of-a-bitch! You goddamn fuckin' liar! You dirty rotten fucker!"

As the ranting continues, Tom prepares the bedroom for the inevitable. He is lying in bed quietly reading his political-science book and without once moving his eyes from the page, he reaches to his right and slowly opens the window. As the bowl of pistachios hits the living-room wall, Tom swings his legs over the side of the bed, gets to his feet, and walks across the bedroom. While not missing one word of the Whig party's influence on the New England states, he opens the door and executes a fine Veronica pass on Mitch, who goes thundering past on his way to the window.

Mitch has the deck of cards clutched tightly in his fist as he stumbles across the unkempt bedroom. He toes an imaginary line in front of the open window, and in perfect shot-putter's form he flings fifty-two of the fucking cards. The pack travels together until it hits the outside wall of the elevator shaft. Then it explodes on contact, merrily sprinkling kings and queens and their entire families onto the same common grave that has claimed hundreds of their forefathers and foremothers.

But Mitchel bears no ill feeling toward me. The cards are the culprits, and once he has ejected them, his animosity, as always, begins to turn to himself. The ranting is over and thus begins Mitch's soliloquy.

"Why? Why do I do this? My father gets up at six in the morning. He works twelve hours a day to earn enough money so I can go to school, and how do I repay him? I'm a shit! I'm nothing but shit. I'm less than shit. I'm not going to get into medical school. I won't even graduate from college. My parents gave up everything for me. And how do I repay them? By being a no-good bum. I don't study. I don't open a book. I play cards all night long and eat those fuckin' potato chips."

Up until this point Tom has remained at the door still reading his political-science book. At the mention of "fuckin' potato chips" he looks up at Mitch and then silently walks into the living room while the soliloquy continues.

Meanwhile I am trying to compute the totals and am at a disadvantage since I'll never know how many points were in Mitch's hand. The gin alone was enough to put me out, so being the great sport that I am, I assess only one point, which brings the grand total to $128.50. I am not overly smug because I know that the higher the debt, the harder it is to collect.

"We won the football game," Tom says in a voice completely detached from the fact that less than ten feet away a friend is spilling out his guts.

"Yeah?" I couldn't care less about the goddamn football game. I have a gnawing feeling of anxiety, and until it's resolved, I can't talk with Tom. My number-one concern is the size of the debt. Somehow I must discuss it with Mitch.

Maybe Tom will mediate the discussion. His great legal mind and his sense of fairness might help us resolve the problem. God, I hope so! I've worked too hard to lose this money! Speaking of God, that's exactly what Mitch is doing now. He is asking His help in becoming a better person. Perhaps between the four of us, we can knock out a workable solution. After all, if Mitch pays his debt, he will be well on his way to becoming a better person.

My second area of concern involves the pistachio shells that are still in my mouth. If I can spit two shells into the bag I will break the all-time record. With great deliberation I let go with a high arching shot that barely misses the ceiling and slips cleanly into the gaping mouth of the bag.

"Did you see that, Tom? I just tied the record. Now watch this next shot!" I place another shell between my teeth and shoot a hard line drive in my attempt to break the record. It banks off the wall, catches the front lip of the bag, and falls in. I'm so proud! "What do you think, Tom?" I ask.

As Mitch drones on about parental love and self-respect, Tom looks deep into my eyes and says, "I think that you are a fool!"

I laugh hysterically, and my next instinct is to call to Mitch. But I hold back since he is now making a new pact with God, and I wouldn't dare disturb him. Besides, I have plenty of time . . . it's only October.

●●●

It was the Fall semester of senior year at Keystone State
University. 1960. Eisenhower was still President . . . no sex,
no grass, no riots, no Beatles, no nothing. The only thing my
friends were really into was card-playing and stealing.

For example, Al Carter stole from the Student Book Exchange—pens, pencils, notebooks; you know, harmless stuff
like that. He was head buyer of the store and there was no
salary. For compensation, therefore, he stole supplies. He rationalized it pretty well. He stole only what he required for his
own consumption and never sold any of the purloined merchandise. Occasionally he would give gifts to his good friends,
but he never stole for monetary gain. Well, almost never.

One semester he stole eleven textbooks, but he didn't call
that stealing. His greatest coup was when he made the biggest
single purchase in the history of the store. He bought three
hundred gross of one style pen. Now that was one shitload of
pens. The manufacturer, in gratitude, gave him two color TVs
and a free trip to the Orange Bowl.

Don't think Al was not concerned with the seriousness of
the situation. He shouldered the entire responsibility of moving
the lot. He was acutely aware that a large investigation would

reflect on his ability to buy properly. He immediately got the ball rolling by taking a few thousand pens for his personal use.

I'll never forget the day he tried to give a pen to Tom. "Al, I really appreciate the gift, but I can't accept this pen," Tom said apologetically.

"How come, muh man? You can't use a pen?" Al was from Philadelphia, and when he talked he held his arms straight out from his shoulders. He rotated them backwards and parallel to the ground while he took short rhythmic steps laterally and then to the rear. This little dance is called a "mummer's strut" and is peculiar to the Philadelphia area, where every year thousands of men, women, and children dress up like ostriches and march in string bands, while they play "I'm Looking Over a Four-Leaf Clover" on their banjos. I'm not sure how this tradition was started or why it is peculiar to Philadelphia, but I'm sure the mummers had a great influence on W.C. Fields.

"Sure I can use it, but, Al, I know how you got this pen and I just couldn't accept it. Do you know that my uncle could prosecute you for this? What you've done is no better than—"

"Are you saying I stole the pen? Is that what you're saying, Tom?" Al was not strutting anymore, but merely shifting his weight from one foot to another.

"Did you pay for the pen?"

"Yeah, I paid for the pen. By working in the store for nothing. By making executive decisions for the Exchange. You're fuckin' A right I paid for the pen!"

"Al, you're rationalizing. You accepted your position at face value. You did it for love, for the experience, whatever. But certainly stealing is not a fringe benefit of your job."

"They know what goes on. They accept it," Al said, and for the first time in the conversation, his feet were still.

"Al—who are 'they'? Don't you understand? It's *you* who must set the standards. *You* call the shots. *You* set the example. *You* are they!"

Al's expression was not easy to read, but there seemed to be some measure of understanding. Tom was president of the

Young Democrats on campus and the New Frontier was about to begin. He was infused by a rampant, idealistic honesty, and when he rode his white horse, it was difficult to resist his magnetism.

"I guess you're right," Al answered in a conciliatory tone, "but I'm in this thing up to my ears. I can't change overnight."

"It's never too late to change. The fact that I got through to you means there's some hope," Tom said, doing his best to smooth over the rough spots.

"Look, Tom, I know you can't accept this gift, and now I can understand why. But would you have any objections to my sending a pen to your mother? If it makes a difference, I'll even buy the damn pen."

"My mother? Why my mother?" Tom asked curiously.

"In gratitude."

"Gratitude for what?"

"For everything she did for me."

"What did my mom ever do for you?"

"Tom," he said softly, "your mother was the best goddamn fuck I ever had."

Jerry Peter Zuckerman was not a thief. He was, primarily, a prick. Guys would say, "J.P. Zuckerman's a prick." And he really was. Years later, when we'd have our reunions and the wives would sit in one corner of the hospitality suite and discuss their children and how fulfilling their unfulfilled lives were, the guys would talk mainly about J.P. and how he really wasn't as bad as he seemed. But he was. Make no mistake about it. The man was a prick and a mean one at that.

I didn't know J.P. Zuckerman when he was a young boy, so I really have no proof, but I have a feeling he pulled the wings off butterflies and burned cats. When I met him during my junior year, it immediately hit me that J.P. was not just your average mean bastard. In those days R.O.T.C. was compulsory and J.P. was my drill sergeant. He specialized in scaring the shit out of me.

Do you remember the Joker in Batman comics? Well, Zuckerman had a smile very much like the Joker's—a wide, toothy, sardonic grin framed by flaming, skinny red lips. The face was powdery white and the hair was dark black and oily. The most distinguishing characteristic of the entire repulsive ensemble was J.P.'s big fat ass, a monumental affair which completely dominated his pants. If there was a shred of humor in J.P. Zuckerman, it had to be in that fat ass, waddling to and fro, suggesting that J.P. could never quite wipe all of it clean.

His favorite prey was girlfriends. "What do you hear from my little Carol?" he'd ask as he straightened my tie. "Is she as good as she used to be? Man, I enjoyed her!" And the big bulbous ass sashayed down the line of bored R.O.T.C. cadets, who were sweating and stinking in the blistering heat.

God, I hated that bastard. I raged inside. This was not like an ordinary attack on someone's mom, which in those days was something you would do to a friend . . . Al was always doing it to Tom.

But when J.P. Zuckerman joked about Carol, it was different. I'm certain he never took her out, but dammit, there was always that possibility. And it wasn't only my Carol, but all the Carols I've ever loved. There's something about Carols, you know—tiny noses, luscious breasts, dark hair, light skin, slim waists, and pliable asses just a fraction larger than the norm. God, I loved them! God, I hated him!

One night, Mitch decided he would take a break from the gin game. He had received five rejections that day, including one from a school of podiatry in the Canal Zone. He needed more than potato chips to stifle his anger and hunger, so he took off early for a local pool hall. Tom, as usual, was at the library. It was too early to sleep, so I wrote this poem about J.P.

> *J.P. Zuckerman draws near*
> *Sinister and insincere*
> *Caution those that you hold dear*
> *J.P. Zuckerman draws near.*

> *J.P. Zuckerman comes by*
> *Strong men cower, weak men cry*
> *Women whimper, flowers die*
> *J.P. Zuckerman comes by.*
>
> *J.P. Zuckerman drops in*
> *Evil-glaring, steeped in sin*
> *No one asks where he has been*
> *J.P. Zuckerman drops in.*
>
> *J.P. Zuckerman is here*
> *Time for hate and time for fear*
> *Little children, don't come near*
> *J.P. Zuckerman is here.*

I typed it neatly and added the following postscript: "Zuckerman, you are a fat, fucking mean bastard and I hate you!" I mailed it, but, of course, I didn't sign it.

Two days later J.P. appeared at the door of my apartment. "Arthur," he said, "I got your little poem." He waddled past me and placed his fat ass on the faded, catsup-stained couch.

"What do you mean, J.P.?"

"Cut the shit, Arthur! I know you wrote that poem. No one else has a way with words like that, and nobody but an asshole like you would waste the time."

"I'm really sorry, J.P.! I didn't mean anything by it. I don't know why I wrote that stuff."

"Don't apologize, Arthur! You hate me and so does everyone else. You think I'm a bastard, don't you?"

"No I don't, J.P. You're a decent guy. I was just telling Mitch today what a real friend I have in Jerry Peter Zuckerman."

"Arthur, I really liked that poem."

"You liked it, J.P.?" I asked incredulously.

"Arthur, no one has ever done anything nice for me. All the guys hate me. Even Tom hates me. The sad thing is that no one ever takes the time to try and understand why J.P. Zuckerman is the way he is."

Now I know what you're thinking . . . that for the first time in his life J.P. really let his oily hair down . . . leveled with me, as they say. That his father died when J.P. was seven; that his mother was an alcoholic; that he lost his brother in the Korean War; that his sister was a cripple; that I really came to know and understand J.P. and we began a friendship that started that night and lasted long after we left the ivy-covered walls. BULLSHIT! J.P. said nothing that night that in any way changed my thinking about him. We did not become friends and I continued to avoid him as much as possible.

"I'm going to do something very nice for you because of that poem," he said.

"And what might that be, J.P.?"

"Are you getting much, Arthur?" he asked.

"Much what, J.P.?"

"Ass, Arthur. Are you getting laid?"

"That's none of your goddamn business!"

"Now don't get yourself all hot and bothered, Arthur!"

The familiar brackish waters swirled through my head as J.P. probed my sex life or lack of one. The humming ache which I could not explain at the time would in later life be recognized as pure anxiety. It was my defense mechanism, and the roar of the sloshing waves blotted out the sound of this fat malignancy that had invaded my unkempt room and screwed-up mind.

I don't know how long J.P. chatted before he actually disclosed the nature of his favor. At times I'm sure I was close to losing consciousness. The sweat beaded on my forehead and I alternated hot and cold, but I managed to avoid hearing most of the bile that poured from that venomous mouth.

Dip, Dip, Dip, Dip, Dip, Dip, Dip, Dip, Boom, Boom, Boom, Boom, Boom, Boom, Get a Job! I sang lustily in my mind, in order to drown him out. But at the end of each bar there would be old J.P. asking if I ever went "all the way" with Carol. An unseen headset pumped the music from ear to ear while I drummed my fingers on the remains of the coffee table and rhythmically stamped my feet.

Sha-na-na-na—sha-na-na-na-na!

"Well, aren't you getting any at all?"

Bah-doh

"Does she let you get in her pants?"

Bah-doh

"You're letting those nice tits go to waste, aren't you, asshole?"

Sha-na-na-na—Sha-na-na-na-na

"Arthur," he said, leaning forward on the couch and opening his eyes in anticipation, "have you ever done anything sexual with Carol?"

I wanted to shout, "It's none of your business, you fat motherfucker! Just leave me alone!" But instead, I remained calm, and with the greatest deliberation I, too, leaned forward and said, "Hey, Dip, Dip, Dip, Dip, Dip, Dip, Dip, Dip, Boom, Boom, Boom, Boom, Boom, Boom, Get a Job," being certain to slowly enunciate each of the eight Dips and six Booms.

"Arthur," he said, looking deeply into my wildly bouncing eyes, "you are a very sick person!"

As I said previously, Zuckerman was a prick. My sex life was not his business. But what really bothered me was that my sex life seemed to be none of my business either. There were problems that I just could not face and deep feelings that were completely unmanageable. How, for example, could I possibly mix love and sex? Oh, sure, by today's standards the two go together quite nicely. But in the early sixties it was like oil and water, at least on a premarital basis. After marriage? Well, that was a different story. Sex and love became the Bobbsey Twins of postnuptial fame—Siamese Bobbsey Twins, to be more precise. You can't have one, you can't have none, you can't have one without the uhh-uhh-uhther.

You don't remember? You say that this was the dawning of the sexual revolution? Well, maybe I overslept, but for reasons unknown to me, I took no part in the revolt. Actually I didn't even know there was a war going on. It's a funny thing with revolutions, eras, and ages . . . you just don't know when you're in them. It's easy enough when these periods are over, and some smartass says, "Hey, that was the age of understanding," or "what a nice era of good feeling."

In the ninety-ninth year of the Hundred Years' War, a person couldn't even take a breather and say, "Wow, only one more year of this shit!" Unfair, I say.

Sex was just something you didn't have with a Carol, especially if you were in love with her. Love was for Carol, Nancy or Sue, no matter how sexy she really was. Sex was with Angel, Darlene, or Daisy. Too bad! If only I had known about the revolution. I missed a lot of good times.

And now the irony of ironies! I have the distinct impression we are now in a *new* sexual revolution. I have the feeling that fourteen years from now, when I'm hopelessly mired in the depths of middle age, J.P. Zuckerman will come to me and say, "Shmuck, you mean you didn't screw around? Every one of your friends did. Man, Arthur, you are a real asshole. The nineteen-seventies weren't exactly the Dark Ages. You were right in the middle of the Extramarital Revolution.

"Why would you think that sex had to be limited to one person? By the way, how *is* Carol? I don't understand you, Arthur. You don't order steak every time you go out to eat. Why limit yourself? All those luscious friends of yours and Carol's! Why, any one of them would have gone to bed with you. But you never swapped. You're the only one who never swapped. You don't have to be madly in love with someone just to sleep with her. Can't you separate sex from love? You really surprise me, Arthur!"

I don't know what song will be popular in the last decade of the twentieth century, but I'm sure I'll be singing it when J.P. comes to call. In the meantime, Carol and I are both checking the newspapers for some sign of the Revolution. When it comes, if in fact it is not yet here, we are prepared to enlist immediately. We want to do our share!

5

Thrice now have I said that J.P. Zuckerman was a prick and now I shall tell you why. The favor he spoke of was, quite simply, a piece of ass. The ass belonged physically to Daisy Boyle, but it had been public property for a long time.

Daisy really wasn't the town whore (make sure you pronounce that 'hoor'), because she rarely charged for it. Not that she wouldn't accept a couple of bucks for a trick. She could always use the money. It was just that she was so crazy about fucking that she would do it for nothing.

Daisy specialized in gang bangs. One guy certainly could not satisfy her. Two or three were not too much better. Daisy needed at least a basketball team, which she could handle with ease. She actually preferred a baseball team, and later she eventually worked her way up to a football team, and I mean both platoons.

There were many stories speculating why Daisy was that way. The most popular version was that a boyfriend had accidentally given her a massive dose of Spanish fly. He found her impaled on the gearshift of his car shouting, "Fuck me, big boy! Give it to me, big boy! Aaaayyy! Arrrrh!" But it is my contention that she experienced a fairly normal initiation to sex, found that it was extremely enjoyable, and decided to fuck because she liked it. The fact that the numbers were so great meant only that she liked it more than most.

Daisy was like one of the guys. She really fit in well with the group. No bullshit, no airs. You didn't have to dress up or take her to a prom or a fancy restaurant. And it was just as well. It's not that easy to get a table for twenty-five people.

With Daisy you could always be at ease. During a session you could really have a nice time. I mean it. Pleasant conversation, joking, and all that. And when it was over or in between rounds, everyone would share a pizza and a couple of sixpacks. Good fellowship. Really nice!

I have thought of Daisy more than once since graduation, and the thoughts are happy ones. The only sadness is when I speculate on where and what and how she is now. She must have been thirty-three or thirty-four then, which means that today she is approaching fifty. Now that's sad. They should canonize Daisy Boyle. She carried the ball for all the girls who either didn't want to or just weren't given the chance.

J.P. and Daisy both grew up in Harrisburg, the capital of Pennsylvania, located one hundred miles south of the Keystone campus. During high school he had taken part in several gang bangs with Daisy, and for reasons that were never entirely clear to me, she took a liking to this malcontent. Their friendship really flourished after J.P. went to college. He somehow convinced her to let him run weekly junkets down to Harrisburg, expressly for the purpose of screwing Daisy Boyle.

So, now we learn that J.P. was not only a prick, but a pimp as well. Every Saturday at 5:00 P.M., the fat, ugly, green Citroën (the car had taken on most of the features of Zuckerman himself) left for Harrisburg. The car's grille seemed to snarl and the chassis had the power to raise and lower itself at will, as Citroëns are wont to do. It was a thoroughly despicable car and it suited its owner well.

Here was the deal: each of the five riders paid $12.50. This fee covered the cost of the motel suite, the cost of Daisy, and, of course, the cost of Zuckerman himself. The only additional expense was the pizza and beer which, when split among five guys, amounted to very little.

The arrangement seemed to please everyone. Daisy was happy. She could always look forward to a Saturday night with five fairly intelligent, fairly clean college students in a fairly clean motel room with some fairly decent pizza and beer. Zuckerman went with the deal, but as I said, Daisy didn't find him offensive.

The deal was good for us. We got an evening of fellowship, brotherhood, and sisterhood, and had a genuinely good time, all for the low, low price of only $12.50. Of course, Zuckerman was part of our deal, too.

And the deal was certainly good for J.P. We didn't know it at the time, but Daisy did not charge for her services. The junket grossed $62.50, so after deducting $12.50 for the suite, J.P. turned a nice $50.00 profit. He didn't even pay for the gas, which was compliments of his father, Monroe T. Zuckerman, who owned a chain of movie theaters in central Pennsylvania. (I always got a big laugh at the advertising of Zuckerman the elder . . . "See you tonight at the Zuckerman" or "The Zuckerman, a nice place for nice people.") And along with the $50.00, J.P. enjoyed everything we enjoyed without the depressing problem of having to contend with J.P. Zuckerman.

●●●

I was to be J.P.'s guest of honor and the $12.50 charge was waived for me. As a further display of his newfound affection, he let me ride "shotgun" (right front window), and he allowed me to choose the other four riders who would accompany us on our mission.

Naturally, Tom, Mitch, and Al were my first three choices, and all of them accepted, Tom with some reluctance because of a political-science exam the following Monday. We agreed to let him study while waiting his turn. Mitch's only reservation was that he didn't have the $12.50. Since I was going gratis, I agreed to advance the money on his behalf and duly noted the increase in his debt, which now had risen to $305.50.

My fourth draft choice was a surprise pick. Charles M. Wickers was a tall, skinny kid from Newton Center (he pronounced it Newton Centah), a suburb of Boston. None of us really knew him that well. In fact, until three weeks before the trip, quiet Charles Wickers had said only one thing to me and that was, "Boston won, seven to three." I had no idea what he meant by that remark. I don't know if he was referring to hockey, baseball, or football. But I just didn't care, so I merely nodded and thanked him for volunteering this important information.

Then two weeks before Harrisburg, he stopped me as I was entering my music-appreciation class. I was at the top of the stairs when he called, "Ahthuh!" He leapt upwards, taking two or three steps at a time. When he reached the top and came face to face with me, he could hardly catch his breath. "I just wanted to tell you that Peter Gunn is on tonight," he said.

I stared at him in disbelief. This was the most insane, worthless bit of information I had ever received. For an instant I desperately tried to determine if there might be some secret meaning to his statement. Maybe Wickers was an undercover agent and I was to reply in a manner befitting my station, or perhaps he had mistaken me for someone who had once expressed an interest in that insufferable program. I never found out, because I merely nodded and thanked him for volunteering this important information.

One week before Harrisburg, Al Carter and I were sitting in the coffee shop of the Student Union Building discussing my chief preoccupation, Mitch's debt. Wickers was sitting by himself on the other side of the room, and luckily he had not seen us. To assure that he continued not to see us, I turned my chair so my back was toward him.

"What pisses me off, Al, is that he makes no attempt to pay off the debt. And if that's not bad enough, I end up paying most of his bills. Today the phone bill came. As usual he had no money, so he asked me to pay it. 'Just add it to my bill,' he says. I'm really sick of his shit."

"Speakin' of sheeyit, Art, guess who's comin' this way?"

"Not Wickers! God, don't let it be Wickers!" I begged. This was not the time to cope with an insipid person like Wickers.

"Hello, Ahthuh. Hello, Albut," said Wickers, and this tall, improper Bostonian stood at our table, with coffee cup in hand, waiting, I'm sure, for an invitation which did not come. "Do you gentlemen cayuh if I join you?" he asked, still standing at attention.

"We're talking some private stuff, muh man. Maybe some other time." But as if he never heard Al's reply, Wickers just plunked himself down beside us. He sat rigidly, staring intensely at us, often giggling at pieces of our conversation that were not the least bit funny. It was disconcerting and downright spooky. Finally we stopped talking.

"Well, Charles," I said nervously. "Al and I have to go now. We'll be late for class."

"Do you gentlemen cayuh if I join you?"

Minutes later the three of us were quietly walking down the beautiful Keystone Mall. I was still inhibited by our new companion and found the peaceful campus, resplendent in its late autumn attire, a welcome respite. It was Wickers who finally broke the silence.

"Ahtie, Albut, I hope you can help me with a serious personal problem."

When he called me "Ahtie" instead of the usual "Ahthuh," laughter erupted from my throat. He apparently felt that something had brought him closer to me, at least close enough to call me Ahtie. I was immediately sorry for the outburst when I realized there was anguish in his voice. I was instantly stripped of any remaining bits of hilarity. I assured him that Al and I would help him in any possible way.

"In spite of my façade of maturity," he said, "I'm really quite inexperienced in sexual matters."

"Jesus Christ," I said to myself. "Now I'm to become father confessor to this lunatic." We were crossing Campus Avenue, and to emphasize my change in attitude, I viciously kicked a stone clear across the road. But I had already committed my ear to him, and he was determined to get some black depression off his chest.

"I have never been what you would call—intimate with a

girl. I guess I never had the nerve. During summer vacation some old friends of mine from Framingham asked me if I would like to 'know' a woman.

"They fixed me up with a girl who 'went all the way.' I guess they all must have slept with her at one time or another. She must have been hahd up or they wouldn't have fixed her up with me. God knows, I'm no bahgain."

I looked at Al to get his response to Wickers's sad tale of self-degradation. He was staring downward and he avoided my glance. Apparently he must have felt the same twinge of embarrassment.

"We met at her apartment, and in only a few minutes she asked me to come into her bedroom. I guess my friends must have made all the arrangements beforehand. I was pretty nervous, but she told me that everything would be all right. By the time I got over to the bed, she was completely naked. Completely naked, Ahtie! Not a stitch of clothing. Do you know what I mean?"

I, of course, knew goddamn well what he meant. In fact, it was starting to piss me off a little that this demented man should get any ass at all.

"What do you think of that, Al? Completely bare-assed!" I called to Al to make sure he was still listening. Lately, Al didn't listen too well and tended to drift off during a conversation. Probably the pens were weighing heavily on his mind, since he still had thousands in stock.

"Hey, muh man," Al said, "my class is in Simmons. That's right at the end of this block. So how about trying to finish your story? Knowadamean?"

"I'm really sorry to trouble you guys with this. Why don't we just forget about it?" Wickers said gloomily.

Both of us assured Wickers that we were more than pleased to listen and help if we could, but that he should be as brief as possible.

"Okay. There's not too much more. She helped me take off

my clothes and in a second I was in bed with her. It seemed that both of us were ready for sex. We engaged in some, oh, what you would call foreplay, I guess. You know, we touched and stroked and—"

"Yes, goddamit, we know what foreplay is," Al said impatiently, and he rotated his finger parallel to the ground to get Wickers moving with the story.

At this point Wickers' accent seemed to thicken and his voice rose an octave, as he got to the good part of his story.

"Then she said, 'Now, now, oh now!' I knew that her moment was approaching, so I lifted myself in order to mount her. When I was on top, but had not yet made penetration, she began pushing my head downwahd. I thought perhaps I had made some mistake, so I proceeded again in my quest for penetration. Again she countahmanded me by pushing my head downwahd, this time with a little more force. For the third time I tried to have coitus with her and for the third time she again pushed my head down. This time her strength was so great that my face dragged across her breasts and was down to her navel before I regained control of the situation. I quickly climbed off her body and by this time I was in a state of detumescence and I was quite angry, too.

" 'Just what do you think is going on here?' I asked her.

" 'Maybe I've made a mistake,' she answered, 'but ahn't you ALBUT CAHTAH, the MUFF-DIVAH?' "

"Sheeeyit!" Al screamed.

"Jesus!" I shouted.

In the middle of Center Avenue, Albert Carter, the muff-diver, broke into the greatest mummer's strut I have ever seen. All of Philadelphia would have been proud. He danced wildly into the street and then back onto the sidewalk. He cakewalked and highstepped backwards and laterally, too. He strutted up the steps of Simmons, and when he disappeared into his class on the second floor, he was playing "I'm Looking Over a Four-Leaf Clover."

Wickers walked me to my music-appreciation class, which was on the next block. He now had his usual deadpan face.

"So long, Charles," I said, turning to go inside. "See you around."

"Good-bye, Ahtie, and don't forget—tonight is Peter Gunn."

Now we were the Harrisburg Six—J.P., Mitch, Tom, Al, Wickers, and I. Eagerly we looked forward to Saturday night to break the tedium of a lackluster week, and this one was going to be something special.

But there was something that superseded our trip to Harrisburg. Something that united the entire Keystone Campus—faculty and students, intellectuals and greasers, even J.P. Zuckerman and me. Football! If Saturday night was the essence of college life, then Football had to be the quintessence. It was Football and Saturday night, in that order, that made it all worthwhile.

On a raw Saturday afternoon in November, a few hours before leaving for Harrisburg, we sat high in the bleachers of Whitney Memorial Stadium, watching Keystone play West Virginia. An early snow had chilled the air and our bodies, but not our spirits, which we fortified with ample amounts of Jacquin's Blackberry Brandy. Flasks of this cheap booze had been passed freely since the kick-off, in spite of ordinances posted throughout the stadium prohibiting the use of alcohol. By halftime we were squirting brandy out of Mitch's large, tan wineskin—all of us except J.P., who drank only from his own private stock of Chivas Regal, and Tom, who said it was a little too pedestrian for his taste.

Al spent much of the game under a scroungy brown afghan, making out with a young townie he had picked up at the gate. He had bullshitted her into believing he was a scout for the Pittsburgh Steelers and had gotten her in with one of the many free passes he had acquired at the BX. There were strange noises emanating from under the afghan, but every time our boys made a sparkling play, Al's head popped out. And when the Green Band played our great Fight Song, Al was on his feet, singing with the rest of us.

Football was more than a game. It was a way to let out all your frustrations of the week. No boredom here. The frenetic stamping of feet during the kickoff, the mass hysteria after a Keystone touchdown, the camaraderie in cheering for a common cause.

It was now halftime, and K.S.U. led West Virginia ten to seven. The Keystone Green Band was performing its salute to American Politics and had just delineated all of Mount Rushmore on the playing field. I thought of Saturday night for the first time that afternoon. "Who's number one?" I asked.

"Key-stone! Key-stone!" shouted Tom and Wickers. Mitch was too busy searching for the hot-dog vendor to answer, and Al and his townie were still groping under the afghan.

"No," I said, "I'm talking about tonight—with Daisy. Who'll be first?"

"Let class show, muh man," said Al from underneath the cover. "Gotta lead with the best!"

Mitch said, "Daisy likes big guys."

"Teddy Roosevelt," said Wickers, giggling aloud. He was still engrossed in the band's formation and he beamed with delight. I stared at him as he rocked back and forth and began to doubt the wisdom of my selection. "I'm the guest of honor. I think that should—"

"Gentlemen," said J.P., who sat in the row behind us. "This inane dialogue is purely academic and I'd like to put an end to it right now. There is one hard-fast rule on the J.P. junket. *I* am first with Daisy!"

The crowd roared as our team dashed out onto the field. I shouted and began the rhythmic stamping of feet, but at the same time, J.P.'s words stayed with me. Zuckerman was to be first. Oh God! But as I looked down on the field I was able to overcome my problem temporarily with some pretty fancy rationalizing. Better it should be J.P. in there first than the entire defensive squad of the Keystone Bears.

"Loan me a buck, Art!" said Mitch, who had finally located the hot-dog man. "Just add it to the bill!"

"Everybody up for the Alma Mater!" said Tom.

As we stood at boyhood's gate
Shapeless in the hands of fate
Thou didst mold us, Keystone State—into men, into men!

Was I truly being molded into manhood? This was my last game at Keystone and I still seemed to be at boyhood's gate. I thought of graduation in June. Only seven months away. Then what? A rush of sadness, followed by a shot of anxiety. Then I looked down at the dozen nubile cheerleaders lifting their legs as they led the Alma Mater. Were they also being molded into men?

It was a great game. The lead switched back and forth in the second half, and with less than a minute remaining, West Virginia scored to go ahead, twenty-one to seventeen. But our Keystone men were not dead. They methodically moved the ball down the field to the West Virginia ten-yard line, using their last time-out to stop the clock. The next play would be the finale. Key-stone! Key-stone! The pace of the cheer accelerated. KEY-STONE! KEY-STONE! The words had lost all intrinsic meaning and were now only a symbol of total devotion. I looked around and captured the hysteria. The wild eyes, the flowing banners, the bright colors, the costumes, the screaming.

The Keystone quarterback raised his hands for silence and the fifty thousand partisans quickly obliged. The ball was centered and the quarterback rolled out to pass. There were no receivers, and desperately he lunged toward the goal. At the six he picked up a block, and at the one he hurdled two West Virginia defenders and landed in the end zone.

KEY-STONE! KEY-STONE! The crowd charged onto the field and the Green Band broke into a joyous rendition of the Fight Song. Complete chaos! In the bleachers co-eds were passed up and down the rows, flasks were drained, throats were strained—and I embraced J.P. Zuckerman.

The dirty, green Citroën pulled into the Harrisburg Motor Lodge at 7:15 P.M. With Captain J.P. Zuckerman, young scion of the Zuckerman Theater Empire, at the helm, we had arrived in search of our Holy Grail. Naturally, J.P. handled the details. He had rented a suite under the name of Anthony Terescavage. We started in on the pizza and beer and waited for Daisy, who was due to arrive at 8:00 P.M.

We had forty-five minutes to work out some important details. There was the unshakable, irrevocable premise that J.P. Zuckerman must be first. That was a house rule. It was choosing the other five positions that could deadlock us for hours.

We argued close to twenty minutes before someone finally suggested that we defer to the infinite wisdom and scrupulous fairness of Tom Nelson. After all, you could always trust Tom to make an equitable and impartial decision. He heard all the arguments and then he began his deliberation. When Tom was asked to mediate for us, he demanded strict compliance with his decision. No bullshit! No complaints! The decision of the judge would be final. We all agreed.

While Tom was deliberating in the corner of the room, Mitch and I began our gin game. He was somewhat handicapped without his potato chips, as I was without my pistachios. But, in a few minutes we had drunk enough beer so that nothing really mattered except Tom's decision. Al was doing his mummer's strut, only now it was more of a stagger. Wickers was sitting quietly and watching Lawrence Welk. Charles had come a long way in the last week. He had told his story at least twenty times, changing the punch line according to his audience; there was Jerry Petah Zuckahman the muff-divah and Thomas Hahvey Nelson the muff-divah and Mitchel Howahd Cahpentah the muff-divah and even old Ahtie himself the muff-divah. It seemed there was no end to the evah-growing list of muff-divahs.

Lovable J.P. Zuckerman spent his time calling acquaintances in Harrisburg. He also telephoned the three Zuckerman Theaters in the area, noting the feature movies and their starting times.

Finally Tom announced that he had come to his decision and that if Lawrence Welk were turned off, he would deliver his opinion.

"My fellow classmates," Tom said, "this decision was not an easy one. But these are not easy times. You have offered me the mantle of responsibility and I have not refused. Compromise is an enigma to me. How many times have we been too far apart on issues but then found some middle ground?—and like a miracle, the spirit of compromise has brought us together. On the other hand, compromise can be a dirty word. Neville Chamberlain compromised; France compromised. The whole free world—"

"What kind of fuckin' shit is this?" Mitch shouted.

"Mitch, you agreed that my decision would be binding," Tom replied.

"I said I'd agree to what you decided, but I don't have to listen to a fuckin' speech. What is this, the Supreme Court?"

"I thought it was quite interesting, the way Tom was leading up to his decision," Wickers piped in. "If you ask me—"

"No one asked you, Old Mister Boston!" said Mitch.

Things were getting out of hand. Mitch was losing in gin and was losing his self-control as well. To his everlasting credit, J.P., of all people, managed to calm everyone down. He asked Mitch to give Tom just a few minutes more and he asked Tom to try and come to the point.

"Wickers will be sixth," Tom said, and when he saw the downcast look on Wickers's face, he tried to cushion the blow. "Now, Charles, the reason for this is that you are the newest member of our group. May I suggest that instead of considering yourself number six in the first round, why not think positively? Try to picture yourself as number one in the second round."

"Arthur will be number two. He is the guest of honor and selected all of us to join him on this trip. We owe him something."

I had mixed emotions over this decision. I didn't want to be last, but it was no comfort to know that I followed J.P. Of course, I said nothing.

"Mister Big Mouth will be third," said Tom, looking at Mitch. "He and Arthur will be playing gin throughout most of the evening and I see no reason to interrupt their play unnecessarily.

"I have chosen myself to be fifth since I want to finish my political-science chapter without interruption. That leaves the fourth slot for Al. Thank you very much for your time."

Tom returned to his political-science book and we went back to our own activities.

Omens tell me whether to be elated or depressed. That's why I usually make an omen count before I decide how to feel.

Daisy was over an hour late . . . bad omen. I was beating Mitch easily in gin . . . good omen. But Mitch had no money, so it really didn't matter . . . bad omen. J.P. didn't seem too concerned about Daisy's lateness . . good omen. I was getting pretty drunk . . . bad omen. Daisy finally arrived at 9:15 P.M. . . . good omen. She was wearing a hideous stole made of a myriad of snarling fox faces . . . bad omen. Omen count was tied: three bad, three good. No projection at this time, but based on the count, I had the distinct feeling that the evening would have its ups and downs.

Daisy was a caricature . . . peroxide blonde, long false eyelashes, heavy red lipstick, slightly overweight. She wore a short red chiffon cocktail dress that was so tight that she walked knock-kneed and her thighs made a loud rustling noise when they tried to bypass each other.

"Boys, I want you all to say hello to Daisy Boyle," J.P. said, and I felt I was in a Western movie. J.P. was the head of the gang and I fully expected him to say, "Daisy, here, is gonna be ridin' with us for a while. Anybody have any objections?"

"Gee, Miss Daisy, it sure is good to meetcha," I said in my best imitation of any one of a thousand nameless characters I had seen in the movies. I affected a great limp and spat several times on the floor.

"Arthur, don't be a schmuck," J.P. said. "Don't pay Arthur no mind, Daisy. He's had a little too much to drink and he tends to become obnoxious."

"Hiya, boys," Daisy said in a throaty, guttural voice, quite reminiscent of Sophie Tucker. "Sorry I was late but I was at a basketball game at William Penn."

I was convinced that this was a euphemism. What she really meant was that she had sexually scrimmaged the high-school team. The joke was on J.P. Instead of being first, he would be sixth, and poor Wickers would be eleventh and maybe even sixteenth, depending on whether she had included the second team.

J.P. didn't waste any time. He took her by the hand and whisked her away into the adjoining room. Twenty minutes later the door opened and J.P. waddled out. He pointed at me from across the room and waved me on.

"She's all yours, Arthur," he said with a shiteating grin. "Don't disgrace me!" He chuckled hideously and slithered across the room, depositing his girth in an easy chair. He sat next to Wickers, who was now deeply engrossed in *The Return of the Werewolf.*

One of my best impressions has always been the Wolfman, and what better time could there be? I jutted my bottom teeth, lowered my eyebrows, and shifted my eyes from side to side. I let my arms swing apelike and proceeded to run around the TV, all the while growling, "Help me! Won't someone please help me? Oh, God, help me!"

"That's quite good, Ahtie," said Wickers, barely lifting his eyes from the real Wolfman on Channel 7.

"Arthur, you're wasting everyone's time, including Daisy's. Now would you kindly get your ass in there!" J.P. said. Anything that smacked of humor disgusted him.

The truth was that I really didn't care to go into that room. Somewhere along the way I lost interest in the whole demeaning project. Now the moment of truth was finally here and I was the fool walking in where J.P. Zuckerman had just trod. If this was what they called sex, then I much preferred to be the Wolfman. Finally, with great reluctance, I threw a gnarled claw against the door and amidst the laughter of my comrades, I entered Daisy's den.

It took my eyes several seconds to get accustomed to the dark room. But gradually I was able to determine that the half-dozen sets of white teeth and the dozen green eyes staring at me belonged to the emaciated fox-head stole that hung over the back of a desk chair. Then I made out the pair of silver pumps at the side of the bed. Then I saw Daisy's red cocktail dress on the bureau. And finally I saw Daisy. She wore her working clothes and she had assumed the receiving end of the missionary position.

She held an index card which she had just removed from the night table. She looked at the card, then up at me as I stood at the foot of the bed.

"Arthur, right?"

"Yeah," I answered, "and you must be Daisy. I've heard so much about you." I assumed that my name was written on the card and I wondered how detailed a dossier might have been compiled on me.

"J.P. says you're very clever," she said.

"Thank you. He also speaks very highly of you."

The absurdity of the scene hit me. There I was, fully clothed, having light conversation with a completely bare-assed woman. This certainly could not be the prelude to a sexual encounter. It was more as if I was the gynecologist and she was the patient.

"Okay, Daisy, would you mind slipping your feet into the stirrups?"

"J.P. also says you're a little off the deep end. Why don't

you just cut the shit now and take off your clothes? Let's get on with it."

"I'm really sorry, Daisy," I said, removing my shirt and placing it carefully over three of the grinning foxes. "Sometimes I say whatever just happens to pop into my mind." I took off my pants and covered the faces of the remaining three creatures. I had no intention of performing before an audience. When I had removed everything but my socks, I approached the bed.

"Aren't you gonna take your socks off, Arthur?"

"Daisy, I hope you can keep a secret; I'm terribly susceptible to athlete's foot. I always keep my feet covered, even when I go swimming. I know that if I walked barefoot in this room, I'd—"

"Arthur," she interrupted.

"Yes?"

"Would you get your ass into this bed?"

To this day, I'm not sure what the problem was. Maybe it was the booze. Too much alcohol will do it. Maybe it was those goddamn fox faces grinning at me from only a few feet away. Sure they were covered, but I knew they were still there. Maybe it was J.P.'s presence that still lingered in the room. Maybe it was the Wolfman shrieking outside the door or silly-ass Wickers' hysterical laugh. Maybe it was all of the above. But, whatever the reason, there was no way that I was going to make it.

Now, it's true that Daisy had an unusual capacity for sex. And you might think that if one guy out of ten or twenty couldn't get it up, she wouldn't give a damn. You're wrong. Daisy cared! She figured that if *she* could do it six times, then doing it once was the least I could do.

"What the hell's wrong with you?" she asked.

"I really don't know." I was now on my back, lying next to her and staring at the ceiling, occasionally putting a foot on the floor to steady the spinning room.

J.P. knocked on the door several times. "You might be the guest of honor, Arthur, but you can't spend the whole night in there."

"Keep your pants on, J.P.," Daisy shouted back, "we're about to set a new world's record."

Although it seemed like hours, I'm sure that it could have been only a minute or two that Daisy was quiet.

"Arthur," she said finally, and she propped herself up on an elbow, "do you have a steady girlfriend?"

"Why do you ask?"

"Because I want to know."

"Yes, I have a steady girlfriend."

"What's her name?"

"Why do you ask?"

"Because I want to know."

"Her name is Carol."

"That's a very nice name."

"Thank you."

Daisy reached over to the night table and drew a cigarette from the pack. She placed it in her mouth and said nothing. I assumed she was waiting for me to light her up. I slapped my naked hips and then my bare chest. There were no matches in either place. Daisy managed to locate a match in the drawer of the table and was now sucking the smoke deep into her lungs.

"What does Carol call you when you two make love?"

The question was more loaded than I was. How could I possibly explain this to a woman who had been laid by half the male population of Dauphin County?

There was just no way I could escape from Daisy. When J.P. talked about Carol, I could blot him out with a song. But this was a different story. When you're lying naked with someone, you're vulnerable.

I had never been in bed with Carol, but I had on several occasions been in car with her and even on beach with her. We had never "gone all the way," but we had put on some mileage.

Necking, petting, making out, "doing things," as we called it. I was, therefore, able to give Daisy somewhat of an answer.

"She calls me Art."

"That's all?"

"That's my name. It's not as if it's not my name."

"Doesn't she ever get passionate? Doesn't she say 'Art, baby' or 'Art, darling?' "

I was really trying my best to remember, but this was a most unconventional witness stand. "I think she says 'Art, honey.' "

"Well, Art honey, you and I are gonna make love."

Daisy mounted a ferocious attack. And booze is strange— where only a few minutes ago it had rendered me impotent, it now yielded the exact opposite reaction. Daisy's waist seemed to become slimmer, her breasts a little larger, her skin a little lighter, and her hair a little darker. Her voice lost its guttural sound and took on that familiar sweet tone, as she gently coaxed me into action.

"Oh, I love you, Art, honey. You're so good, Art, darling."

At one point I opened my eyes and stared at her. I could not believe it. It was Carol in that bed. I swear it! I whispered her name and began to float higher and higher. There was no stopping now.

Minutes later, while I was removing my pants from the fox heads and placing them on my bruised body, the idea hit me.

"How would you like to do a little favor for me?" I asked the chameleonlike creature who again was Daisy Boyle. She was now smoking another cigarette and waiting for Mitch.

"It seems to me that I already did you a favor, and a big one at that."

"That's true, and you have my undying love and admiration. But you're a person with a sense of humor and I'm sure you'll enjoy this." I buttoned my shirt and stood at the side of the bed.

"Well, Art, honey, just what do you have in mind?"

I sat down on the bed. "Well, Daisy, I have this plan." I

lowered my voice and she listened intently to every word. When I was finished she smiled and nodded her head.

"You're a nice lady, Daisy. I just want you to know that. And I want to thank you for everything—and I mean *every-thing*." I took her hand, and to the amazement of both of us, I kissed it. Then I stood up, zipped my fly, and elatedly opened the door and rejoined the group.

The next hour went according to schedule. Mitch followed me and took as little time as possible. He was anxious to get back to the gin game. I had "loaned" him another $3.00 for his share of the food and added it to his bill.

While Al took his turn, I added another $26.50 to Mitch's bill. The debt was getting completely out of hand. Mitch was making absolutely no effort to pay, and at that moment I had a suspicion that the debt was beyond the collectible stage. There was only one good omen. Mitch was still throwing the cards, which meant that he might still have some interest in reducing his bill.

Tom emerged from the smoke-filled room. He straightened his paisley print tie, put on the alpaca boatneck sweater his people sent from Bergdorf's, and headed for his political science book. When he was comfortable in the easy chair, he whipped off his glasses and said, "Guys, there is something inherently inequitable in this situation."

Mitch paused long enough in the gin game to give his customary imitation of Tom. He rolled his eyes, shook his head back and forth, and in a falsetto said, "Inherently inequitable." The rest of us were in no mood for a sermon and remained quiet.

"I say, this situation is unfair," said Tom.

"You jay-ohin' me, man?" said Al. "You're the cat who made the battin' order. So cut dat inequitable sheeyit!"

"Mister Carter, I'm talking about the exploitation of Daisy Boyle."

"Tom," said J.P. with an evil grin, "I notice your conclusion came after you sampled the merchandise. You should have said something before you got your whistle wet."

"I'm only human, J.P. I'm not immune to sins of the flesh. In this way I'm no different than the rest of you. But now I've seen the error. The important thing is that we try to benefit from our—"

"Let me tell you how I benefited from a similar situation," said Al. "It also involved a woman—an older woman, too. Someone you know, Tom."

"Bastard! You bastard! I will not listen to your despicable nonsense. My mother does charitable work. My mother is president of the D.A.R. My mother is the first lady of Belvidere. Tell him, Art! You know my mother. Tell this ignoramus!"

"Uhhh, yeah. Tom's right," I said to Al, who was now doing a half-strut in the corner. Half, because he was doubled over with laughter. "Mrs. Nelson is a very nice lady," I added.

"Play the fuckin' game!" said Mitch.

"And let's get on with our game!" said J.P. "Charles, do you think you might see Daisy now?"

Wickers was watching *Cry of the Vampire* and Lon Chaney, Jr., had been replaced by Bela Lugosi. "One second, J.P. Let me just see this scene!"

"Charles," I said. "You seem to be somewhat of an authority on vampires. Why is it that some of their victims die and others become vampires?"

"I don't really know, Ahtie. I'll have to look it up," he answered and stared intently at Count Dracula. Then he rose slowly and, keeping his eyes on Bela Lugosi, he carefully backed his way to the door. Finally he said, "Ahtie, watch the movie and tell me what happens!" Then he disappeared into the other bedroom.

I don't know the exact sequence of events. I am neither an eavesdropper nor a Peeping Tom. But I was sure it went something like this:

Wickers was quite nervous as he entered Daisy's bed. She said very little when he undressed and he assumed she was just a little tired from the evening's activities. After all, he was number six. Some of his courage returned when the preliminaries went fairly well. But he was totally unprepared when he felt the sudden, powerful, viselike grip on the back of his neck. His first thought was that one of us had snuck in the room and was playing a joke on him. He twisted his neck what little he could under the immense pressure, and to his horror he discovered that the powerful hands on him were Daisy's. He felt intense pain as he tried unsuccessfully to free himself. The pressure was now pushing downward to his shoulders and he was being forced down toward the foot of the bed. As his face was pushed lower, he suddenly realized what was happening. He gasped and his eyes opened wide in terror. The firmness of her grip had lessened somewhat and with some newfound super-strength, he managed to reach around and pull her hands off him.

"What's going on heah?" he shrieked.

"What are you so upset about? Aren't you CHARLES M. WICKAHS, the MUFF-DIVAH?"

We were prepared for the worst. We heard the shouting and the thud of his feet on the floor. Two seconds later the door was flung open and there stood Wickers, naked as the day he was born and in an obvious state of detumescence.

"That was funny, Ahtie," he said calmly, "really funny . . ."

He stood there in the doorway for what seemed like an eternity. His eyes pierced mine and I knew that a thousand tiny wheels were whirring behind that glazed look. I was instantly sorry for conspiring with Daisy and I prayed that his psyche had not suffered any permanent damage.

"You know, Ahtie," he continued, "I've been thinking. The victim dies if he loses too much blood. And he becomes a vampire if the blood loss is not too great. I'm not sure just where the dividing line is. Maybe it varies from victim to victim. I'll look it up." Then he shut the door and went back to Daisy.

The evening was grinding down. At 11:00 P.M. Daisy announced that she had a previous engagement. She retired to the bathroom for what she called some "freshening up." Actually it was more like a general overhaul. Ten minutes later she emerged "as fresh as a Daisy," as Wickers so aptly put it. And after he said it, he laughed hysterically for several minutes. I considered it a gross overreaction to something that was not particularly funny. Perhaps he was making up for an evening of unbelievable underreaction. As Wickers giggled on, I shot a glance at Mitch, who was playing solitaire and winning back most of the money he had lost to me.

Mitch caught my look and just shrugged his shoulders. "Fuckin' clown!" he said, referring to Wickers, and he peeled the top layer of cheese and tomato off a cold pizza slice, rolled it carefully, and popped it into his mouth. He flicked his fingers rapidly and then wiped them on his pants.

Daisy adjusted her dress, said her good-byes, threw her moth-eaten menagerie around her shoulders, and was out of the door.

"Sheey-it!" Al said. "It ain't fair we done pay dis room for duh night. We only used it four hours."

"If you are suggesting that we leave without paying, you can count me out," said honest Tom. "When we took possession of the room, we made a de facto contract."

"Tom, why don't you stick your de facto contract up your de facto ass," Mitch said.

"You know, Mitch, you have no respect for anyone or anything."

Mitch did another Tom imitation. He waved his hands and contorted his face. "No respect for anyone or anything," he mimicked.

Wickers was staring intently at Victor Mature, who was now smiling through a torture session administered by the

Roman Legions. But he had not missed one word of our conversation. "Actually, gentlemen, we have a bit more than just a de facto contract. It was my understanding that this room has already been paid for. Isn't that true, J.P.?"

"Yes, I paid for the room. But if you want to head back, I'll get the money back . . . all of it."

J.P. spoke with such conviction that it was hard to doubt him. And yet, I wondered how he could pull it off.

"Then let's get the hell out of here!" Mitch said. "I sure could use the cash."

"Mitch," I said. "You didn't put up any money, so if a dividend is declared, you won't be sharing in the proceeds. I'm really sorry!"

Mitch took on a very hurt look. "Please, Art, I'm a little short. Couldn't you just add it to the bill?"

"Well, if we're all in agreement, let's clean up the room and get our things together. Would anyone like to take in a movie before we go back? I'll get you a special price on tickets."

All of us assured J.P. that we didn't care to finish this nice evening at the Zuckerman Theater, the nice place for nice people.

"Then let's move out!" J.P. said, and he waddled toward the door. His troops broke camp and followed behind him.

J.P. drove over to the motel office. He parked the car just outside the front door. It had turned out to be a warm night, and only a screen door separated us from J.P. and the desk clerk. We would have a bird's-eye view of the confrontation and we waited anxiously.

J.P.'s back was toward us as he approached the desk. He hunched over and he drew his chin in to his chest, giving a crestfallen appearance. He stood at the desk and waited for the clerk.

"Yes, sir, may I help you?"

"Yes, I . . ." J.P. started to reply, but his voice choked off. He sounded like a wounded animal.

"Sir, is there something wrong?"

J.P. managed to compose himself to some degree. He fumbled in his pocket and finally withdrew two room keys. He laid them on the counter in front of the clerk. "Room 213 and Room 214. I'm checking out," he said in a cracking voice.

The clerk took the keys and went to the filing cabinet. He pulled out the sheets that said "Anthony Terescavage."

"Mr. Terescavage, you just checked in here a few hours ago."

"Yes, I know, sir. Is there any chance you might be able to refund my money?"

"Mr. Terescavage, this is highly irregular. Just what's going on?"

J.P. leaned closer to the man. "I just called my home in Pittsburgh . . . A few minutes ago, my father was killed in a car accident. I must get back immediately."

"Oh, dear Jesus," cried the clerk, holding his forehead. "I'm so sorry!"

"I'm still in a state of shock. He was killed instantly."

"Oh, God, Mr. Terescavage, I wish there were something I could do to help. This is such a tragedy!"

"You could really help a lot by just giving me a refund. This happened so suddenly and I need the money to get home. I'm leaving right now for Pittsburgh."

"Of course, Mr. Terescavage. Oh, I'm so terribly sorry," he said and staggered to the register. He took out a twenty and a ten and pressed the bills into J.P.'s open palm. It was more than twice the amount J.P. had paid for the room. "I wish there was something more I could do."

"Thank you," J.P. said. "I'm lucky to have my good friends going back with me." He threw a thumb over his shoulder to indicate the five of us in the car. "Good-bye and thank you again."

J.P. turned and waddled toward us. Tears were streaming from his red eyes, tracing a crooked path to the red lips which now framed the widest, most monstrous smile I had ever seen.

And with every step J.P. took, the poor clerk continued to shake his head and mutter things like, "I'm so sorry, Mr. Terescavage. I wish I could help, Mr. Terescavage. Godspeed, Mr. Terescavage. Good-bye, Mr. Terescavage."

As the Citroën pulled sluggishly onto the darkened highway, the five riders sat in shocked silence. We had totally underestimated the cruelty of this man. For a few lousy bucks, he had killed his father.

As we were leaving the Harrisburg city limits, the huge billboard suddenly appeared on the roadside, punctuating the end of this horrendous evening. It was a giant picture of the "late" Monroe T. Zuckerman, all decked out in top hat and tails. "Visit Your Nearest Zuckerman Theater, a nice place for nice people."

I looked at the frightening face on the sign, which was a replica of the one on the animal at the wheel. I stared only for a split second, but the image stayed with me a long time.

For most people, Monday is the worst day of the week. It's Blue Monday. It's back to work, back to school, back to whatever you hate most. But for me, there's no day that's quite as bad as Sunday. Sunday is that gray day when broken dreams, pointless present, and nebulous future join forces. Sunday is the day for crying, moping, and self-deprecation.

And on that Sunday, every thought, every action was overshadowed by my depression. I thought about poor Mr. Zuckerman. I felt that he really was dead. I was relieved when I saw no mention of his passing in the paper. Then I realized that the paper had already gone to press at the time that J.P. was committing his infamous act of patricide. I listened to the all-news radio station for an hour, but still there was no mention of Zuckerman.

I was alone. Mitch had borrowed my car and had driven to Williamsport to visit his parents. Tom was studying at the library. This was a perfect opportunity for me to prepare for the week that would be crashing down on me in a matter of hours.

It was always a terrifying experience to be alone with my

work, especially on a dreary Sunday afternoon. So I did then what I have been doing ever since whenever things get too tough. I slept. Right there on that shabby gray couch. With a pile of badly neglected textbooks by my side, with a bunch of unresolved problems in my mind, and nothing to keep me from either, I took the familiar, easy way out . . . I slept.

The first telephone ring, which I heard only subconsciously, told me bad news was coming. The second ring said that Mr. Zuckerman of Harrisburg had been instantly killed in a head-on collision on the Pennsylvania Turnpike, ten miles east of Pittsburgh. The third ring said that the late Mr. Zuckerman was survived by his wife, the former Alma B. Ernst, and a prick, Jerry Peter, who was his son. I stumbled across the room and clipped the fourth ring in midair.

"Yes?" I gasped, my heart pounding in anticipation.

"Arthur? Is that you?"

"Yes," I said in a barely audible whisper.

"Arthur, are you all right?"

"Yes, I'll be all right." My teeth were chattering uncontrollably as I slowly sat down at the kitchen table.

"It's Mother," my mother said.

"Yes, Mother," I said.

"Arthur, what in the world is wrong with you?"

"You have some bad news for me, don't you?"

"How did you know?" she asked.

"It's Mr. Zuckerman. He's dead, isn't he?"

"Arthur, what are you talking about? Who is Mr. Zuckerman?"

"Monroe Zuckerman, J.P.'s father."

"Arthur, I don't know any Zuckerman. I called to tell you that we received some very sad news today."

No matter what that sad news was going to be, I could not help feeling some sense of relief. Zuckerman was alive and well.

My mother's sad news was the untimely passing of Aunt Gert from Scranton. She was only eighty-nine and she hadn't even been that sick. Of course, she had been in the Home for three years and she did have a heart condition, you know. Mary had been with her just last week and she was fine, you know. You just never know. It really was a shock, you know.

"You just never know," I agreed, really warming up to the situation now. "How is Uncle Henry taking it?"

"My God, Arthur, what is wrong with you? Uncle Henry died two years ago." She really was quite disgusted with me.

"Jeez, that's right. I'm so upset about Aunt Gert, I don't even know what I'm saying."

I suppose the apology was accepted. There was a pause in the conversation and a definite shifting of gears.

"Have you been studying, Arthur?"

"Oh, sure. I was studying when you called." The opening gambit was always the sad news. Then the studying. Now she would ask about the dating. I rested my chin on my open palm and discovered that the couch had left its checkerboard imprint on my face. I pondered the ridges and valleys.

"Have you been going out?" she asked. It was her greatest fear that Carol would eventually do me in. She was insistent that I date as much as possible so that I would become a comparison shopper. It didn't matter who or what I took out. Just so I dated. She wanted me to climb every mountain, ford every stream.

I thought about the stream I had forded on Saturday night. "Oh, sure," I said. "I had a date last night. A girl from Harrisburg."

"Oh, who fixed you up? Aunt Elizabeth?"

"No, no. A good friend of mine lives in Harrisburg. A couple of guys drove down there and he fixed us all up. Real nice time."

"Oh, I'm glad. Did you call Aunt Elizabeth?"

"No, I didn't have a chance. It was really a busy evening for me."

"Will you be taking her out again?"

"I don't know, Mother," I said, suddenly thinking of the

grinning foxes. "Daisy was very nice, but I'm not sure I want to get all that serious right now."

"Well, if you change your mind, we certainly wouldn't object to your bringing Daisy home for the holidays. We'd like to meet her."

"Yeah, that would be nice. I'd like to introduce her to some of my old friends, too. Let me think about it."

I wondered if my mother would really prefer Daisy Boyle to Carol. I toyed with the idea for a few seconds. But it was now time for the standard close, which consisted of the great achievements of family and acquaintances. This part of the phone call was the biggest put-down of all. I felt it was designed to lessen my own accomplishments. I braced myself.

"You remember Stephen Baker, don't you? That's Aunt Dorothy's youngest son."

"He's dead," I blurted out, confusing her standard close with her standard opening.

"That's not very funny, Art. As a matter of fact, Stephen graduated magna cum laude from Penn. He was accepted at a dozen medical schools. He'll have his pick of the litter."

I thought of poor Mitch barely able to find just one graduate school to take him in. And here was this goddam smug bastard, cousin Stephen, who would easily ooze his way into any medical school.

"I saw Harriet Snyder yesterday. You know, Craig's mother," she said.

I couldn't imagine what Craig could accomplish in life. His parents sent him to a country-club college in Florida, a school where no one flunks out. And he flunked out. Craig's only attribute was a unique ability to belch at will.

"What did old Craig do?" I asked. I knew there would be nothing like medical or law schools. This would be the very general success story.

"He went into the wholesale lumber business and he's doing fantastic."

Always a great line. A one-dimensional summing up of a person's life. The fact that his father spent the last thirty-two years in lumber meant nothing. "Doing fantastic!" A new T-Bird, a natural-fitting charcoal-gray suit by Brooks Brothers, and most important, a fiancée with a lot of money. Just fantastic! I wondered if he could still belch once every twenty seconds. That, to me, would still be a more important credential.

Of course, all of this was really a prelude to the inevitable question—"Have you made any decisions concerning your career?" she asked. "It's only a few more months, you know."

"Well, nothing concrete, but I have a few irons in the fire." I lied about the irons in the fire. There were none. But I was telling the truth about there being nothing concrete.

"Have you had any job interviews?"

"A few coming up, Mother." Another lie.

"Well, everyone here sends their best."

"Mother, I really am sorry about Aunt Gert. She was a nice lady."

When the call was over, I sat and thought for several minutes before returning to the couch. The familiar depression was not there, despite the untimely passing of Aunt Gert. She had been a grand old lady, and she had made the supreme sacrifice. She laid down her life so that Mr. Zuckerman might live.

Do you know about the drear? You may not know it by that name. You may not even be consciously aware of it. But I just cannot believe that I am the only person in the world who has felt its presence. Drear is a feeling, a sixth sense, a combination of atmospheric conditions and perhaps a touch of loneliness. But it is very real to me . . . It comes once a week, always on Sunday when late afternoon is fumbling the ball over to early evening.

Drear is gray and brown and black and bleak. Drear does

not creep in on little cat's feet like fog. It's more like a tidal wave in slow motion. Drear is unbearable in the late fall when the days are the shortest. And it is always much worse in colder climates. Drear is at its peak in Atherton or the Keystone campus in late December. You just know you're going to have the shit end of the stick for a long, long time.

The worst way to face drear is alone. It's an incredibly lonely experience. I would have even welcomed J.P.'s presence, which is really scraping the bottom as far as companionship is concerned.

I thought about my future. Uncertain, frightening. Teachers teach. Preachers preach. Doctors and lawyers practice, hopefully till they get it right. But what the hell do I do? What is liberal arts anyway? A smattering of unrelated horseshit. A little bit of this, a little bit of that. But not enough to really sink your teeth into. Great for pre-law, great for pre-med, great for pre-anything. But how about if you're not going on to anything else? What if the first four years are the be-all and end-all?

Well, I know enough Spanish to tell you who the five most famous Mexican bandits were: Villa, Huerta, Carranza, Zapata y Obregon. Great, huh? And I can talk for hours about Herman Melville's works. Some people feel that Captain Vere was God and Billy Budd was Christ. Impressive? I can even discuss *escherchia coli, bacillus subtillus,* lifo, fifo, and why the League of Nations failed. Did you know that the contrabassoon is the lowest-pitched instrument in a symphony orchestra? I know all about diagrams, diaphragms, pentagrams, the Pentagon, and the Parthenon. I can talk about Aristotelian logic, but tell me, where is the logic in the following? In six months they're going to give me a sheepskin, saying that for four years I have successfully matriculated in the Collegium of Liberalis Artisis. BIG FUCKIN' DEAL! Now what? Just where do I go from here?

The drear is a perfect time for heavy thinking, but my life's ambition, or lack of it, was not what I would call resolvable. However, there was a problem that might be resolved. I stood at the kitchen window and threw the drapes to the side, just in time to catch a wipe-out wave of drear. It lifted me, carried me across the room, and sat me at the kitchen table. I dialed Carol's number.

●●●

I met Carol during the summer vacation after my freshman year at Keystone. In a way, we had half of a storybook romance. She was either Harvest Princess or Class Sweetheart at Newburg College. But I was not the quarterback, editor of the newspaper, or president of my class at Keystone.

The most amazing part was that she loved me. Why? Why me? She could have dated anyone. She could have had the nicest, richest, smartest, best-looking guys around. But she either refused to go out with them or was so miserable on a date that she was not asked out again. All because of me. Simply incredible!

I concluded that she was a hopeless monomaniac. Her sickness was me. There was a thin, rose-colored, protective shield around me, and when she looked at me, she saw only good things. "You can be anything you want to be, Art. You can do anything you want to do."

If I wrote a few paragraphs, I was a writer. My piano playing was better than any professional's. I could take my pick of any career. Anything I wanted.

Carol told me how happy she was that with all the beautiful girls after me, I still chose her.

I gripped the phone tightly.

"Hi, Carol."

"Art!" She had the sweetest, crystal-clear voice. It was always reassuring to hear her. It's a pity that I can't reproduce voice timbre, because it is infinitely important that you understand this voice. She was soft and quiet and melodic. It was exciting to hear her say my name. It was not just a salutation. There was a genuine fondness and longing there. A consuming happiness that poured through because of me and at the same time a bittersweet kind of sadness . . . also because of me.

I was determined, at long last, to open up with her.

"How are you?" I asked with no emotion.

"I'm fine, Art. I miss you a lot," she answered with emotion.

I wanted to say that I missed her, I loved her, I wanted her. I wanted to say that I wanted to be with her and on her and in her. But the integral part of my goddamn, crazy-ass conspiracy was either to say nothing or to say nothing of consequence. When I had a particularly strong emotion, I would go the exact opposite way. Interest yields disinterest. Feeling yields callousness. Sexual attraction yields a complete inability to look a person in the eye for more than two seconds at a time. Don't open up, Art! As Mitch would say, "Just play the fuckin' game!"

"What's new, Carol?" Now isn't that a great line? Lots of feeling. Lots of warmth.

"I think about you a lot, Art."

One last chance, you goddamn, fucking clown. She's giving you a chance. Tell her. Get rid of the lump, the knot, the bone . . . get rid of whatever it is that is holding you back, not only from Carol, but from everything else that you want.

The perspiration beaded, the throat constricted, and the right words almost came.

"Hey, I was just sitting around here thinking. May twenty-first is Senior Weekend. If you have nothing else to do, maybe we could get together?"

"Would you like that?" She tried to extract at least some

small measure of sensitivity from me . . . even a tiny show of tenderness.

I pictured her sitting in the big, red Naugahyde chair. I really should say lying, her neck on one arm of the chair, her ponytail draped down, and her legs hanging over the other side. I could see the long brown wool skirt with the fluffy French poodle and the tan, tight-fitting cashmere sweater. I loved her.

"Why do you always answer a question with another question?" I was gruff and tinged it with enough animosity to produce some instant self-hatred.

"I just wondered if you really wanted me to be there!"

"Well, I asked you, didn't I? I wouldn't have asked if I didn't want you here."

"Do you?"

"Yes, I want you here!"

"You could say it like you mean it," she said. She was struggling to hold back the tears.

"C'mon, Carol, stop it. I honest-to-God don't understand what you're crying about. I really want you here. Will you please stop it?"

"I miss you, Art!"

"I miss you, too." I really meant it. I missed her terribly, but the answer was just that . . . an answer. If she had said "thank you," I would have said "you're welcome." If she had sneezed, I would have said "God bless you."

"I love you, Art."

"I love you, too." Another answer. The most amazing thing was that I had the colossal nerve to call J.P. a "prick."

"I'd love to come up for Senior Weekend."

"Okay. I'll write to you. I'll send you all the details."

"Okay. Good-bye, Art."

"Carol . . ." I was choking now and I paused to steady myself. "I can't wait to see you. I really want you to be here." Hooray! Three cheers for Arthur! Perhaps there was hope after all.

Dealing with Mitch was an altogether different ordeal.

"You got one hell of a fuckin' nerve, Art!" Mitch was really pissed off. He now owed me $340 and I had just confronted him with the figures.

"*I* have a lot of nerve?" I was truly amazed. "Why do *I* have a lot of nerve? It's not like I'm asking you for *your* money . . . I'm asking you for *my* money!" I was really hot. All the frustrations of the past twenty-four hours were being unloaded on Mitch, but after all, he did owe me the money.

"Are you inferring that I'm a fuckin' crook? Is that what you're saying, Art?" His voice was getting louder. His eyes darted around the room until he found the bowl of potato chips on the remains of the coffee table. They had been sitting there for over three days, but that didn't seem to bother him. He leaped from his chair, knocking a pile of Tom's papers to the floor, and moved quickly toward the chips. I was sitting on the couch and, thinking that a bodily attack on me was imminent, I threw my hands up in front of my face. I was relieved to see both of his hands sink deeply into the soggy chips. He was so upset that he couldn't wait for the condiments.

When he had forced at least seven or eight of the chips into that cavernous mouth, I continued the dialogue.

"Mitch, let me see if I can explain a little English grammar to you. The speaker implies and the listener infers. Do you follow? Do you know what I mean? In other words, *I* would *imply* that you are a fucking crook and *you* would *infer* that you are a fucking . . ."

I never finished the sentence. This time the attack came. His greasy hands were around my throat and were squeezing my life away. He was screaming incoherently about fucking, smart-ass bastards, and potato chip crumbs were spewing out of his mouth in all directions. His face was as red as mine.

It was Tom who indirectly saved my life. During the entire argument and up until the assault, he had been sitting at his desk, quietly writing his term paper on the merits of a capitalistic society. As my eyes bugged out of their sockets, Tom said, "You know, Art, I've never seen Mitch this angry before!" Then he lowered his head and went back to his work.

Tom's words brought Mitch to his senses, and the viselike grip was relaxed.

As I slowly caressed away the red fingerprints from my aching throat, Mitch stood up, bolted down a chip or two, and moved toward his studious roommate. "I'm going to tell you once and only once," Mitch said, his index finger pointing close to Tom's nose, "mind your own fuckin' business, Mr. Clarence Darrow, and put your nose back into your fuckin' torts!"

"You know, Mitch, you're a big baby. If you don't mind, I'm going to see what's going on next door," Tom said. He folded his papers and snapped off the desk light. With a quick push of his shoes against the wall he forced his chair backwards and stood up.

"Oh, *I'm* a baby!" said Mitch in his usual mocking tone.

"Yes, you are," Tom replied as he walked toward the bedroom.

"Not you though. You're not a baby, are you?"

"No, just you," Tom said. He disappeared into the bedroom and slammed the door.

"Well, I'll tell you something, my mature friend," Mitch shouted at the closed door. "While you're being the Peeping Tom, Tom, kindly jerk off in your own bed!"

"Seeing what's going on next door" was a euphemism, a catch phrase that meant Tom was going to spy on a young married couple who lived six and a half feet from our bedroom window. Most of Tom's study breaks were spent watching, but in all the countless hours of peeping, Tom never saw anything more than a good-night kiss. But he never gave up hope and would sometimes keep his lonely vigil for hours. Deep down he felt that eventually he would see something. For him it was worth the wait.

With Tom out of the way, Mitch returned somewhat sheepishly to the center ring. "Now, where were we?" he asked me. He sat on the edge of Tom's desk, and I detected that he was just a little bit sorry for his irrational, childish behavior.

"Well, let's see. You were in the process of strangling me. You got mad because I asked you to pay on the debt. You owe me the money. I won it fair and square."

"You called me a fuckin' crook and it pissed me off," Mitch said.

"No, sir, I didn't call you a fucking anything. I merely said that it's beginning to look like I'm getting screwed."

"And how are you getting screwed? I'm the one losing all the money."

"No, goddamit, you are not the one losing all the money!" I was not getting through to this madman and I was frustrated. I was determined to explain it till he understood. I leaned forward on the couch and concentrated hard on my next move. I paused momentarily as I carefully selected the right words. I did not want to get choked again.

I lifted my right forefinger perpendicular to the floor and pressed my lips together for courage. "Mitchel," I said in a serious voice.

"Arthur," he said, and from his mildly humorous tone I knew that some of his madness had left.

"Mitchel, you haven't lost one nickel to me. Do you want to know why?"

Mitch nodded.

"Because you haven't paid me one shit-picking nickel. Am I coming through to you, Mitch? You see, losing, the way I see it, doesn't mean that we play a little gin and I just happen to score better than you. Do you know what I mean, Mitch?" I was speaking gently now. "Losing, at least the way I see it, means that when I score higher than you, we assign a certain monetary value to these points, and you, being the loser, reimburse me accordingly."

He seemed to understand because he was nodding his fool head off.

"And now, Mitch," I continued, "I look over the records and find that you don't ever reimburse me. You never pay me anything. So it's really not like losing at all, is it? Do you follow what I'm saying?"

He hung his head and stared at the floor. I assumed that this was the equivalent of an affirmative reply.

"And now I must tell you the worst part. Not only do you not pay, but you continue to borrow from me and add it on to the debt. This compounds the felony, Mitch. You lose to me in gin, so I loan you money which you don't pay back. And this doesn't make any sense to me.

"Now I have a very big problem of my own. I can't seem to make up my mind what I'm going to be doing for the next forty years or so. Actually, this really has nothing to do with you, Mitch, but believe me, it's causing me a great deal of anxiety. Chances are that I'll wind up in my father's business. Now this is not the most exciting prospect in the world, but I just don't have the drive to do anything else."

"What's the point?" Mitch's attention span was short and his eyes were now scanning the room in search of food. I knew I would lose him if I didn't close quickly.

"The point is this. If I'm going to be a businessman, I must start applying some sound business techniques. And I'm going to start right now.

"I want some money! Now! Even if it's only a token payment. Then I want you to present a plan to me . . . a workable plan explaining how you are going to reduce this debt. There will be no more cards, no more loans, and no more bullshit until you make this attempt to . . ."

"Okay, okay, I get the picture. Keep your fuckin' shirt on. You can start by taking four dollars off the debt right now."

"Fine! That's a good start," I said, and I held out my extended palm. Four dollars was more than I had hoped for. I was elated.

"No, no! I'm not actually going to give you the four. Just take it off the debt," Mitch said.

"I'm not sure I understand." The tingling started in my forehead.

"I put four dollars' worth of gas in your car today."

"So what! You borrowed my car to go to Williamsport. Did you forget? You used *my* car, you ingrate. Of course you put gas in the car. *You* used the gas to drive *my* car to visit *your* parents. Now what kind of shit is this? You want me to reimburse you for this? That's a pile of shit! Isn't it enough that I loaned you *my* car? Why should I pay for *your* gas?"

"I'm not asking you to pay!" he said, and he was getting indignant as if I had offended him. "You don't have to reimburse me at all. Don't you see? This is a start like you wanted, Art. You don't have to come up with the money. Just take the four dollars off the debt." He was really proud of himself, and his eyes glowed. He smiled beneficently.

I stared at him for a very long time, while he basked in the aura of his new-found glory. I ritually removed all the sandy particles from both eyes with my forefinger. Then I did the same to my ears, this time employing my little finger. With my little finger I then cleaned out the corners of my mouth. I was now ready.

"You know, Mitch, I'm really sorry about the misunder-standing we had before. But I really didn't call you what you said I did."

Mitch closed his eyes, smiled serenely, nodded rapidly, and whispered, "It's okay, Art. It's okay. I understand."

"But, Mitch, I hope you'll truly understand what I'm going to say to you now. Listen closely! It's not easy for me to ex-press my inner feelings. No more misunderstandings. Okay?"

He nodded again.

"Mitch, you're a big, steaming pile of shit. Do you under-stand what I'm saying? And most important, and I hope you don't misunderstand this time . . . YOU ARE A FUCKING CROOK!"

I didn't care if he choked me or not. I stood up and quickly walked past him. I turned the corner and disappeared into the bedroom, leaving Mitch by himself. He deserved his own company.

December was bad. Real bad! Mitch and I reached a new low in our relationship. But I stood by my pledge. No more gin-playing until he came up with a workable payment plan. His conversation with me amounted to a few social amenities such as "Pass the fuckin' peas!" and "Turn off the fuckin' TV!"

One night in January, Mitch woke me up at three in the morning. Since we really had not been talking, I assumed it was Tom who had finally seen his married couple in action. But, it was Mitch, all right. I lifted my head and stared at him.

"Art, I've been wondering."

"For Christ's sake, it's three in the morning. Why don't you do your wondering in around five or six hours?"

He was not to be put off. "Do you really think I'm a crook?"

"Of course not, Mitch! Just give me a workable plan and I'll be happy. A workable plan, that's all I want." I turned away and yawned.

"That's why I woke you up, Art." He was whispering so Tom wouldn't be disturbed. "I just came up with a great idea!" He paused for me to get suitably excited, which I did not. We both waited for the other to speak. There was a heavy note of expectancy in the air, and knowing that I would not get back to sleep until his plan was heard, I finally gave in.

"All right, Mitch, what's your plan?"

"Why don't we put on a show?"

I really hadn't expected much, but this bit of news was less than even my lowest expectations. I pretended to drift back to sleep.

"Did you hear what I said, Art?"

"Yes, I heard you," and as groggy as I was, I still couldn't hold back the irritation.

"What do you think?"

"I think we should talk about it tomorrow," I said.

"C'mon! I want to know what you really think."

"Mitch, I really think you're trying your best, but quite frankly I'm amazed to hear a suggestion like that coming from you. I feel like I'm talking to an asshole like Wickers. No one in real life puts on shows to raise money; that's Hollywood bullshit. That's Andy Hardy crap. You asked me what I think. Okay. It's stupid! It's worthless! It's a shitty idea!"

"No goddammit! Not that kind of a show, you fuckin' creep. I'm talking about showing a stag film. Right here. In this apartment. I have a great stag film at home. I'm sure we could get at least fifty guys that would pay a buck to see it."

At least Mitch was trying. As far as I was concerned, there was nothing to lose. The possibility of finally reducing the debt was quite appealing to me. It would be good to end the cold war we had been waging for over a month.

Now I felt ashamed over the way I had treated him. He was really trying, and I felt that maybe some sort of apology might be in order. I vacillated and finally decided against it. Any show of weakness on my part might suggest that I was ready to play cards, perhaps right then, at 3:00 A.M.

"What do you think, Art?" He was asking for approval or any tiny show of support.

I had decided against an outright apology. There was just

no need for it. But certainly a small kind word wouldn't hurt. "I think it's a fair idea. It just might raise some money."

"Do you consider it a workable plan?"

"Yeah, I think it is. We'll talk about it in the morning." I fluffed up my pillow, turned over, and was asleep in seconds.

I thought I was dreaming. I heard the quick, repetitive shuffle of cards. I opened my eyes. It was no dream. Mitch was shuffling only a few inches from my face, and I felt the breeze and smelled the plastic odor.

I was getting pissed off. "Mitch, I'm not going to play now!"

"You said, 'Give me a workable plan,' and that's just what I gave you. Now play the fuckin' game!" He was now rapidly dealing the cards, some of which hit the hills and valleys of the blanket and fell on their backs.

It was useless to resist any longer. "One game and that's it," I said.

"Across the board?"

"Okay, across the board." I sat up against my pillow and rubbed the sleep from my eyes.

"Play the fuckin' game!" he said.

I'm not quite sure what happened. Mitch sat on the edge of his bed and I remained under the covers of my own. The playing field was my rumpled blanket, which had to be smoothed periodically to clear off the potato-chip crumbs. We played by candlelight, giving the game an eerie, clandestine effect.

I can't help thinking that I may have taken a dive. After all, nothing could have been gained by my winning. Another loss for Mitch might have even depressed him enough to put a damper on his great, new "workable plan." The cards just didn't come and I just didn't care.

When it was all over at 4:00 A.M., Mitch had whipped my ass for $32.00. I had very little strength left, and I didn't give a damn about losing. But I felt I had to "play the fuckin' game" for his benefit. I contorted my face into as horrid a grimace as I could muster and ordered him to give me the cards.

I opened the window and flung the cards against the elevator shaft while I yelled things like "fuck," "shit" and "goddamn." I even threw in "piss" for good measure. He thoroughly approved and his big red face beamed. I couldn't quite work up a good whimper, and I discussed nothing with the Lord of Hosts, but I did manage to fall dramatically on to my bed and I sighed for several seconds.

My last bit of noise jolted Tom out of his deep sleep, and he shot up straight in the air. He sized up the situation incorrectly. He quickly flipped over on his stomach and barely lifted his eyes above the cold iron bar at the head of his bed.

"Douse those lights!" Tom whispered, not taking his eyes off the darkened window across the way. "Did you see anything? Were they doing things?"

"Go back to sleep, asshole! We were just playing a little gin!" Mitch said, and I never saw him looking so happy.

The candles were extinguished and in a moment Tom was asleep again. I was just dozing off when I heard Mitch's voice.

"Art?" It was sort of a question to see if I was still awake. I made up my mind to answer only if he asked a second time.

"Art!" Not a question this time and a little bit louder.

"Huh?" Half-feigned sleep, but half-real, too.

"Art, we didn't straighten out."

I assumed he meant that we had not taken the $32.00 off the debt. It was rare that he won. I smiled and was genuinely happy for him. "I know it was a big win for you, Mitch, but can't it wait till morning?"

"Hey, Art, of course it can wait till morning. I'm not pressing you."

"What?"

"I said I'm not pressing you for payment. Hell, your credit is good. Don't worry about it. Pay me when you get the money. I trust you."

My jaw fell open and I stared at the ceiling for at least thirty seconds. Then I shifted to my right side and stared in Mitch's direction. Either he was joking or he was a complete asshole or I was living in an asylum. If I could just see a smile on his big face, I would have some inkling. But it was dark in the room and I could see nothing. It was after four and I just didn't care to pursue the matter any further. So I closed my eyes and slept.

12

● ●

I must admit it really was a "workable plan." We invited all
of our fraternity brothers to see the movie and we told them
the truth. The show was being run as a benefit for Mitch, who
had fallen upon hard times in his gin-playing. We didn't pub-
licize it outside the fraternity because of the space limitations
of the apartment. The projector and screen were loaned to us
by the Political Science Department. Tom had gone to his
professor and got the equipment at no charge . . . he had
explained to them that it was for educational use. It was out of
character for Tom, who rarely lied, but in a way the movie was
educational.

The turnout was good—much better than we had even expected. Forty-eight of the "brothers" showed up at our apartment and five of them even brought dates. And then, of course,
there was Wickers. Now that's a hell of a good turnout.

While Tom was saying hello and Mitch was saying thanks,
I made damn sure that I was in complete control of the most
important part of the afternoon. I personally collected the
money.

I felt that if I didn't make the actual collection, there would
be a shrinkage of the proceeds. Mitch wouldn't just take the

money. That would be too simple. He'd make up some out-landish tale. Or he'd find some unforeseen expense. I wanted to avoid all of this, so I announced that I would be handling the money. Surprisingly, there were no objections.

"Okay, Tom," Mitch said. "Show the fuckin' movie!" The line got a long, nervous laugh.

I watched the people in the audience. I was nearing the end of my college career, and this might be my last opportunity to see all of my friends together. For my first three years at Keystone, it was the fraternity that was the focal point. The fraternity was where my friendship with Tom and Mitch began. We pledged together during our freshman year. Mitch got his bid because he was a jock, or at least the brothers thought he was a jock. He certainly looked like one. Mitch told them he had wrestled in high school. A jock was a prized possession for a fraternity—even a third-rate jock like Mitch, whose only sports were eating, drinking, and gin-playing.

Getting Tom Nelson, Jr., was a real coup for the rushing chairman. Tom was the number-one pick—dean's list, debating team, student government. And he was good-looking, came from the right kind of family, wore the right kind of clothes. Tom had class!

I really don't know why I got a bid to pledge Delta Pi Beta. When the brothers asked the question "What will Arthur do for the House?" I can't imagine what the answer might have been. I was not a jock or a great student. I had no campus activities, so I must have come through on my own merits, whatever they might have been. Maybe they thought I was clever or humorous or musically inclined.

These were not the same guys that were there when we pledged Delta Pi Beta. But the faces were the same . . . generally good-looking. They were slender to medium-build and had short hair. All wore the same costume—khaki chinos with belts in the back, button-down oxford shirts with a button in the back, argyle socks and black-and-white saddle shoes with nothing in the back, and most important, a tan Barracuda jacket. The engineers in the group adorned their belts with slide rules, but engineers were kept at a minimum because they were dull.

I stationed my chair near the door of the apartment which placed me a few feet behind the screen. I stared at the faces that stared at the screen and I was not sidetracked by Candy Barr, who had begun her tricks. As the flickering lights reflected on the wide-eyed faces, I sat and reflected on fraternity life at Keystone.

"Okay, you jack-offs, this is it!"

The brothers had burst into our pledge meeting, wielding heavy wooden paddles. Their faces were not unlike those of Nazi storm troopers. We were immediately aware that Hell-week was beginning and that our long, tedious pledgeship would end in a few days.

"Grab your jewels and assume the position!" Translation: We are about to beat the shit out of you. We are going to give you something meaningful so that you will always remember your pledgeship at our beloved Delta Pi Beta. Therefore, in the age-old manner, prescribed by years of brotherhood, you may bend slightly from the waist. Get a good grip on your balls because they might drop down and be sent into orbit.

Tom Nelson, Jr., was our pledge president. He guided and counseled his pledge brothers. We were on an arduous journey in our search for the true meaning of fraternity, and Tom constantly tried to buoy us up. Sometimes he was criticized by the other pledges, but he never wavered or lost his genuine interest in us.

In the midst of the paddling, a somber-faced Tom would weave in and out between brothers and pledges, bringing us hope and solace. While each man was screaming, Tom would bestow his benevolent look—a knowing smile—upon him.

Tom said, "The paddling is important in our search for true fraternalism. We don't understand it now—but we will. I promise you, we'll know someday. When we're brotherized, we'll have all the answers. Just bear with it! You won't regret it!" Then he continued on his mission of mercy.

He would catch our eye and get that mystical look. Then he'd close his eyes halfway, nod his head rapidly, and move his fingers up and down. He said nothing, but the message was loud and clear—"Don't give up! Don't be too upset! Hang in there! Soon you'll know!"

After I had absorbed a particularly vicious whack which sent me flying, Tom was there to catch me. "Trust me, Art," he whispered. "When they put that Delta Pi Beta pin on you, you're going to know!" I looked at this good person and trusted him.

For six days we competed in relay races, putting out fires by urination or spitting some vile concoction. But the climax of Hellweek was the "garbage" game. We were told to lie on our backs in metal coffin-type containers that were normally used for mixing mortar. Then the brothers poured honey, vinegar, and oil on us. When we were drenched with this foul mixture, they coated us with chicken feathers. The screaming reached a crescendo when they began dumping real garbage—directly from the can. The Master Frater embellished the festivities with his own tour de force. He mounted a stepladder high above us and cracked raw eggs together, directing the mixture into our open mouths.

Now let me remind you that this was not an insane asylum or a witch's coven or the My Lai Massacre. The brothers were newspaper editors, members of honor societies, debating-team captains, class presidents, and R.O.T.C. officers, and all of these classy guys worked themselves into a frenzy shouting obscenities at us. They elbowed each other profusely and slapped their knees and thighs. They rocked back and forth convulsively and laughed so hard that tears filled their eyes and their throats ached. It was their finest hour and they loved it.

The highlight of these festivities came on the seventh day when we stood solemnly, holding large, unlit candles. On the far end of the darkened rathskeller, where we had recently reclined in a trough, now stood the Master Frater, resplendent in a beautiful, flowing white robe. The hands that previously held raw eggs now clutched a flaming torch and a Bible.

"Come, ignite your candles with the eternal flame of brotherhood!" When we had all touched our candles to his torch he said, "By the sacred powers vested in me, I now proclaim you brothers of our beloved Delta Pi Beta. Welcome, welcome, thrice welcome!" And from the brothers came exuberant shouts of " 'Tis well!" and "Yea, verily yea!" Then the Master Frater attached the fraternity pin to our blue blazers.

The lights came on and Tom came running toward me. He extended his hand and I clasped it. Despite the tears in his eyes, he smiled broadly and nodded his head. He whispered, "*Now* you know, Art," and he winked. Confused, I spun around to take in the entire rathskeller scene. All of the other brothers, both old and new, were also smiling, nodding, and winking. But dammit, I still did not know. I wanted to scream, but everyone else seemed to know. Maybe I missed something. So I smiled, nodded, and winked too. And afterward I got very, very drunk.

13

· ·

Why did I pledge Delta Pi Beta? Why did I spend close to five months of my life as a modern-day slave? At best, my pledgeship was a steady flow of worthless tasks. Why did I go through that bullshit? It was bad enough that I finished the whole degrading mess, but it's even worse that I never even considered quitting.

What in hell attracted me to the House? I don't even remember hearing a political discussion there. I can't recall any arguments on civil rights or women's rights. There were no marches, rallies, strikes, or protests.

I can recall only one occasion when the brothers displayed a degree of interest in current events. When the Holy Father, Pope Pius XII, lay dying in Rome, the brothers kept a constant vigil at the television set. They had organized a betting pool as to what hour the pontiff would pass on, and interest ran high because of the $24.00 that would be won by the lucky brother when the unlucky Father expired.

When I think of this docile, uneventful style of living in the House, it is difficult to understand how or why there was Hell-week. Why did a group of mindless young men whose interest ran low in important areas build up such a raging enthusiasm in the basest sort of activity? I don't know the answer. That was just the way things were in those days, and you just didn't question it.

Candy Barr was completing her tricks. She was now doing her last scene, which involved some pretty fancy group techniques. I stared first at the brothers, who were shouting their approval, and then at Charles Wickers, who was laughing in that high-pitched cackle. It was at this moment that I made a very important observation.

I determined that Wickers was the strangest person I had ever met. He definitely heard things that were inaudible to everyone else—voices, I assumed. There had to be voices talking to him constantly. This would account for his totally unpredictable behavior and would explain his silly giggle when others were sober-faced, the sad countenance during an otherwise hysterical scene, and the seemingly foolish, unrelated statements that popped into his conversation. There just had to be voices.

The movie was over. The brothers were buzzing among themselves and moving toward the door. Any lingering doubts I may have had about having moved out of the House and renting the apartment were firmly erased from my mind. My only regret was that I hadn't moved out sooner.

When the last brother had left, babbling some nonsense about how I should visit the House more often and renew old friendships, a great sense of relief overcame me. I was pleased to be rid of them and looked forward to the quiet hours I might spend by myself. I closed the door, turned, and was quite startled to see Wickers still sitting in my living room.

The room was still dark, and this single person sitting with his back toward me was an eerie sight. He sat erect in the chair and there was absolutely no movement in his body. Either he was transfixed in some sort of hypnotic state or he was dead. I hoped that it was not the latter. The recent proceedings had completely enervated me, and I was not in the mood to cope with the death of Wickers. I approached him cautiously from the rear, and when I was abreast of him, I was relieved to see that he was alive, although he did appear to be under a spell. He was staring at the blank movie screen. Despite my intrusion into the periphery of his wide-eyed scan, he remained completely still.

Perhaps the stag movie had triggered him into a catatonic condition. I stood silently and looked at this strange person, hoping he would soon come out of whatever he was in.

Then, after ten long seconds had elapsed, Wickers said, "Ahthuh, what's your favorite kind of soda?" When he spoke, his eyes never moved from the empty screen. It was like watching a blind man.

"Coke, I guess," and I suppose I should have added something like, "why do you ask?" But by now I had become used to his madness. It went along with my "voices" theory, and I just didn't care to pursue the matter. I thought longingly of my bed, the most perfect way to end the afternoon, and this oddball was keeping me from it.

He stared at the screen. Finally, he got up and walked toward the door. I stopped him before he opened it.

"Charles, tell me something," I said. "What is it about you that I like?"

He thought for a moment. "I really don't know, Ahthuh."

"That's just it, Charles. Neither do I."

14

● ●

You have met some of the grandest masters of deceit. And along with the liars you have seen sadists, a nymphomaniac, a prick, and several assorted lunatics. But with the exception of Al Carter's pen fiasco at the student bookstore, I have not talked about any thievery. And Al would give you a pretty convincing argument that what he did was not actually stealing.

But Mitch was a thief. No question about it. He was a shoplifter and he was quite good at it. Like Al, he rationalized that he really was doing nothing wrong. But in Mitch's case, there were no shades of gray. What he did was outright stealing, and while morally it was the same as Al's escapades, in the eyes of the law it was quite different.

Mitch was a specialist. He stole food at the Save-a-Penny Food Store, a medium-sized supermarket near the Keystone campus. He liked the friendly personnel there, and he felt they sold high-quality products.

At first, Mitch never discussed his peculiar method of food shopping. He would always go alone to Save-a-Penny and "buy" only for himself. This way he was able to keep his stealing from Tom and me. He was familiar with Tom's holier-than-thou attitude, and he didn't want any lectures.

I discovered his secret by accident. One day he had borrowed my car and had forgotten to return the keys. I was in a hurry to get to the car, and Mitch was in the shower. It had been raining most of the day, so I assumed the keys would be in Mitch's blue raincoat, which was hanging in the hall closet.

I opened the closet door and reached into the pocket of the raincoat. Surprise number one. There was no bottom to the pocket. It had been ripped out of the coat. I tried the other side and—surprise number two—the bottom on that side was missing also.

Having one pocket missing could be normal, but the absence of both pockets was too coincidental. There was something sinister going on. My first thought was that Mitch, my wonderful roommate and trusted friend, was a pervert. A man who wore a raincoat as much as he did was suspect to begin with. Almost daily there were stories of men dressed in raincoats who roamed the campus. They would wait for an unsuspecting co-ed to approach, and when they got within a few feet of their prospective victims—Whammo! The raincoat would be flipped open, and to quote the great Charles Wickers, they would expose their members, which would invariably be in a state of tumescence.

I listened to Mitch happily singing the Fight Song in the shower. It was hard to believe that he could be the campus pervert. But he did wear that raincoat an awful lot—even when it wasn't raining. That was one telltale sign of a true pervert. And now there was this business of the two missing pockets—certainly another bit of damaging evidence. Jesus! No pockets! How very convenient for a pervert who specialized in exposing himself.

I didn't know exactly what I was searching for, but again I reached into the bottomless pocket. My hand sank further and further until I was in up to my armpit. I was at the very bottom of the lining. I felt something vaguely familiar, but it just couldn't be. You just don't keep something like that in a raincoat. I began withdrawing the foreign object.

I never heard the water stop. I was too engrossed in my work. I never heard the bathroom door open. Nor did I hear Mitch approach me from the rear. Apparently while I was exercising my sixth sense, he was acting on his as well. He stood behind me menacingly. Now my sixth sense went to work again and I felt his presence. I quickly turned to face him with my right arm still in the cookie jar.

I was shocked to see him standing there, exposing himself. Then I remembered he had just showered, and his costume was perfectly permissible. Unfortunately, Mitch did not feel the same way about my conduct.

"May I ask, what the fuck are you doing?"

I withdrew the object, and my eyes confirmed what my fingers had hypothesized. "Mitch, what is this?"

He looked at my discovery. "Are you blind? It's a fuckin' lobster tail. Now, what are you looking for in my raincoat?"

I thought back to when he had attacked me, and I was frightened. Tom was at the library, so there was no one to save me should Mitch strike again.

"I was just looking for my keys. You did borrow my car, you know." I said it with enough animosity to take some pressure off me. I was in a precarious position and the gambit worked.

He nodded and said, "Here, give me that fuckin' lobster tail!" He walked into the kitchen and I heard the refrigerator door open and shut. Then he went back into the bathroom to finish drying himself.

Dinnertime was extremely quiet. As usual, Tom ate a meager cheese sandwich on white bread, I had a greasy hamburger, and Mitch—well, Mitch had lobster tail. The silence during the meal was reminiscent of earlier days when the gin-playing had stopped and the cold war was being waged.

Mitch broke the ice. "I guess you're wondering about the lobster tail," he said with a mouthful of lobster tail.

"No, not at all, Mitch."

"Fuckin' liar!"

"Look, I don't care if you carry lumps of cowshit or a diamond-studded douche bag in your raincoat. It's perfectly okay with me. You do whatever you want—it's a free country, isn't it?"

"Don't give me your crap! You're dying to know about that lobster tail."

Tom was puzzled. "Hey, what's going on here?" he asked.

"Mind your own fuckin' business!" Mitch said.

"I don't have to sit here and listen to your Gestapo-like tactics," Tom said.

I had a distinct feeling that Mitch was trying to break some dreadful news to us, but just didn't know exactly how to go about doing it. "Our friend Mitch carries a spare lobster tail in his raincoat. He never knows when he might need one."

"It so happens, I got that lobster tail at Save-a-Penny."

"They certainly package their merchandise in a strange way," I said. Both Tom and I began to suspect the worst.

Tom continued the cross-examination. "I'm not sure if I heard correctly, sir. Did you say you bought or got the lobster tail at Save-a-Penny? Please repeat your answer!"

"You little pisspot! I'm not on trial here! Who's the Gestapo now?"

"Did you buy it?" I asked softly.

"Yeah, in a way I bought it."

"Mitch, I have a premonition that we are going to hear an Al Carter story," I said.

"It's a known fact," Mitch said, "Save-a-Penny charges more than any other market in town, anyone will tell you that."

"It seems to me your option is to buy elsewhere," Tom said. "I priced a sport jacket yesterday and I thought the price was too high, but that didn't give me the right to steal the coat."

"But Save-a-Penny is convenient for us. Why should I drive your car a mile or two when I can walk to Save-a-Penny? You should be happy about that, Art."

"Yeah, thanks a lot, Mitch. I really appreciate that."

"And besides, I didn't steal anything. It's true I didn't pay for a couple of lousy lobster tails, but I paid the full price for all the other items. And as I said, Save-a-Penny overcharges for everything. It averages out."

Tom was outraged. "You know, Mitch, your moral code, or lack of one, is really amazing. Now you can twist things as much as you want to suit your own conscience, but in my mind you're nothing more than a petty thief." He got up from the table and began to walk away.

"A petty thief, huh? You're full of shit, Tom. You're really full of shit!" Mitch shouted the last few words at Tom, who was now sitting on the living-room couch, reading the newspaper. Then he continued in his own defense. "I'm no thief, Art. My parents are not wealthy by any means. I'm on a limited budget. You know that. I don't steal everything in sight. I take only food products—and only what I can eat—and only from Save-a-Penny. You better believe that, Art. It's the truth. Let shit-fingers in there think whatever he wants. But I'm no thief."

I once heard a similar argument from a hunter. "I don't kill at random," he had said. "I eat everything I shoot. Nothing is wasted." And to emphasize, he pompously added, "Hunting is man's way of harvesting nature's overproduction."

I applied the hunter's words to what Mitch had already rationalized and came up with an entirely new image of my roommate. He was no petty thief, tearing through the stores of small independent businessmen on a wild plundering spree. He was a romantic figure in blue, and it was always harvest time at Save-a-Penny, the citadel of business treachery. Mitch was a modern-day Robin Hood, taking from the rich and giving to the poor, which in this case was himself. He didn't steal indiscriminately, and like the hunter, he ate everything he took.

My mind was whirring now. How could I best channel this new-found energy to my advantage? A lot of time had elapsed since we showed the stag film, and in spite of this successful venture, the debt had risen again. We were at the point where I might again call for a new workable plan.

"Mitch, I certainly don't condone stealing, but I have to admit that it doesn't sound so terrible the way you describe it." I was leading into my own workable plan. In the living room, Tom rattled his newspaper and shook his head, but Mitch was pleased that I wasn't going to lecture him. "You're right," I continued. "Goddamn Save-a-Penny does overcharge for their merchandise."

"Fuckin' A!"

"But there's one point I want to get clear. I have one question for you."

"Ask away, Arthur." Mitch was completely relaxed now. He leaned back in his chair and picked a large piece of lobster meat out of his teeth.

"You say that it's okay because you don't steal indiscriminately."

"Right!"

"You eat everything you take, so there's no waste. And of course you do pay for some items, so it's not as if you're really stealing that much."

"Right! Right!" He started on his dessert—a bowl of potato chips—and I wondered whether they were part of the Save-a-Penny harvest.

"Do you believe that your actions are moral because *you* eat the food or because the food is eaten?"

"You jay-ohin' me, man?"

"No, I'm perfectly serious."

"Well, what kind of dumb fuckin' question is that? It doesn't make any sense."

"Let me put it to you in a different way. Let's say you took some food and another person—a friend for instance—helped you eat the merchandise."

"You, for instance?"

"Me, for instance."

"Jee-zuz, Art, are you nuts?" Tom shouted from the living room. "That would make you as big a crook as he is."

"Disregard Tom," I said to Mitch. "Suppose I shared a lobster tail with you from time to time. Would *my* eating the food affect your plan?"

Mitch was silent for a moment. "What's in it for me?" he asked finally.

"I'll get to that in a minute. But first let me show you why I think your plan would remain intact. You wouldn't be stealing indiscriminately. All of the food would still be eaten—the only difference is that two people would do the eating. You'd still be harvesting some of Save-a-Penny's profits, but we both know they overcharge. Of course, you'd still pay for some items just like you've been doing all along. No difference whatsoever. What do you think?"

"I think you're a fool," Tom said as he stood. He was upset. "Mitch is an animal, but you should know better."

"You little pipsqueak! I'll kick your fuckin' head in!" Mitch said, and he pushed his chair backward.

"Save your strength, Mitch. I'm leaving. I have no desire to spend any more time in your company. Yours either, Art. You're both crooks." He walked across the living room and entered the bedroom, slamming the door behind him.

"Just stay in there, Tom, and watch your people! See what's going on next door!" Mitch was shouting loud enough to be heard through the closed bedroom door. "Just remember this, you little creep! Peeping is just as much a crime as shoplifting!" Then Mitch turned to me and again said, "What's in it for me?"

"It will be your new workable plan and it will be even better than the last one. Don't get me wrong! The movie was a great idea, but it was only a one-shot deal. This is the only way you can finally pay off the debt. Finish it. Get it and me off your back for all times."

Mitch seemed to be absorbing my speech, and I was certain he would go along with my wishes. He popped a chip into his mouth. He stared at me while he digested the chip and what I had said. He was ripe and needed just a bit more persuasion.

"You know, Mitch, I feel that once the debt was eliminated, or even just reduced to a moderate level, your card-playing would automatically improve. I'm sure of it. With that weight off you, I know you would play a better game. Without pressure you might even put *me* in the red. Now wouldn't that be nice for a change?"

"What if I'm caught?"

"How long have you been—uh—shopping at Save-a-Penny?"

"Almost a year now."

"Have you ever been caught before?" It was fallacious thinking at its worst, but it seemed to work on Mitch.

"Yeah, I guess you're right."

Now it was time for my coup de grace. "And do you want to know the best part? You won't have to do anything more than what you're doing now. The routine will be exactly the same— only the size of the harvest will change. Now, is it a deal?"

"It's a deal," Mitch said, and we shook hands.

Mitch and I were cleaning up the kitchen while Tom checked on the people next door. Mitch, for reasons which I now was able to understand, enjoyed some elaborate meals. So he headed the clean-up committee and I gave him some very minor assistance when I wasn't napping. Both of us were elated with the new agreement and had been running through some of the details.

I knew the big question would come up eventually, so I decided to get in the first licks. "Mitch, have you given any thought to how we'll apply the food to the debt?"

"What are you getting at?"

"Let me repeat what I said before. I don't in any way consider this to be stealing, but in the eyes of society you'll be giving me stolen goods."

"What's the point?"

"You know what a fence is?"

"I sense a con job coming on."

"It's no con job. We have to work out the discount."

"You're out of your fuckin' mind! I'm not giving you any discount!" he said.

I tried to restrain myself. "Mitch," I said softly, "I'm going to be fencing stolen merchandise. There's not a fence in the world who would pay the retail price for stolen goods. You must discount the merchandise."

"You goddamn prick! A fence resells the goods. You're not going to resell anything. You're going to eat it—all of it. So don't give me that fence shit! Try to be honest for once in your life!"

I bristled from his last remark. It was farcical coming from the mouth of the number-one charlatan in the state of Pennsylvania. But I finally had my fish on the line and I wasn't about to let him off the hook. "Let's be fair about this thing, Mitch. You're going to be paying me in lobster tails. Right? I assume that's your specialty and that's fine with me. I really like lobster tails. As food goes, I don't think you could find anything finer."

"Fuckin' smartass!"

"Yes, but as I was saying—"

"You're not funny, Art!"

"Okay, I'll be serious. As much as I like lobster tails, I'm sure you'll agree they're not the primary rate of currency in this country. I can't buy a shirt with a lobster tail. I can't pull into a gas station and say, 'Two lobster tails' worth,' I can't—"

"Don't talk down to me!"

"I'm sorry, Mitch, but you lost money to me in a gin game. It was understood that you'd pay me in *money*. I've agreed to accept lobster tails in lieu of cash, and I feel I should be compensated for that."

I had talked to him in a kind way and I thought I had made my points well. I was surprised when he slammed his fist down on the kitchen table, which I knew was a prelude to a barrage of indignant remarks. That's why I welcomed the knocking at the door.

I ran quickly across the living room and opened the door. It was Wickers. "We're in space, Ahthuh," he said. It was a typical Wickers thing to say, since it had nothing to do with anything he and I ever spoke about before. Months ago I would have been puzzled by such nonsense, but now I just didn't give a shit.

"That's good, Charles. I'm happy for you," I said, closing the door in his face. Apparently one of his voices had asked him where he was and that was his perfectly logical answer.

"Who was that?" Mitch shouted.

"No one—absolutely no one. Don't worry about it." Then I had a change of heart. "Ah, shit!" I turned and walked back to the door. I just couldn't do it—even to a madman like Wickers. I opened the door again and saw he hadn't moved. "Come on in, Charles!"

He followed me back into the living room. "Isn't it exciting, Ahthuh?"

"Yeah, it's really great!"

He looked around the room. "Aren't you watching it on TV?"

"Watching what, Charles?"

"The space flight. We put our first man in space—a three-hundred-mile suborbital flight. May I?" His hand was on the TV set. I couldn't care less about a space flight. But if watching it on TV kept Wickers away from me, I was all for it. I nodded to him and returned to the kitchen.

The TV account of Commander Alan Shepard's historic flight formed the background for the remainder of our own historic argument. Of the two, the latter is by far the more vivid in my mind.

"Society considers my actions illegal—right?" Mitch jumped right back in, but at least he was relatively calm now. The short pause in the action had defused him.

"You better believe it!"

"If I were caught I'd be in trouble."

"No doubt."

"Most likely I'd be thrown out of school."

"Good chance of it."

"Might even be sent to jail."

"Oh, it's a possibility, I guess. But as a first offender, I doubt very much that—"

"Look, big shot, the point is that I'm taking a risk—a big risk. And that's more than I can say for you. If I get caught, absolutely nothing happens to you."

"Mitch, there's no earthly reason why I should take a risk. This is no joint venture. We're not in this together. I want you to pay your debt, and this is how you've decided to do it."

"Getting caught would keep me out of medical school. I may never practice medicine because of this."

I thought of the rejections that continued to pour in daily. Graduation was only a month away and this silly ass didn't have a prayer to get into medical school. He would be lucky enough just to get out of college. "Mitch, the risk is the same whether you steal—uh, shop—for yourself or for both of us."

"Fuck you!" Mitch said. Now I was in trouble. As long as the argument had been flowing on logical or even semilogical grounds, I had a chance. But now the debate had taken an ugly turn. There was no way to argue against a "Fuck you!"

"What kind of thing is that to say? 'Fuck you'? You just don't say 'Fuck you' to a person when you're in the middle of a serious talk."

"I'll say 'Fuck you!' whenever I want. And I'll say it again— 'Fuck you!'—and once more—'Fuck you!' Any objections?"

"I suppose our little talk is at a close," I said.

"No, it isn't. I'll go ahead with our deal," Mitch said. "But I want the lobster tails valued at twenty percent above the price marked on the package."

"Fuck you!"

"Oh, now it's 'Fuck me'! I see. It's okay for you to say it but not for me."

"You have absolutely no justification for adding on to the price," I said.

"I have every justification. First of all, I'm taking a risk. Secondly, this is a gambling debt, and I don't give a shit what you say—a gambling debt is *not* the same as any other debt. You didn't lend me any money. You didn't sell me anything either, so it's not the same. You thought you wouldn't be paid at all. So be happy with the plan. Twenty percent *above retail,* that's it."

It certainly was a great philosophical debate, but I feared that we were now hopelessly deadlocked. The great Save-a-Penny harvest would never get off the ground and the debt would not be paid.

Then Mitch said, "Wait a minute. I have a great idea!"

"Let's put on a show!" I said.

"No, let's call on the great mediator. Let him settle it. Let Tom decide."

"That is one hell of a good idea. We'll defer to his scrupulous fairness."

We were elated with the idea and went marching through the living room on our way to meet the Wonderful Wizard, Tom Nelson. But a funny thing happened on the way to the bedroom.

As we went by Wickers he said, "This is a great day for America."

"Stick it up your ass!" Mitch said, and we both laughed.

Wickers was not to be put down. "In less than ten years, we'll have a man on the moon."

In perfect unison both Mitch and I said, "Big, fucking deal!" This time we broke into hysterical laughter and were exceedingly raucous when we smashed open the bedroom door.

The bedroom had been uncommonly quiet. But we could hardly be expected to consider the polite way to enter a bedroom—especially when our minds were so preoccupied.

We poured into the darkened room, bringing light from the living room and a lot of boisterous shouting. "Tom, we must talk with you!"

"Knock it off! Jee-zuz Christ!—And shut that goddamn

door!" It was a shrieking, anguished animal noise that came out of Tom's mouth—so very different from his normally calm voice. I had never heard him swear before, so I was instantly aware that we had stumbled in at a most inopportune moment. He had been lying prone on his bed and he propped himself up on an elbow when he turned to silence us. Now he was again flat and low on his stomach, and he shifted his eyes back to where they had been before our rude intrusion.

We followed the path of his stare out through our open window, across the six and a half feet to the other open window, into the other bedroom, and right on to Tom's people. Both man and woman were naked. He was lying on his back and she was kneeling at his side, striking a pose reminiscent of the famous Marilyn Monroe calendar. It looked like the beginning of a torrid sex scene.

Tom, after months of striking out, had finally hit pay dirt. Or, I should say he was on the verge of it. But, because of our loud entrance or Tom's excited reaction to us, the couple knew they were being watched. They looked at us. In a flash, a luscious pair of breasts went flying toward the window, while the man in the background shouted obscenities. She pulled the cord and the venetian blinds fell to the window sill, cutting the scene before it really even began.

"Damn!" said Tom. "Damn! Damn!" He stood up and threw his political-science book to the floor. Then he sat down on the edge of the bed and held his head in his hands. He was the picture of utter dejection.

"We're really sorry, Tom," I said.

"We didn't know," Mitch added.

"Do you know how much time I've put into this? Do you know how many hours I've spent waiting? I was almost there and you guys ruined it!"

Mitch and I sat down on the edge of the other bed. We knew how much this meant to Tom, so we sat quietly across from him, nodding our heads from time to time in commiseration. We were on a condolence call and poor Tom was the bereaved.

Suddenly Wickers stuck his head in the room. "He's in the watah now," he said to the three of us. Tom didn't look up, but Mitch and I turned toward him. We looked at Wickers for a second or two, but said nothing. Then we turned around and faced Tom again.

"There'll be other times, Tom," Mitch said. "You'll get to see them again. I know you will." He reached over and touched him on the shoulder.

Tom slowly shook his head. He was much too distraught to answer. The three of us sat silently for several minutes, while the Navy Band and Charles Wickers sang "God Bless America" to welcome Commander Shepard.

Then Tom gave a great sigh and attempted to pull himself together. He lifted his head and for the first time he looked right at us. I saw that his eyes were red. "No, there won't be other times," Tom said pensively. "They'll never leave those blinds open again. Not while they're in bed, anyway. I've been watching them since September and this was the first time and the last time. I almost had it, but now it's lost forever." He was fairly steady now, and he seemed ready to accept the raw deal that fate had handed him. He stood up muttering, "I was so close—so close," and he walked past us.

"We're really sorry, Tom," we said again, standing up in respect, but the damage had already been done.

Much later, when we felt a sufficient amount of time had passed, we went to Tom again. He was sitting at the kitchen table, eating his bedtime snack of cookies and milk and reflecting on what might have been. Mitch turned his chair backwards and sat down, draping his arms over the back of the chair. Tom just sat quietly staring at nothing in particular, popping one Oreo after another. He sipped the milk, rolled it around until the cookie got soggy, then swallowed. I sat on the other side of Tom. Both Mitch and I awaited each other's opening of the conversation. Finally, Mitch gave me a short nod, indicating that it might be better for me to begin.

"Tom, we'd like to get your opinion on something." There was no answer. "You see," I went on, "Mitch and I are having a disagreement on a matter and—well, we thought you might be able to give us your opinion." Tom sipped his milk, said nothing, and continued to stare at the wall.

"Who the fuck does he think he is? Helen Keller?" Mitch was getting impatient. I shook my head at him. You just didn't treat Tom that way, especially now.

"Tom, I'd like you to listen to our case." I spoke softly. "I'm very serious. We both value your judgment." Again no answer. I lightly touched his sleeve to get his attention. "Tom, do you hear me?"

"You should have knocked," Tom said.

"Yes, yes, of course we should have. It was stupid. We didn't think."

"It's the least you could have done. Just a common courtesy for a friend."

"You're right. Of course, you're right. Mitch, isn't Tom right?" As his answer, Mitch extended his middle finger in the classic gesture. When Tom turned to him, he had already inserted the finger into his ear and was digging away.

"Sure! You're fucking A! I agree with Art. Look, tomorrow is Saturday. If you're still charged up, we'll get a hold of J.P. and ride down to Harrisburg."

"You completely missed the point. That's not what I want."

Sometimes Mitch was so goddamned thick-headed. Instead of backing off, he plunged right in. "Maybe I could arrange to leave the door open when I'm in with Daisy, and you could watch. That would make up for today."

"You're a fool, sir, and an unmitigated ass," Tom said to Mitch.

Things were rapidly deteriorating, and I found myself in the unenviable position of mediating between Mitch and Tom. I decided to make one last attempt.

"For Christ's sake, Tom, will you pull yourself together? Don't let him get to you. And you," I said to Mitch, "will you shut that big fucking mouth of yours?" It seemed to be language they both understood.

"Tom, you had a setback. I'm sorry, but believe me, there'll be other days. You've got to rise above this. You have a promising legal career ahead of you. That's why we came to you in the first place. Now, will you mediate this for us or won't you?"

Tom slowly sipped his milk, and I'm sure he had at least one flash of the kneeling lady with the big jugs. Then he set the glass down with authority and said, "You may proceed with the case."

Both Mitch and I sighed, and I began, "Your Honor, my roommate has, over the past eight months, run up a sizable debt with me because of his complete ineptness at gin rummy." Mitch stopped picking his nose and glared at me, but he didn't interrupt. "Now, Your Honor, we've finally agreed on a workable payment plan. He will be paying off in lobster tails."

"What the hell is going on here?" Tom shouted. "Is this what you wanted me to mediate? This is why you barged into my room? Oh, good God! To think I lost out for this! I won't listen!"

"You agreed. You can't go back on your word," Mitch said.

"You already know how I feel about this. You're a thief! I told you that before. There's nothing to mediate."

Here we were, getting thrown out of court before we even presented the case. The judge was really pissed off, but I held my ground.

"Tom, we're not asking you to judge whether this is ethical or moral or even legal. We've already worked that out between us. That's no longer your concern. We're asking you only to mediate a problem."

"No!"

"Someday you're going to be an attorney. Your clients won't all be innocent. Some of them will be guilty as sin. Will you refuse to defend them? Would you deny a person his rights just because you disagree with him? I hope not. Two friends who value both your friendship and your advice come to you with a problem. Do you refuse to listen because of a silly prejudice you might have against thieves?" Mitch was glaring at me, but he sensed a breakthrough.

Tom was doing some deep thinking. He rose slowly from the table and went to the refrigerator. While he was pouring another glass of milk and his back was toward us, I smiled at Mitch and flashed a V-sign, which in those days meant "victory." He returned the smile and again flashed his middle finger.

Tom returned with his glass of milk. He sat down and deliberated for another ten seconds. Then he said, "You may proceed with the case!"

It was a splendid trial. Both Mitch and I presented our arguments and Tom listened to every word. It was conducted with considerable dignity. And all the while we spoke, the TV droned on about the successful flight of Freedom Seven, punctuated by Wickers' squeals of delight. America's entrance into the space race was completely eclipsed by Mitch's impending race to the Save-a-Penny.

At last, both of us finished our respective arguments. Tom said, "There are several serious considerations involved here— some deep ramifications. I'll need some time to deliberate." He got up from the table and started toward the bedroom.

"Tom," I called after him. "You're not going to check on the folks next door, are you?"

He never turned around, but in a voice filled with new-found inner strength, he said, "No, Art, it's all over—I'll just have to accept it." Then this tragic figure retired to his chambers.

While Tom deliberated, Mitch and I played a few rounds of gin. Card-playing was the best time absorber. If we hadn't had gin rummy, we might have developed some rotten habits like studying or watching TV with Wickers.

Speaking of Wickers, just then he poked his head around the corner. I knew he was there from the scowl on Mitch's face.

"Looks like croziah," Wickers said.

"Sure does," Mitch said quickly. In fact his reply came so rapidly that I thought maybe he knew what a crozier was.

"What did that mean?" I asked Mitch.

"I have no idea, but why get involved with his bullshit?"

"Well, for once I'm going to see what makes this lunatic tick. I say that he's tuned in to something that we can't hear. Voices—I say he hears voices." I played the hand until I picked the card I was waiting for. "Gin!" I said, laying down the cards.

"Shit!" yelled Mitch. "You're really busted! You don't pick a single card the whole game and you go gin."

"Just lucky, I guess. You total it up. I'm going to have a little talk with Mistah Wickahs." I went into the living room and sat down on the couch.

"Charles, what is a crozier—or a croziah, as you put it?"

"The horse, Ahthuh." His eyes remained transfixed on the television set.

"A horse? A crozier is a horse?"

"Yes."

"Well, then what did you mean when you said, 'Looks like crozier?' You see, you caught us by surprise and that just didn't make any sense. In fact, it still doesn't make any sense. What looks like crozier?"

"The Derby—the Kentucky Derby," he said, and during this entire conversation he never lifted his eyes from the TV.

"You mean Crozier is the name of a horse that's racing in the Kentucky Derby?" Wickers nodded. "When is the Kentucky Derby?" I asked.

"Tomorrow, Ahthuh."

"Now we're getting somewhere. You see, a lot of people kind of think you're not all there, Charles. You say some pretty strange things. Actually, what you say is not all that strange. It's just that you say it at strange times. Do you follow me, Charles?

"No, Ahthuh."

"This business with Crozier, for instance. You were merely giving us your opinion on who would win tomorrow's Kentucky Derby. Right?"

"Yes."

"But you see, Charles, we weren't talking about the Kentucky Derby or even horses, for that matter. As a matter of fact, we've never spoken about horses in this apartment. That's why it sounded so strange when out of nowhere you came in and blurted out that shit about Crozier. Can you see now why we thought it so strange?"

"No I can't, Ahthuh."

I was losing my patience. "Dammit, we weren't talking about horses!"

"But I was."

"Ah, *you* were talking about it? You mean, in your mind, to yourself, silently, you were talking about it?"

"In a way," Wickers said.

"Charles, do you hear voices—voices that talk to you alone?"

For the first time in the conversation he turned and faced me. "You might say that, Ahthuh. I suppose I do."

"What do these voices say?"

"They're different all the time. Sometimes they say humorous things. Sometimes they warn me."

"For instance?"

"Oh, once I was driving near Bahston during a thunderstorm, and the voice told me to be very careful. About a mile up the road, I discovered that the bridge had been washed away by a flash flood."

"Then what you have is sort of a built-in premonition system."

"Do you think I'm crazy?"

"Charles, I always thought you were tuned in to something that we couldn't hear. It makes you different—not crazy. I'd like to think that I'm your friend."

"You ah, Ahthuh."

"Fine. Then as a friend I want to give you some advice. Most of the guys are really intolerant. Oh, they're nice guys and all that, but they just don't have the patience for things that are—different. And some of your statements seem to be a little on the weird side. Now I know that a lot of the things you say are prompted by these voices. This explains a lot of things that I just didn't understand before. But I wouldn't recommend telling the guys about the voices. Somehow this might make you seem even stranger."

"What do you suggest, Ahthuh?"

"I suggest you try to preface your remarks. Take this Crozier business, for instance. You had a detailed discussion in your mind about the Derby. Am I right?" Wickers nodded. "Okay. But you must remember that Mitch and I were not in on your discussion. So, when you popped your head into the kitchen and said, 'Looks like Crozier,' it sounded a little strange. We didn't know what the hell you were talking about. When you say things like this, people think you're—nuts. Try to preface a little bit. In this case you might have said, 'Hey, did you guys know tomorrow is the Kentucky Derby?'"

"If I said that, Mitch would have told me to stick it up my eeass."

"Maybe so. I'm just giving you an example. You might have said, 'Anyone interested in the Kentucky Derby?' That would have been a good opening. Then you might have followed up with 'There's a horse by the name of Crozier running' or 'Does anyone have any preferences?' There's so many ways you could have done it. But you just came barrel-assing in there and said, 'Looks like Crozier!' Do you know what I mean, Charles?"

"I'm beginning to, Ahthuh."

He paused for a moment. He seemed to be holding something back from me, and then decided to make a clean breast of it.

"Sometimes I hear a different type of voice. It just hints at something—sort of a riddle."

"A riddle?"

"The voice will say something like—uh . . ." He was thinking and he stared at the ceiling for what seemed to be a very long time. Maybe he was hearing voices at that very moment.

"Charles?"

"Yes?"

"Are you all right?"

"Yes, I'm fine. You'd appreciate this one, Ahthuh. Do you remember Harrisburg?"

"Sure, but I'd like to forget about it. It was a rotten experience with J.P. and his father."

"It certainly was rotten. But, it's funny how you remember that business about J.P.'s father. I remember my own experience much more vividly."

"Charles, I'm sorry. It was a lousy thing to do to you."

"No, no, Ahthuh, you got it all wrong. What you and Daisy planned was funny. What I did was unfair."

"What did you do?"

"Why, that act I put on for you and the guys."

"An act? What the hell are you talking about?"

"Well, it all started with the voice. If you remember, I was talking to you just before I went in to Daisy."

"Yeah, I remember."

"Well, that's when the voice said, 'Et tu, Brute.' "

"The voice said that?" Wickers nodded. "Then this voice is multilingual."

"No, not really. 'Et tu, Brute' is a fairly famous saying. That's what Julius Ceasah said when Brutus—"

"I'm familiar with the saying, Charles," I said impatiently. "But where's the connection?"

"It was a hint that I was going to be done in by my best friend."

I could feel the blood rising to my face. My conduct in Harrisburg was in the true spirit of Delta Pi Beta. The brothers would be proud. At that moment I was not. I wanted to apologize, but the words didn't come. So I sat in mute silence and listened to this unbelievable person tell his incredible story.

"It took me just a few seconds to solve it, Ahthuh. I discussed it with Daisy. She's quite nice, you know. Well, we both thought your idea was so clevah, Ahthuh, we decided to play the play, as they say. It was rotten to play a trick like that on you, but we really meant no harm. We only did it because we knew you and the guys were counting on us and we didn't want to hurt your feelings."

"But we heard you in there."

"An act."

"But you came to the door."

"Just an act, Ahthuh,"

"Well what the hell were you doing in there all that time?"

Wickers blushed. "We were consummating our affayuh, Ahthuh,"

"And when you went back to her?" Wickers nodded. "You consummated it again?" I asked.

"And a third time for good measah," said Wickers.

I didn't attempt to answer him. I just gaped, and for the first time in my strange association with Wickers, I wondered just who was conning whom.

15

• •

We waited patiently for Tom. He had never taken this much time to reach a verdict. When he had been sequestered for one hour, we were slightly anxious, but this was no ordinary case. By the end of the second hour we were really on edge. But because of the bomb that exploded in our faces the last time we had entered the bedroom, we now had an unspoken agreement to leave Tom alone. The television was off and the gin-playing was over.

Wickers was paging through a new issue of *Time* magazine, and it was he who broke the painful silence. "I've been reading an interesting ahticle in *Time*." Mitch looked up from his solitaire long enough to twist his face into a quick series of taunting contortions. I yawned.

"This is sort of hahd to believe, but do you know what one of the fastest-growing fads is on campus?" It was just too tedious to answer him.

"Mitch, do you know?" Wickers asked.

"Muff-diving," Mitch growled back. He licked his thumb as he prepared to turn over his next card in his game of solitaire.

"No, it's not muff-diving, Mitch," Wickers said. "Ahthuh," he said, "would you cayuh to guess?"

"No, I don't think so, Charles." I was still a bit wary of him.

"Let me read this to you—'From the city colleges on both coasts to the sprawling Midwestern campuses, students throughout the country, in an alarmingly increasing rate, are turning to—?' " He still wanted us to guess.

"If you're going to read the fuckin' article, then read it!" said Mitch.

"Ahthuh?"

"Charles, just read it!"

"Suicide!" He cackled for at least ten seconds while we stared at him. When he had regained his composure, he continued. "It's almost like a fad. When there's a suicide at a particulah school, chances ah there'll be another one befoah too long."

"Why the increase?" Mitch asked. I hadn't heard him ask a serious question in a long time. The atmosphere in the room was getting heavy.

"No one knows for suah. Students just seem to be turning to suicide moah than evah. Some do it aftah receiving a setback."

"Like what?" I asked.

"Like failing in something—not reaching a goal, or having an important plan collapse."

"Well, there's usually some advance notice," I said. "I thought every potential victim really wants help. He indicates when he's thinking about suicide. Then someone can stop him."

"Not always, Ahthuh. Last week, a student at Hahvahd had a minor setback—at least according to his friends it was minor. He acted quite normally. Never even gave a hint. He wasn't irrational. Just said he was going to take a little rest."

I looked at my watch and then at the bedroom door. "How bad a setback must it be?" Suddenly Wickers had become the eminent authority on suicide, and he seemed to revel in the unaccustomed attention we were giving him.

"I guess it varies with the individual. You know the old

saying, Ahthuh. 'One man's meat is another man's poison.' "
He cackled and rocked so hard I thought he would fall off the
couch. When he said "poison," I ran a quick mental inventory
of the medicine cabinet. I looked at Mitch, who, I'm sure, had
similar thoughts. He shook his head.

"What seems to be the most popular method?" Mitch asked.

"Of killing oneself? Nothing elaborate. Seems most students are just—jumping out of windows."

For the second time, Mitch and I went smashing through
the bedroom door.

●●

We fully expected to look out that window and see Tom
lying spread-eagled on a pile of queens and kings. We were so
sure he was dead that we ran past the bed where he was
sleeping.

Our loud noises woke him up, and he immediately assumed
his peeping position. But this time it was only for a split
second. He quickly and sadly remembered that it was all over,
and with that realization weighing heavily on him, Tom closed
his eyes and tried to go back to sleep.

"How was I, Ahthuh?" Wickers had poked his smiling face
into the room.

"How *were* you? You're a goddamn lunatic!" I shouted.
"What the hell do you mean, how were you?"

His face fell. "I led into it nice and easy, the way you suggested befoah."

"Honest to God, Charles, will you please make sense!"

"The voices, Ahthuh," he whispered, trying to keep our
secret intact. "Tom was very quiet in here and I thought he
might have done himself in. It does happen, you know. I could
have blurted out something like 'Tom's dead!' But I remem-

bered our little talk befoah. That's why I led into it so gradually. How did I do?"

"What the hell is going on here?" asked Tom, who was somewhat amazed to hear his own mortality discussed so flippantly.

"Tom," I said, "we thought you might be dead."

"Jee-zuz. You guys are a bunch of crackpots! First you devote your lives to crime and now you're planning my death."

"Look, asshole!" Mitch yelled. "You said you were going to mediate. You never came back and we worried about you. We didn't come in sooner because of what happened earlier. You were supposed to retire to your chambers—not to retire for the night."

"I was tired," said Tom.

"Fine. You slept for two hours. You're not tired anymore. Now, goddamn you, mediate!" Mitch said, and he and I sat down on the other bed. Wickers joined us.

Tom sat up in bed, cleared his throat, and prepared to give his memorable lobster-tail decision.

"Gentlemen, may I preface my remarks by again saying that I consider this entire matter to be personally repugnant. In no way should it be assumed that my forthcoming decision condones your actions. I will not be a party to any crime. Nor will I engage in rationalizations. Crime is crime in this and any other case. I will take no part in what I call Orwellian newspeak. I—"

"What is this shit? Give the goddamn decision and be done with it," said Mitch.

"Tell him, Arthur! Tell him now, or I swear I'm going back to sleep."

"For Christ's sake, Mitch," I said, "will you shut up? You know the rules!" Mitch said no more, but he couldn't hold back a quick karate chop with his left hand to the center of his right arm. The gesture had the same meaning as the extended middle finger, which meant he still objected to the judge's decision.

Wickers wore a wide, beaming smile. "I really like this, Ahthuh," he said with real feeling. "I really do." He was trembling with excitement.

"I'm glad, Charles." I was getting weary of all of them. Up until that moment, I had always felt that college had not prepared me for a specific career. I was badly mistaken. If things should ever go sour in my father's business, I now had enough practical experience to be a zoo-keeper.

Tom continued, "I emphatically object to your venture. However, I have agreed to mediate and I will not repudiate my agreement. It is ironic, but in a way the payment is very well suited to the debt. After all, what better way is there to repay an immoral gambling debt than with stolen food?"

I glanced at Mitch, who silently mimicked Tom with a grotesque face. Then I looked at Wickers, who still wore his frozen smile. He hadn't been so intense since he told the muff-diver story.

"But I will speak no more of morals or ethics."

"Thank God!" Mitch whispered. That was all Tom needed. He laid his head down on the pillow, pulled the blankets up to his neck, and closed his eyes. He was packing up his marbles and going home. "No, no, I'm sorry, Tom," Mitch said. "I didn't mean it. Tell him it was a mistake, Art. Go ahead! Tell him!"

"He didn't mean it, Tom. He won't do it again." This whole scene couldn't be happening. It just had to be a dream.

Even Wickers said, "He didn't mean it, Tom." The three of us managed to coax him up to a sitting position.

"You have both agreed on lobster tails as the prime currency rate. The only matter that concerns this court is how we shall ascertain value. Mitch wants a higher value than retail because he's taking a risk. Art says he is doing Mitch a favor by accepting lobster tails instead of money and therefore a lesser value should be assigned. I feel that compromise is the answer. I say that the only value to be assigned is the one that the people from Save-a-Penny have already assigned to their

· 107 ·

products—*the retail price*—no more, no less. And that, gentlemen, is my decision: we use the exact retail price! Now get out of here and let me sleep!"

It was so simple! Why hadn't we thought of it before? Tom just seemed to always come up with the right answer. How very wise he was!

We turned off the lights and filed out of the darkened room. Wickers said, "This is a great day for the free world!" I didn't know if he was referring to Thomas Harvey Nelson's historic decision or Alan Bartlet Shepard's historic ride. Frankly, I didn't care.

17

● ●

Thus began what Tom came to call the "unholy alliance." From the beginning, he regretted his decision to mediate and he always felt personally responsible for creating a monster. But the arrangement worked fairly well and lasted almost to the very end of our senior year, when powers beyond our control caused a rupture in the agreement.

We abided by Tom's decision and valued the lobster tails at the retail price. After each harvest we carefully itemized my portion of the booty and subtracted it from the debt, which had become like the burning bush in the Old Testament—it was never extinguished. Mitch usually managed to lose as much or more than my food was worth.

I went to the Save-a-Penny just to see Mitch in action. He was a master in his craft. He always prayed for inclement weather, which would justify his wearing a raincoat. But mild weather never kept him home. During a heat wave he just waited until after sundown.

He started in produce. He would carefully inspect an apple, shining it on the sleeve of his raincoat. When he found one that met his expectations, he had it weighed and placed it in the shopping cart. He always commented to the employees as he made his rounds, saying trivial things like "Hi, guy!" or "Cold enough for you?" or "How 'bout dem Pirates?" His desire was to have a low profile at Save-a-Penny. He wanted to be seen, but not watched.

It was interesting to watch him work. He would silently debate whether to place an item in the cart or in the coat. The only exceptions were bottles of soda, which he always paid for, and lobster tails, which he always stole. The management never did figure out why lobster sales rose dramatically while profits plummeted.

Our arrangement was a classic case study. If a chart were made of Mitch's behavior, it would graphically show a steady increase in greed and a complete breakdown of principles. But it was gradual, changing slightly every day, and it reflected Mitch's ever-changing ideas of his role at Save-a-Penny. It was our very own microcosm, and illustrated how values and ideas could easily be altered.

At first he took *only* food and ate everything he took. Nothing was wasted and he didn't profit financially. He saw himself as a poor boy struggling to get through college and, hopefully, medical school. Taking some food was the only way he could make ends meet.

Then I came into the picture and the original concept was slightly amended. It was now, "*We* ate everything he took." What's wrong with that? The food still wasn't wasted. Had the profit clause been abused by this change? Mitch said no and I agreed. After all, he wasn't peddling the tails around town. Yes, it was okay. The spirit of the original concept was still intact.

If two could eat what Mitch took, it was only a question of time when three could do it—or four. Nothing was violated. Al, Wickers, and even J.P. came by the second week and enjoyed a lobster tail. Still, no waste and no profit. During the third week Mitch said, "What's really important is that I take only food and that everything is *eaten*."

"You've decided to sell the lobster tails. Didn't we agree there'd be no profits?" I asked.

"You know, Art, it's funny. I honest to God don't ever remember saying that."

"You said it, Mitch. I remember your saying it."

"What I may have said was 'exorbitant profits!' Yeah, I think that was it. No exorbitant profits."

"No matter what price you sell them at—it's one hundred percent profit for you. That sounds exorbitant to me. You're worse than Save-a-Penny. Even they don't make 100%."

"Art?"

"Yeah, I know." The conversation was over. If I had pressed him any further, it would have degenerated into a "fuck you" or an attack on my mother.

There were other changes too. Mitch began to diversify the harvest. At first he stayed with seafood—shrimp, crabmeat, and scallops. Then he gradually branched into meats and poultry. By the fourth week, he asked for special cuts of Delmonico steak. During this time, the cart began to have fewer products at checkout time and the raincoat more. By the fifth week, he was paying for only two or three items.

One day, Mitch said, "My conscience is clear."

"What did you steal now?" I asked.

"It's not stealing. How about taking the price of these Luckies off the debt?" He flipped a carton of Lucky Strikes to me. I looked at the cigarettes, and for the first time, I felt things might be getting out of hand.

"This violates the agreement," I said heatedly.

"Not really."

"We aren't going to eat these cigarettes."

"Eat? Who said anything about eating?"

"The deal was you would take only food and we would eat everything you took."

"No, not quite."

"This should really be good," I said.

"What I actually said was, 'I'll only take things we can consume!' "

"You did say 'eat,' Mitch, but even if you did say 'consume,' I don't—"

"You're some fuckin' English student! Don't you know what consume means? You never heard of oil-consuming nations? You think they eat the oil? Asshole! 'Consume' means 'use.' Just so we *use* everything. There'll be no waste. Isn't that really what it's all about?"

It was a giant step forward, or backward—I wasn't sure which. But it gave great new latitude to Mitch's plan. We were no longer restrained by having to eat the merchandise. Under this new interpretation we were now able to eat, read, smoke, even wear the goods. Just so it wasn't taken indiscriminately, and most important—wasn't wasted.

On May 2, 1961, Mitchel Howard Carpenter brought home a giant red-and-yellow Yo-Yo. On each side was a picture of a clown. When the Yo-Yo went up and down, the nose lit up and the clown said, "Hiya kids! Hiya kids!" I wondered how this item might fit into Mitch's ever-expanding rulebook.

"Mitch?" I merely pointed to the object which had been taken indiscriminately—not from Save-a-Penny, but from a small, family-run sundries store.

"I took it 'cause I liked it," he said defiantly. He didn't add —"Do you wanna make something out of it?" but it was clearly implied. Then he walked into the kitchen to begin preparing the evening feast.

My life at K.S.U. was not just a series of stag films, gang bangs, shoplifting, and card-playing. You must realize that along with the fun and games, there was also some serious cheating.

Dickens so eloquently said, "It was the best of times, it was the worst of times." That's just how it was in my short Spanish-speaking career. Unlike any of my other courses, I had exhilarating peaks and terrible lows. There were no "gentleman's C's" in Spanish. I was never able to slip by unnoticed.

I flunked my first semester in Spanish, and in the process I portrayed the part of the class fool, a role that I had never played before. Later, when I received straight A's, I switched to being the class genius. I was ill at ease in both roles. Throughout my entire study of the Spanish language, I longed for the pleasant, undemanding anonymity I was accustomed to during the rest of my mediocre matriculation.

As a liberal artist I was required to take a foreign language. I chose Spanish because a Wickers-type voice said, "Why not take Spanish? It's the easiest language to learn." Unfortunately, I elected to start my Spanish studies during my semester of indentured servitude at Delta Pi Beta. It was a mistake—both the pledging and the Spanish, and each tended to make the other less palatable. I had scheduled my class at 8:00 A.M., and my mind was never quite clear or fertile enough to nurture the seeds of a foreign language.

I was a master at faking. I faked geology. I went on field trips and never knew what the hell I was looking at. The goddamn smartass girls would look at strata and write down pages of data on their clipboards. They always knew exactly what each layer represented and they scribbled incessantly. All I saw was a bunch of rocks. But somehow, when the examination came, I was able to fake it. I'd make up keys and memorize them. Paleozoic, permeazoic, mesozoic. Then I'd hit the true and false. I seemed to excel in true and false. Any dope could score fifty percent, so by combining my sixth sense with my limited knowledge, I was usually able to score in the seventies.

And that's pretty much how it went in all the subjects. Literature, history, the arts—I was able to fake it in much the same way. Accounting, finance, and economics—a little more difficult. They were troublesome, but I got by. Bacteriology was a problem since I never learned to use a microscope. While my classmates saw amoeba and paramecium, I saw only my eye. Imagine looking through the aperture for hours at a time and seeing only your eye? Once, in a rage, I stuck my finger into a culture of escherichia coli just to prove that there really was something on the slide besides my big, fucking eye. It was a rash thing to do and I regretted it for weeks. Seems I inadvertently transferred E. coli to my crotch. This happened only a few days after my trip to Harrisburg, and the resultant infection caused me a great deal of mental anguish plus a few sleepless nights. But, in the end, I was even able to fake bacteriology.

But, my friends, one does not fake Spanish. One may affect a false Spanish accent or commit a few phrases to memory if one wants to impress some non-Spanish-speaking people. But there is no way to pretend to speak a foreign language when you don't know shit about it. Believe me, I was stripped naked and there was no place to hide.

El Señor Don Ramón Menéndez Pidal (Pee-dahl') was my Spanish teacher. He was a sadist. When he discovered that I had never studied the language before, he came after me mercilessly.

There are two distinct Spanish dialects. One is Castilian and one is not. I never knew what the other was called. Perhaps it had no name at all. But when El Profesor Pidal asked if I learned Castilian in high school, I said "no" because I hadn't. I didn't tell him I hadn't learned the other Spanish either.

That's really where my troubles began. Castilian is basically a lisping type of Spanish. For example, in regular Spanish, the word "civilization" is pronounced *seeveeleezaseeohn,* but in Castilian it is pronounced *theeveeleethatheeohn.* Do you see the difference? Now it certainly is not my aim to teach a Spanish lesson. I couldn't care less about the whole goddamn thing. But it is quite important to understand a few basics.

Castilian Spanish got its start because one of the Kings of Castile had a distinctive lisp. His subjects didn't want to offend him, so they all spoke with a lisp. I don't know if the story has any validity—nor do I care.

But here is the confusing part. Do you remember when I said El Señor Pidal was a sadist? Well, he was also gay, with quite a distinctive lisp as well as a swish. So I never really knew if he was speaking Castilian or the regular version.

In the beginning he asked me a simple question. "Theñor Arturo," he lisped. "¿Eth uthted un ethtudiante de ethpañol?" Translation: Mr. Arthur, are you a Spanish student? Isn't it neat the way they put that upside-down question mark before the question?

Please understand that I had no idea what the man was talking about. But I was still naïve enough to think I could fake out the head of the Spanish department, who now stood directly in front of me, his open hand placed firmly on his slim hip. Like I did in so many other courses, I applied the old "true-false" doctrine. At least I would have half a chance.

"Thí," I lisped back in what I thought would be the Castilian version of "Sí."

"¿Thí?" he shrieked. He had suddenly and unaccountably become enraged. At first I thought I had given the incorrect answer, but I couldn't imagine why a grown man like Señor Pidal should become so indignant over such a small matter. I wondered how important his question may have been, that a simple "yes" answer would have caused such an uproar.

"¿Thí, thí?" He repeated it again and he swished toward the front of the room, turning his back to the class.

"He thinks you're making fun of him," someone whispered.

"All I said was 'Thí.' How am I making fun of him?"

"It's 'Sí,' not 'Thí.' "

"But the Castilian version?"

"That's not Castilian, shithead. He's a homo. Pidal's a goddamn queer. That's the way he talks."

I was in trouble. Pidal was huffing and puffing and making bull-like sounds, although by the end of this exchange he would be the bullfighter and I the bull.

I tried to patch up the difficulties I had caused by my inadvertent slur. "Sí, señor," I said smartly, without a trace of lisp, Castilian or otherwise. But Don Ramón Menéndez Pidal was not about to let me off so easily. He repeated his original question, this time in quite a bitchy tone.

"Are you a Spanish student?" someone whispered. "He's asking you if you're a Spanish student. Just say, "Sí, Señor Pidal, soy—"

So in the little Spanish I knew, I nervously answered, "Sí, Señor Pidal, soy . . . el estudiante de español." I thought I had answered it well. That's why I was amazed when teacher and class alike began a round of hysterical laughter.

Now, I have told a funny story in my day, and quite frankly, the good-natured laughs of friends have always given me a nice warm feeling. But, when I sat and absorbed the deprecating cackles of my peers, I reached one of the lowest ebbs of my collegiate career. I had emerged from a long, comfortable stay in the woodwork, and I was on the wrong end of the joke. At one point, the laughter became so loud and vicious I felt there might be a very real possibility of my being attacked. I was saved by the bell.

On my way out I asked a classmate what had been so funny. "Pidal asked if you were a Spanish student," he said.

"Yeah?"

"You said you were *the* Spanish student." Then he laughed right in my face and continued to howl as he walked down the hallway, apparently reliving the hilarious incident in his mind.

I cursed him and Pidal. In spite of my embarrassment, I still wondered just why everyone had gotten so wild. ¡Caramba! These Spanish-speaking people sure had a strange sense of humor.

I started far behind everyone that semester, and it never got any better. Actually, it got a lot worse. By the end of the first month, when my classmates were conversing quite fluently with Señor Pidal, I was fast becoming a hopeless case. I was so out of it I began cutting class to avoid the ridicule of Pidal and the bastard students that flocked about him to lavish abuse on me. I supplied the comic relief for todo el mundo (everyone).

"Señor Arturo," Pidal said one day.

"Sí, señor," I answered smartly.

"¿Qué se encuentra después de la vida?" Translation: What do we find when life is over? Naturally I had no idea what the question meant. I should have known that you can't fake a foreign language, but I never stopped trying. I took a chance.

"Después de la vida, se encuentra—uh, uh—nada." Translation: When life is over we find—uh, uh—nothing. Light giggles, but at least it wasn't a crazed lynch mob. Perhaps I had unwittingly stumbled on an answer that at least was moderately acceptable.

But El Señor Pidal sensed a killing and was not to be sidetracked. "¿Nada?" He fluttered his lashes in mock amazement. "¡Dios mio, Señor Arturo! ¿Se encuentra *nada*?" And in English he said, "What do you find when life is over?" He demanded a specific answer. For a second, I thought he had finally outsmarted himself by unwittingly giving me the translation.

Now what was that goddamn word for death? I knew it began with M. Oh, God, what was it? Then I remembered. I sat erect and prepared to answer. The crowd was still, sensing the moment of truth was near. They hoped they might at least award him my ear. ¡Olé!

"Después de la vida," I began very slowly, "se encuentra—uh—uh—mierda." This time the crowd went completely berserk. They leapt out of their seats and shouted at me. They were wild-eyed. I looked around at the hysteria that surrounded me. Then I glanced at Don Pidal, who walked in a small semicircle, his hands outstretched to receive the tumultuous ovation.

I felt the sting of the banderillas in my neck and back. What in God's name did I say this time? Whatever it was, I vowed this would be my last day in Spanish under Don Ramón Menéndez Pidal. I was willing to lie down in a vat and have garbage dumped on me. I was content to play the part of a loafer or a bum. But, goddammit, I would no longer be the village idiot for this sadistic son-of-a-bitch and his wolf pack!

"Arthur, you are the best! You, honest to God, are the best!" It was one of my classmates. He shook his head as he passed me in the hall. At least a half hour had elapsed since the uproar and he was still chuckling as he went by.

At least I would discover what terribly funny thing I had said this time. I increased my pace and was now walking with him. "Hey, what is the Spanish word for death?" I asked.

"Muerte," he replied and flashed a wide grin.

"Muerte? Well, isn't that what I said?"

"Nope! You said 'mierda.' " He began chuckling again.

"Which means?"

"Shit!" he replied and laughed hysterically.

Shit? Shit? I repeated it to myself. OH, SHIT! ¡Estúpido! Asshole! Finally I managed to calm myself.

At least my answer was grammatically correct. And who's to say what we'll find after life? Not that son-of-a-bitch Pidal.

You know, things can get plenty shitty during life, too. Just take that Spanish class, for example. That was real shitty for me. Maybe it's pretty much the same when it's all over.

She walked slowly and uncertainly down the narrow, winding path leading from the rocky dunes to the quiet, deserted beach. She took each step gingerly, as if the slightest miscalculation could send her to a most horrible fate. Behind her tagged six screaming children who occasionally broke into wild singing. She cautioned them to be careful, although they clearly were in less danger than she. There were cries of "We won't fall, Miss Webber" and "Don't worry, Miss Webber!" Apparently she was a counselor and she had taken her group on a field trip to the shore of my secluded mountain lake in the Poconos.

As they snaked down the path, the children's squealing broke my concentration. I had been at this beach several times during the month. In a comfortable shady spot amongst the rocks, I'd set up my lounge chair and there studied the shit out of Spanish. This was my first interruption, and I was irritated. I peeped out over my textbook and glared. But when I looked at this Miss Webber stumbling down the hill, my anger disappeared. She was so damn pretty I couldn't believe it. I lowered my book to my lap. I rolled up a notebook paper into a telescope and held it to my eye. I wanted to focus on this beautiful subject by removing her from the chattering circus that followed.

She looked about eighteen. In spite of the terror she was experiencing, the smile still came through. It was the symbol of the sweetness I could see, even from my hiding place, some fifty feet away. Well, this kills the Spanish for today, I thought. Unless she's fat. I'll wait till she takes off that cover-up.

When the caravan was only a few feet from the bottom, she stumbled. I leaped from my chair. I would help her, soothe her—meet her. What an opening! Any one of my cool, smooth fraternity brothers would have been on top of the prey in seconds, saying cool, smooth things like "Hi, there. It looks like you're falling for me already." Goddamn bastards!

I let the moment pass. What would I say? What would I do? I suppose if she were really hurt, I would have gotten my ass over there. But soon she was again laughing and telling the kids to please be careful. I fell back into my lounge chair, praying she would be fat. I had so much work to do. I just didn't have the time to waste.

Now they were on the beach. She balanced herself by leaning on a child's shoulder and took off her sandals. I strained as she unbuttoned the cover-up and then removed it. She had a body too! Dear God, she was stacked! Breasts, legs, ass. She had all of them. There would be no more Spanish this afternoon. Why did she come to this beach?

She played with the kids. They built castles and sang and danced. But she wouldn't let them bury her in the sand. They dug for whatever people dig for on beaches. They found things, too. Every couple of minutes an excited child would shout, "Look, Miss Webber!" or "What's this, Miss Webber?" And she knew. She patiently explained each item to the little urchins. But when they presented her with something that was a little too wiggly, she would leap to her feet, demanding they throw it back into the lake.

I wanted to walk down and introduce myself, but I was afraid she wouldn't be interested. Probably had a hundred boyfriends. Suppose she snubbed me. Then what? Finally, I worked out a brave plan. I would casually walk to the water and skip a few stones in the lake. Then I would look over and notice her for the first time. I could nod and maybe even mumble a "Hi!" When I had finally convinced my legs to move, she suddenly jumped up and ran toward the water. I wasn't prepared for such a move and I fell back into the chair.

She ran until the water reached her knees. When she realized how cold it was, she turned and ran back. She's probably meeting some guy later. Some sharp fraternity bastard has all this. Suddenly she began running in my direction. My heart pounded. I feared she was about to talk to me. But she fell on her blanket. Then she lifted her head and I thought she looked right at me. She smiled and at that moment I felt I might be in love with her. I must get up and talk to her immediately. I reached for my Spanish book.

I strained at my leash as she combed out her long, lustrous hair. I admired her when she began taking pictures of the kids. She looked very professional just snapping off one after another. Then she looked in my direction, and when she began walking toward me, I panicked.

I looked right at the camera and she snapped. "I just couldn't resist," she said. "You really make an interesting study—sitting here so seriously." She smiled. "I'm sorry if I disturbed you."

Now I was almost certainly in love. I shook my head and grunted, "No, it's okay."

"It looks like you're writing the Great American Novel."

"No, not really. Just trying to study."

"And I disturbed you. I'm sorry."

It appeared I was going to lose her, and in desperation I said, "No, it's okay. Don't leave."

She turned her head and glanced at the children, who were playing and getting along reasonably well. "Okay, but not too long. I have to get the kids home soon." And she sat down.

I can't remember one thing we talked about for the remainder of the afternoon. I do remember that I stared at her a great deal, and most important . . . I was definitely madly in love with her. No question about it.

The brats started pestering her. "When are we going, Miss Webber?" . . . "I'm hungry, Miss Webber." And "I have to make tinkle, Miss Webber."

"It's about that time," she said. "It was nice talking to you."

"Yeah, same here." My love was leaving and I was mutely helpless. Say something, dummy. Say something, big shot . . . dumb ass. "I don't even know your name."

She laughed. "I'm sorry . . . I'm Carol—Carol Ann Webber."

"Hi, Carol," I said, and I introduced myself.

"It was nice meeting you, Art."

Throat constricted. "Yeah, same here." I'm losing her. Say something. Those little bastards . . . those goddamn, mewling Lilliputians are carrying her off.

I managed to lift my paralyzed arm and held out my hand. She took it. I looked at our clasped hands and then at her. "Come back," I blurted.

"I will," she said. Then she and her brood were gone.

We both returned to the beach the next day, and the next and the one after that. And for the remainder of the summer vacation, I studied Carol and Spanish in that order. And it came to pass that I loved them both—in that order.

It was the last night of the vacation. Tomorrow I would be going back to war, to do battle with Don Pidal. There was an air of desperation. We were the last outpost—a garrison state isolated from the rest of the burning world. We had met on that beach, so it was fitting that we close out the summer there, clinging desperately to each other and hoping that time might at least be slowed down.

It was a clear, cool night, and from somewhere on the other side of the lake came the mournful sounds of a husky saxophone, leading an amateur combo in a sad farewell to summer. Carol and I were making out. It was more intense than any of our previous times. This would be the finale.

Under the blanket, we had removed our clothing from the waist up. As we embraced, I realized that neither of us had spoken about tomorrow. I would be returning to school and there had been absolutely no discussion of our relationship. Would it continue? When would I see her again? Would she date others? God, I hoped not. That would have been too much for me. I never told her I loved her. It was crystal-clear—even then. But telling her was another matter.

As we clutched and grabbed, I ran it through. I would tell her. Okay, tell her. Should I say, "I love you, Carol," or "Carol, I love you?" I'll tell her now . . . or maybe now. Okay, I'll count to ten and then I'll tell her. You goddamn jerk! Tell her! I looked at her, kissed her, touched her, but— I didn't tell her.

Hours had passed and still we held on. Soon the sun would be up, and in only a few hours I would be leaving. Time was running out and I had not told her. Suddenly Carol said, "Oh, Art—I love you, too." She filled with emotion and kissed me. It touched off a massive chain reaction of "I love you" and a frenzied round of making out.

Up until that night I thought I knew what nice girls did and didn't do. But now it was confusing. I was losing control. It really was nice loving the one you loved. More than nice. Outstanding even. Everyone must be crazy! It was really good, loving someone you loved. What a unique experience. Why didn't anyone think of this before? You really didn't have to stand in line for three dollars a throw or con some poor pimply-face to do it in your car. It really was okay to open your eyes and see someone beautiful. Make love with your love! What a revelation!

We were nearing the point of no return when I displayed a superhuman show of stupidity. I rolled off her and placed my hands on her shoulders. I pushed her away. And in the tradition of Emmett Kelly and all of the other great clowns, I whispered, "No, we're not ready for this!"

She was confused and hurt. I assured her it was in our best interest to wait. Her eyes filled with tears. I wanted to show her I really loved her in spite of my strange behavior. "Here, put this on," I said, shaking the sand out of her blouse and helping her into it.

"Don't you like my body?" she asked.

"Sure!" I paused as I lifted my own shirt and removed the Delta Pi Beta pin. "But I think it would be much better to pin this on your blouse."

"Oh, Art," she screamed, and hit me with all of her 114 pounds, knocking me down into the sand. I regretted stopping what might have happened a few minutes ago, but at least she was happy now.

After I fumbled with the pin, we held tightly. The tears were rolling down her face again. I thought of my leaving her in a few hours and soon I was crying too. But our faces were pressed tightly together, and I'm sure she never knew.

20

●●●

I had really studied the shit out of Spanish that summer and had become an expert on the subject. I was obsessed with the desire to speak it fluently and flawlessly. And constantly fueling this lust for knowledge was my overpowering hatred for Don Pidal. For every mile of my return trip to Keystone, his pink face loomed in front of me, and his taunting, lisping voice echoed in my ear. Don Ramón Menéndez Pidal, I'm going to get you! Don Ramón Menéndez Pidal, su madre vive en una casa de putas. (Translation: Your mother lives in a whorehouse.) Y su padre está allí también. (Translation: And so does your father.) Señor Pidal, you're not going to have to wait till life is over. I'm going to give you a living death. And not only muerte, Señor, but a lot of mierda, too.

I returned to campus ready to be the conquering hero. I was Don Quixote and was fully prepared to do battle. Unfortunately, the son-of-a-bitch of a windmill didn't show up. I sadly learned that Señor Pidal had taken a sabbatical and would be away from the university for an undetermined period of time. But the department assured me Pidal had not taken another job and advised me to schedule with another professor. They assured me El Señor Pidal would return to K.S.U. by the time

I would be studying advanced Spanish. They smiled at my insistence on having him for my teacher, and the office secretaries threw knowing looks back and forth. They were aware of Pidal's sexual preferences and completely misinterpreted my enthusiasm.

I considered explaining how wrong they were. It was not love that drove me to their office. It was pure hatred and my savage yearning for revenge. I was embarrassed by their looks and I flushed. In those days homosexuals were not gays. They were queers. Goddamn queers. Fucking queers even. But I didn't want to tip my hand—not yet. Let them think whatever they wanted to. I would wait for my man.

That semester I simply knew everything there was to know. I was not a smartass and I volunteered absolutely nothing. But in perfect Spanish I answered every question that was asked.

While Pidal was in Spain, Mexico, or wherever Spanish professors go on their sabbaticals, I went from an F to an A. My teacher, a gentle woman named Señora Paz, said it was a pleasure having me in her class. I was now *the* Spanish student. Fuck Pidal!

My experience in intermediate Spanish was similar. My grasp of the language was increasing all the time. I impressed teacher and class alike. There never was any doubt that I would be first in the class. So, while Señor Pidal did whatever Spanish professors do on their sabbaticals, I sailed through intermediate Spanish with a high A average.

The time had finally come for advanced Spanish—my last chance for a crack at Pidal. I had studied hard for a year and a half. I had paid my dues. After all, studying was not why I was in college. It was completely alien to my character, especially when it was at an obsessional level. But I was now fully prepared for him. I returned to the office of the Spanish Department.

As I approached the front desk in the office, I had the premonition that something might be wrong. Things had gone too well for me. I had focused on this moment for a long time. I had thought about it repeatedly, and in my long preparation I had become totally attached to it.

"I'm sorry, sir, but I'm afraid I have some sad news for you," the man said.

"Yes, Mother?"

"I assume you haven't heard about Señor Pidal?"

"No, Mother!"

"I'm sorry to have to be the one to tell you this, but—you see, Señor Pidal is—"

"Dead, the son-of-a-bitch is dead. I knew it!" I was shouting and pounding my fist on the counter, and the clerk was frightened. "What happened to him? How did he die?"

"He didn't die. I didn't say he died."

"Pidal lives? You're telling me now he's alive?"

"What in the world is the matter with you, fella?"

"You said you had some sad news concerning Professor Pidal," I said in a much calmer voice. "I thought you were going to tell me the man was dead."

"Christ, man, you are sick! You better get hold of yourself or someday they're going to come after you."

"Yes, all right. Fine! I'm sorry. I've gotten hold of myself. You said you had sad news." There could only be one thing worse than Pidal's death. Far worse! That would be his not returning to campus.

"Señor Pidal is not returning to campus."

"¿Qué?" I shrieked. "¿Qué?" I shrieked again, and I was far more agitated now than when I thought the bastard was dead. "What do you mean, he's not coming back? Goddamn you! They promised me! They assured me he would be back. Now where is that son-of-a-bitch?" I made what he thought was a menacing move toward him, and he jumped back.

"Señor Pidal is in Bolivia," he said quickly. "He is still on his sabbatical."

I was trembling. I had been deceived by the department.

"Would you care to sit down for a minute?"

I disregarded him. I was not about to be given the run-around by a pisspot clerk. I had too much of an investment in this project, and for once I was not going to play my usual passive role. "Is he coming back or isn't he coming back? Don't bullshit me!"

"I really can't say."

"You can't say, or you don't know?"

"I don't know!"

"Well, goddammit, you get someone out here who does know!"

He retreated into one of the back offices and was gone for a minute or two. I nervously busied myself by looking at the Spanish and Mexican art objects on the wall. There was a watercolor of Barcelona, an oil of Chapultepec, an aerial photograph of Tehuantepec, and last, but certainly least, a large portrait of the elusive Pidal. He sat in one of those tilted poses, looking wistfully toward the camera. He held a cigarette in one hand, its smoke curling lazily upward past his smiling, thin-lipped mouth. How utterly stupid he looked, reclining on the unseen velvet pillows! In the bottom right corner, angled at the same degree as Pidal himself, was Pidal's flowery inscription—"Fondly, D.R.M. Pidal." Fucking asshole! It was a lasting tribute to my great self-restraint that I did not spit on his incredibly asinine face.

"Arthur?" I quickly spun around to the familiar voice of Señora Paz. Apparently the clerk had told her about his encounter with a madman, and when she saw that I was el hombre loco, she was genuinely puzzled.

"Hello, Señora Paz," I said in the calm, pleasant voice I knew she would remember. "¿Cómo está usted?"

"I'm fine, Arthur. Just fine. But you seem to be having quite a problem." Her voice was soft and kindly. She did not want to believe the clerk.

I knew she was fond of me. I rid my mind of the rancor I felt for Pidal and his stooge. I contorted my face into a boyish look and in a boyish voice I said, "Señora Paz, you know me. I'm not a troublemaker."

"That's true, Arthur. That's why I don't understand just what is—"

"Señora, all I want to know is if and when Señor Pidal will be returning to campus. I don't think I'm being unreasonable. I want to schedule advanced Spanish with him. That's not asking too much, is it?"

"Arthur, why is it so important to have Señor Pidal as your teacher?"

She was a good person, and I decided to tell her my story. Of course, I was extremely careful to edit the story for her consumption. I left out the episodes about "mierda" and "el estudiante" and anything else that would suggest a vendetta. It was a masterful job. I left the impression that I had failed freshman Spanish and had subsequently devoted a large part of my college career to bettering myself. The only way I could reach my goal was to again have Pidal for my teacher.

She understood. "Señor Pidal asked for and received an extension of his sabbatical. He is still in Bolivia."

"When will he be back?" I asked, bracing myself.

"In one year."

"Señora, I can't wait another year. I'm due to take advanced Spanish this semester. If I lay off a whole year, I'll lose my momentum."

"Arthur, if it means that much to you, why not schedule a few semesters of Spanish literature? It would keep you in practice, and you might even find it interesting."

"What assurance is there that he'll be back in a year? In one year I'll be starting my last semester; I'm running out of time. I'm a terminal case at this university."

"I can't give any assurances. I'm telling you all I know. The extension of his sabbatical is for one year only. My personal feeling is that he will return for the spring semester of 1961, but I can't guarantee that—"

"Gracias, señora. I appreciate your help." There was no point in pushing her. I wanted to keep her friendship. I would wait one more year.

"De nada, Arturo. Good luck to you."

I turned and walked toward the door, passing the clerk without comment. There was still one unanswered question.

"¿Señora Paz?"

She looked up at me. "¿Sí?"

"What is a sabbatical?"

"Pardon?"

"A sabbatical. What is it? And what does one do on a sabbatical?"

She smiled a lovely smile. "Why not ask Señor Pidal when you see him next year?"

"You know, señora, maybe I'll do just that." I smiled back and then left the office of the Spanish Department for the last time.

21

●● ●●●

Spring Semester, 1961.

I sat in the classroom anxiously awaiting the entrance of
Señor Pidal. He had returned from Bolivia and was scheduled
to teach this class. My only fear was a last-minute change. It
happened from time to time, but I had never been concerned
before. The professors had always seemed as meaningless to
me as the subject matter they attempted to teach.

I was Inspector Javert in *Les Misérables*. He had searched
continuously for Jean Valjean. For years he relentlessly pur-
sued his man, waiting patiently at times, but often being driven
to the brink of madness by his obsession. Just as he cried out,
"Jean Valjean, I will catch you!" I called out "Menéndez
Pidal, I'm going to break your ass!" The only part of the analogy I didn't like was Javert's suicide after he had finally caught
his man. I couldn't possibly foresee my own suicide unless, of
course, Pidal had not returned.

I sat and waited. I had done my homework well. All I required now was his presence. If he showed up, I would have
him.

The door opened slowly. It was an agonizing climax to my
long battle. I swear I heard trumpets playing in perfect two-

part harmony, heralding the triumphant return of Don Ramón Menéndez Pidal.

I had positioned myself inconspicuously in the rear of the room. I needed the luxury of watching him while I remained unwatched. I rolled up a sheet of notebook paper and held it to my eye. I was able to shut everyone else out. I held him firmly in the crosshairs of my scope and savored every second of it. Electrified with nervous energy, I followed his swishing path from the door to the front of the room.

He placed his attaché case on the desk and took a long wide-eyed look at the class. I put down my scope and stared back. I was sure he hadn't seen me. Perhaps he wouldn't even remember. After all, it was a long time since I sat in his class as a lowly freshman, and perhaps those events had had a lasting devastating impact only on me.

As he wrote his name on the board in the same flowery script I had seen in the Spanish office, he said, "Soy Don Ramón Menéndez Pidal." Big fucking deal, I thought. He held his hand high in the air and then let his wrist go limp, dropping the chalk into a container on the desk. As he rubbed his hands together to rid them of chalk residue, he glided gently around to the front of the desk. Then, using his hands as support, he nimbly lifted his tiny ass and placed it on the edge of the desk. He withdrew a cigarette from a fine gold case and tapped it with quick, animated movements. After lighting up and inhaling several times, he daintily lifted one knee on top of the other. Then he leaned over on one hand and supported himself. He sat in this tilted position and the smoke drifted upwards. I brought back my telescope to zero in on this absurd recreation of his ridiculous portrait in the Spanish office.

Apparently this whole bit had been a warm-up before his opening monologue. He cleared his throat and began to speak in the lisping voice I well remembered. "This is Advanced Spanish. We in the department sometimes refer to it as Conversational Spanish . . ." He rambled on about the values of understanding a foreign language and speaking it fluently. He talked about all the countries where Spanish was spoken. As he spoke, he dangled his legs from the desk while his eyes panned back and forth across the class. Like a searchlight his glassy stare darted in front and in back, somehow just missing me each time. This was the first time I wanted to be on center stage, and I had a spotlight of my own, ready and far more powerful than his. I softly whistled Ravel's *Bolero* and did a fine drumming accompaniment on my desk.

He was now making concluding noises. "And so, class, this will be one of the few times I will be speaking to you in English. From now on, our talks will be en Español." Just as he said "Español" his eyes met mine, but then quickly moved on without incident. There was absolutely no sign of recognition. All my work had been for nothing. My eyes fell to the desk and I stopped my drumming and whistling routine.

"It is my fondest hope," he continued, "that by the end of this semester—" He had stopped suddenly. I looked up and was amazed to see him staring at me. I had given up too soon. Apparently I had looked away just before he did his double take. Now there could be no mistaking it. That bastard remembered.

He began his monologue again, but he never lifted his eyes from mine. His words were detached and had a hollow ring. Luckily for him, it was a canned speech. His mind was now somewhere else—on me. "It is my fondest hope that by the end of this semester, you will not only converse in Spanish, but think in Spanish." After he spoke this line, he lifted himself off the desk and walked around to his attaché case.

Except for the few seconds that he was checking inside the case for my name on the roll call, he never stopped staring at me. After he had confirmed his suspicions, he closed the case and placed it under the desk. He was ready for business and he was smiling.

But I had made contact too. I was ready for him and I braced myself. Again I was whistling and drumming *Bolero*.

I neared a climax—of *Bolero,* that is. And, of course, I was smiling too.

He started with some basic questions.

"Señora Berkowitz, ¿cuál es más grande, la ciudad de Pittsburgh o la ciudad de Harrisburg?" Translation: Which is larger, Pittsburgh or Harrisburg?

"Pittsburgh es más grande, Señor Pidal."

"Bien, Señora."

"Señor Yamosuka, ¿cómo se llaman los Reyes Católicos de España?" Translation: What are the names of the Catholic rulers of Spain?

"Fernannnnnnnnnndo e Isabel." Translation: Ferdinand and Isabel.

"Muy bien, Señor." Pidal was thrilled with the answer, especially when the Japanese señor held the n so long.

"¿Cuándo vivieron los Reyes, Señora Koznofsky?" Translation: When did the rulers live?

"Hmmm, acerca de mil cuatrocientos noventa y dos." Translation: Hmmm, about 1492.

"Muy bien, muy bien, Señora."

He flitted his way up and down the aisles, seemingly happy with most of the answers he was receiving. From time to time he glanced over at me, perhaps to make sure I was still there. Finally he stopped only a few feet from my desk.

"Ah, Señor Arturo!" Translation: Ah, Mr. Arthur!

"Ah, Señor Pidal!" Translation: Ah, Mr. Pidal!

The class laughed nervously. Pidal smiled and spoke to the other students. "Mis amigos, Señor Arturo es *el* estudiante de español." The class laughed, this time not so nervously. They were getting into the spirit of things. It was not the same group I sat with years ago, but people were funny—all people. Like a pack of wild animals, they would turn on anyone at the first sign of weakness.

Y Señor Pidal es el prick de español, I thought. What I actually said was, "Es verdad, mis amigos, soy *el* estudiante de español." Translation: It's true, my friends, I am *the* Spanish student.

And again the class laughed nervously.

Pidal gave a mock look of surprise, arching his eyebrows and pressing his lips tightly together. "Ahora, una pregunta, por favor." Translation: Now, one question, please. "¿Qué se encuentra después de la vida?" I'm not translating this one— you know what it means.

God, it was just too good to be true! After all those years, he had even remembered the exact question. His impression of our confrontation must have been as intense as mine. I wanted to hold this moment for as long as possible. "¡Repítalo, por favor!" Translation: Please repeat that!

He asked the question again and shook his head disparagingly. I had waited so long and I just didn't want it to end. Like a 78 rpm record played at 33⅓ rpm, I finally began to answer. "Después de la vida se encuentra ah—ah—"

"¡Rápidamente, señor! No tengo todo el día!" Translation: Quickly, sir! I don't have all day!

I had held back as long as I could. Now I could no longer contain myself. It came out in short, staccato bursts, "¡Cálmase bastardo, y oye lo que tengo que decir!" Translation: Keep your shirt on, you bastard, and listen to what I have to say.

He was caught totally off guard, and this time his face turned white with the real look of surprise and shock. My outburst threw him up against the window, where he would remain motionless until my lecture had ended.

"Usted me tiene hasta la coronilla." Translation: I'm absolutely fed up with you.

I waited until the noise died down and then I continued in fluent Spanish. "Your question is not a simple one, Mr. Pidal. There really is no concrete answer. A more important question is, 'What do we find *before* death?' I'll give you an answer to both questions— SHIT! Yes, SHIT! Mister Pidal. You heard me right! You gave me a lot of it and now I'm returning it with interest. I suggest you think about my answer this time. Don't laugh it off like you did before!"

When I packed up my pencils, papers, and notebooks, Señor Pidal was still backed up against the window, motionless, looking down at the floor.

"Buenos días, señor," I said cheerfully as I skipped out of the room, but he didn't look up. Perhaps he was still thinking about my answer.

22

● ●

After I defeated Pidal in a manner far sweeter than in any of my dreams, there was just no place to go. He became an obsequious bootlicker. My new role of star and prodigy was nearly as loathsome as the part of the fool I portrayed so well in freshman Spanish. I was certain I would never be the fool again. But this mantle of genius was a cross, too. Every tough question was thrown at me. I should really say "served" to me by Pidal. He treated me with great respect and cringed when I spoke. When I answered flawlessly, Pidal would fawn. It was all such a pain in the ass. I longed to be in a class like sociology where no one bothered me, where I would lull myself into a stupor, or draw bowling scores in my notebook or just pick my nose without the interruption of a "¿Señor Arturo?" with that fucking inverted question mark.

Soon I had second thoughts about how I did him in. No doubt I had cause to despise him. Revenge is powerful stuff. I liked it while I was throttling him and I still liked myself when I left his class. I was high for a day or two, but after I replayed the scene for the tenth time, the doubts started to set in. At first it was a nagging, pulsating sore that I just could not isolate, but in the middle of my biggest and quite possibly my only victory in a long series of ties, I knew I had already climaxed and was beginning to come down.

Soon I realized I didn't like ripping people apart and making fools of them. It may have been great for the brothers or J.P. Zuckerman or Pidal himself—but it wasn't for me. I should have just answered his stupid questions. He would have instantly recognized my new-found knowledge and now I wouldn't be bothered with him. I wouldn't have to close my eyes at night and see his pathetic figure, cowering against the window, staring disconsolately at his own feet.

23

● ●

The BX was just the way Al Carter liked it—busy. It had been a great week for business, and Al was personally responsible. Soon he would be graduating and there were still thousands of those fuckin' pens in stock. In desperation he had decided to sell two pens for the price of one. He promoted the idea in the campus newspaper, and now the Annual Two-for-One Pen Sale was a success. Al stood beside the cash register and surveyed the activity in the store. He was pleased.

"Gotta hand it to you, Al," said one of the female workers. "You really know how to run a sale!"

"Thank you, momma," Al said, and he threw his arm around her shoulder. "It was real easy, baby; I just planned muh work and then I worked muh plan."

"That's cute."

"I'm-oh-tell you sumpun' else dat's cute." He looked at her ass and slid his hand down toward it.

She pulled away from him. "Al, wasn't the advertising just a little bit unethical?" she asked.

"Whatchoo mean by dat?"

"Well, you called it the *Annual* Two-for-One Pen Sale."

"Ain't dat what it is?"

"No, it's not an annual sale. The BX never ran a promotion like this before."

"Sheeyit, this is the *first* Annual Two-for-One Pen Sale. It's so successful, they'll run it every year. Knowadamean?"

"Great idea, Al," said another worker as he approached the register. He held up a fistful of pens. "We got rid of a shitload of your pens."

"Just cool it, muh man. We ain't runnin' dis sale to sell pens. We calls it a 'leader.' We're using duh pen to sell other merchandise. Knowadamean?"

"Sure, Al!"

Al saw a good-looking girl in the store and he strutted out from behind the register. "Hi, baby. Can I give you a hand?"

"That's your biggest problem, Al. You're all hands."

"C'mon, baby. I'm-oh show you duh famous pens we is sellin' Two-for-One."

"Sheeyit," she said in a remarkably good imitation. "You was givin' dese pens away for nothin'. Knowadamean?" She threw a light punch to Al's upper arm.

"Al Carter!" shouted a girl at the register. Al turned around to face her. "Phone call for you!" She lifted the phone in case he hadn't heard above the noise in the crowded store.

"Excuse me, baby," and he did the stroll down the aisle toward the phone.

"Carter here," he said into the phone. "Hey, man, speak up. Lot a noise here." Al cupped a hand over his other ear and tried to concentrate on what the caller was saying.

"Ramirez Carrega," repeated the caller in a deep, thick Spanish accent.

"What the fuck's goin' on? Speak English, man. I don't dig dat French shit."

"Thees ees Ramirez Carrega, the como se dice—uhhh, gymnast."

Al was quite impressed. Ramirez Carrega was a very big man on campus. The Mexican had competed in the 1960

Olympics and was rated one of the top gymnasts in the country. "What can I do for you, Señor Carrega?" asked Al.

"I theenk I can do something for you, Meester Carter. I have something that will eenterest you."

"I'm listenin', muh man."

"Tengo en mi casa—excuse me. I have in my house a copy of the como se dice—uhhh, final."

"The como se dice final? What the fuck you talkin' about, man?"

"The Spanish test, Meester Carter. The final examination."

Al removed his hand from his ear and slapped it down hard on the phone. He put on his best cloak-and-dagger face and his eyes darted from side to side. He whispered, "You want to give me a copy of the Spanish final?"

"Not quite, Meester Carter. I want to *sell* it to you."

"You want to *sell* it to me?"

"Sí."

"How much?"

"One hundred."

"Pesos?"

"Dollars, Meester Carter. One hundred *dollars*."

"Oh. Jesus Christ, Jesus Christ," Al said rapidly in an extremely agitated voice. He wiped the sweat from his forehead and began jumping up and down on the balls of his feet. "I don't have a hundred dollars."

"I'm sure you'll como se dice—uhhh, manage. Meet me at my apartment. I live at mil noveciento, excuse me—1900 Penn Drive. If you're not there weetheen thirty meenutes, I'll find someone else."

Al heard the loud click. "Carrega," he said, "you're a como se dice—uhhh, motherfucker." Where do I get the money? J.P.! I'll ask J.P. No, that's no good. The prick will want eight hundred percent interest. Tom's worthless. Little creep would lecture me on the evils of cheating. Mitch is too poor. He'd talk about his parents and all that. Art?—Perfect! Art won't let a friend down. He has the money. He'll help me study too.

Trouble is, how can I do everything in only thirty minutes? I'll have to make a temporary loan.

The bell on the busy cash register interrupted his thinking. "Sheeyit!" he said with a big smile. He removed five twenty-dollar bills from the drawer and casually slipped them into his pocket. He said good-bye to the workers, picked up his attaché case, and started for the door.

"Hey, Al," called his assistant. Al turned around. "Al, I think the register is short."

"How much?" Al asked coolly.

"Looks like about a hundred dollars."

Al immediately sized up the situation as only a minor problem. "Refunds, muh man. A lot of those pens are sheeyit. I had to give the people back their money. That's where your hundred dollars went. Refunds." Then he opened his case and withdrew several hundred pens. He handed them to the startled assistant. "Funny thing," Al said. "There's really nothing wrong with most of them. But you know the old saying, 'the customer's always right.' Just put them back in stock; nobody'll know the difference." Then Al lifted his arms to a full-height mummer's-strut position and was off to his rendezvous with como se dice—uhhh, Ramirez Carrega.

Upon entering the apartment, Al's first sense to be stimulated was his sense of smell. "Sheeyit! It stinks in here!" he said softly as he walked through the foyer, and his nose twitched involuntarily from the pungent odor that permeated the place.

"Een here," shouted Carrega from the bedroom.

When Al entered the room he got a concentrated blast of the odor. Carrega, wearing what appeared to be the bottom half of a woman's bikini, was working out on the parallel bars. There was no ventilation in the hot, dusty room, and Al was instantly aware that the cause of the stench was Carrega himself.

"Make yourself at home," said Carrega, and the muscular little man continued his routine. "I'll be done in meenute."

"Thanks a lot," Al said, and he gagged. He placed a hand-kerchief over his nose and mouth and staggered around the perimeter of the room, looking at the impressive collection of trophies and awards.

"Preety nice, huh, Meester Carter?"

"Yeah, sure. Pretty nice," Al said, and again he gagged.

The last object on the wall frightened Al. It was a gold-framed, autographed picture of Don Ramón Menéndez Pidal.

"Oh, my God!" Al said. He grabbed his case and started toward the door.

"Hey, where you going?" shouted Carrega.

"I'm-oh get da hell out of here."

"You leaving?"

"Fuckin' A!"

Before Al reached the front door, Carrega had done a per-fect dismount, scrambled through the apartment and overtaken him. He grabbed Al's sleeve and said, "Hey, what's wrong, amigo?"

"There's been a misunderstanding," Al said.

"No meesonderstanding. I sell you the Spanish final, no?"

"No!"

"¿Qué pasa?"

"Muh man, I saw that picture on your wall."

"Pidal?"

"Yes, Pidal. The head of the fuckin' department."

"But Menéndez and I are cómo se dice—uhhh, friends. Good friends."

It was hard for Al to believe. "Pidal and you?"

"Sí."

"Good friends!"

"Sí."

"Then he knows about the Spanish final?"

"¡Dios mio! Of course not. I took it from the wastepaper basket in Pidal's office. He knows nothing about it. Come, we'll finish our deal."

The close proximity of Carrega caused Al to gag again, and he brought the handkerchief back to his face.

"A cold, Meester Carter?" said Carrega as he walked back toward the bedroom.

"Allergies,"Al said as he staggered behind him.

Carrega handed the examination sheets to Al who, no longer able to stand, sat on the edge of the bed. "One hundred dollars, por favor!"

"Hey, muh man. Hold your horses. I wanna be sure this is really the test."

"Take your time, Meester Carter. I'm not going nowhere." Carrega sat down on the bed. Al got a whiff and turned green. He reached into his pocket, grabbed the twenty-dollar bills, and threw them at Carrega. Then he quickly stood up and grabbed the attaché case. As soon as he stepped outside and began to breathe in the fresh air, his spirits returned. After reading the first few lines of the test, he lifted his head and laughed out loud. In no time he was strutting up Penn Drive, playing "Happy Days Are Here Again" on his banjo.

24

••

When Tom's number-one leisure-time activity was termi-
nated, he turned to bowling. For him it was something to do
during a study break. For me it was just another activity to
relieve the monotony. I often wished he had turned to something else. Although he was wise in most matters, he sure
picked a loser of a sport. But I felt somewhat responsible for
alienating the couple next door, and I was anxious that Tom
find something new to occupy his time. So there we were in
the foul, cigar-smelling atmosphere of Kelly's Bowlodrome,
bowling our asses off and saying shit things that bowlers say.
Things like "Pretty shot, Art." "Tough shot, Tom." "You
missed by a coat of paint, Art." "You missed it by a cunt hair,
Tom." "You're as hot as a pistol; I'm as cold as a witch's tit."
We talked about turkeys, blind pins, pockets, jerseys, cherries,
and all of the other crap that bowlers talk about.

While we recited the bowling litany, Al Carter appeared. At
first he sat in the spectators' area, watching us from a distance.
He seemed to be debating whether to approach us and unload
whatever he was carrying. He cracked his gum feverishly and
his eyes darted from side to side. He dangled a cigarette from
the corner of his mouth and periodically jerked his head side-

ways to see if he was being followed. I glanced back at him, saw the obvious intrigue, and wondered who might be after him. Perhaps the administration was finally onto his pen fiasco and was closing in on him.

Al was years out of South Philadelphia, but he just couldn't shake that hood look. He no longer had the D.A. haircut, but his hair was a little too long for the times and there was still a suggestion of grease. It's true that Keystone was not the Ivy League, but it wasn't Calvin Coolidge High either. But there was old Al looking like he just came off American Bandstand, complete with turned-up collar and cigarette pack tucked tightly under his rolled-up shirtsleeve.

I had just made the 9-10 split and I walked back to the scorer's chair. Al had stopped twisting and jerking long enough to have seen the shot. I thought he would be impressed, but he had something else on his mind. He disregarded my expertise. "C'mere!" he whispered, and he began jerking his head backwards in a horrible twitch.

I did what I thought was a pretty good imitation. I jerked my head back toward the pins and whispered, "I'm bowling. C'mon down here!"

I sat down and Tom was preparing to throw the ball. Al extended his thumb and jabbed it several times toward Tom, making it clear that he did not want Tom in on the conversation.

It was a disagreeable chore just to be bowling. I didn't have to play Al's silly game too. So I gave him my best "Don't worry about Tom—he's okay" look and turned back to mark Tom's score. Al decided to play his cool number. He got up and began walking down toward us, clapping his hands in front, then in back of him. He even added something new to his routine—a rhythmic snapping of fingers. When this one-man band arrived at the scorer's desk, Tom was sitting there, and I was addressing the same pins in the same absurd set-up I would look at some thirty or forty consecutive times during the evening. God, bowling was a bore!

"How's your mom, Tom?" Al asked.

"You know, Al, I really don't see the humor in that. It's not funny at all." Since Harrisburg, the two of them rarely spoke, except for Al's occasional momisms.

Now I was returning from my latest round with the pins. I had just missed the 8 pin in the 2-4-5-8 combination, and as custom dictated, I cursed the "mother-in-law," which in bowlers' jargon is the unseen 8 pin in the rear. Tom handed me the pencil and we exchanged positions.

"We got the test!" Al said in an excited whisper.

I was genuinely puzzled. "We got the test—we got the test," I said, hoping that the repetition might shock me into remembering something. Nothing clicked for me, and while Al sat, nodding his head and cracking his gum, I got up to bowl again. As I raced down the approach, it occurred to me that a little bit of Wickers had rubbed off on Al.

"Okay, we got the test," I said as I returned. "Just what test have we got?"

"The Spanish final, Art." He quickly looked from side to side, making sure he hadn't been heard. "We stole the Spanish final," he said triumphantly.

Unfortunately, Al had spoken a little too loudly. It was again time for the changing of the guard, and the self-appointed trustee of virtue was at that moment returning to the chair. And he heard.

Al made a feeble attempt to put Tom off. "Why don't you bowl a couple of extra frames while Art and I—"

"Jee-zuz, Art! You're not listening to him, are you?"

"Tom," I said. "I don't know any more about this than you do. I can't imagine what he wants with me, but certainly we should at least let the man finish. You especially should know that every person is innocent till proven guilty. Even Al is entitled to his day in court."

"Seems I heard that line before." Tom said, thinking back to his famous, but regrettable, lobster-tail decision. But I had hit at Tom's ultimate weakness—curiosity. We took a bowling recess and he sat down with us to hear the details.

Al enjoyed acting out his little intrigues and managed to squeeze every ounce of drama out of a situation. To prep himself for his story, he hunched his back so his chin was down almost level with his navel. He snapped his fingers and increased the frequency of his gum-cracking. He looked over his left and then his right shoulder. When he was sure he had not been followed, he began whispering.

Tom and I hunched over in similar positions, straining on every word. It wasn't that Al was so terribly interesting, but he had an irritating habit of speaking just below the average person's threshold of hearing.

"Your friend Pidal makes no secret 'bout his sexual preferences."

"Pidal is not my friend!" I said adamantly. In the early sixties, homosexuals were perverts, and one had to vigorously deny any association with them. I had a genuine hatred for the man, and it had nothing to do with his homosexuality. I hated him strictly because he was a rotten bastard and not because he was a goddamn queer.

"Hey, I was only kidding. Everyone knows Pidal's a fruit. I know you're not his friend. Just the opposite, right?" He stopped snapping long enough to throw a light, good-natured punch up near my shoulder. He desperately needed my help in his venture and he didn't want to antagonize me.

"Al, why don't you just get on with it?" I said.

"Okay, okay." Then he paused long enough to create a new dramatic mood, which wasn't easy on the thirty-first lane of Kelly's Bowlodrome. He stopped his St. Vitus dancing, hunched a little lower, and in a voice tinged with great suspense, he whispered, "Ramirez Carrega." Then he sat and waited for my response.

I stared back at him with an expression that mirrored exactly what was going on in my mind. I spoke fluent Spanish, but the words "Ramirez Carrega" meant absolutely nothing. "Al, talk sense," I said.

"You've never heard of Ramirez Carrega?"

"What is it?" I asked.

"The gymnast. Christ, Arthur. You're really out of it. Everyone knows Ramirez Carrega."

"Except me. I'm out to lunch, right? Fine! Now stop the riddles and get to the point, Al, or we're going to start bowling again."

"Okay, Art. Cool it! In plain English, Carrega is Pidal's girlfriend."

"They're lovers?"

He smiled and again punched me in the arm, an action that I interpreted as an affirmative answer.

"Carrega's no fairy!" Tom said indignantly. "I don't believe it!"

"Tom, there were certain things I didn't believe about your mom either."

Tom immediately stood up and began walking away. As he passed me, I grabbed his shirtsleeve and said, "C'mon, Tom, he didn't mean it. Stick around!"

"I don't see the humor, Art. Jee-zuz, it's just not funny. Would you explain what's so damn funny about it?

We assured him it really wasn't funny, and both of us struggled to hold the laughter back. Finally, Tom sat down.

Al continued. "Okay, Tom. Let's put it this way—Carrega is close to Pidal. They spend time together. A lot of time together. But you're right. I don't know what they do in private. But I don't think that's even important."

"Just what is important?" I asked impatiently.

"The important thing is that Ramirez Carrega removed a copy of the final examination from Pidal's office yesterday, and he's willing to sell it for a hundred dollars."

"Just why am I being forced to listen to this?" Tom asked.

"And what do you want from me?" I said.

"Personally, I don't give a shit if you listen or not," Al said to Tom. And to me he said, "Art, I thought you'd want a piece of the action."

"Are you nuts? Why would I want the Spanish final? I already know everything there is to know about the goddamn language. I'll get an A without cracking a book. And you want me to pay for it, too? That's like an ass-man paying Daisy Boyle."

"Okay, forget the money," Al said quickly, and I realized he never had any real hope I would pay. "Come in for nothing."

"If I don't pay, what do you need me for?"

"I'm flunking Spanish, Art. If I don't get at least a high C in the final, I won't graduate. It all hinges on that test."

"So study the stolen test. You don't need me."

"Art, I don't know shit. Most of those questions need answers in Spanish. If you don't help me, I'm finished, even *with* the test."

Al was telling the truth. Having the test was not enough to pull a dumb-ass like him through, especially if he needed a high C. My mind churned feverishly.

"Jee-zuz, Art, you're not going to listen to him. Don't be a fool!"

Tom had seen me stray before, and he now was my self-appointed conscience. It was going to be Armageddon as Tom and Al struggled to capture my soul. I had to consider all the possibilities. On the surface it seemed like an overpowering case against going in with the cheaters. It was stupid, worthless, and dangerous. But somehow, pulling Al and the rest of the dummies through the final would get me some additional revenge on Pidal. And also—it was always good to get Tom pissed off. Oh yeah, this was just going to be perfect for me. Now all that remained was to twist it around with some ridiculous rationalizations—for Tom's sake, of course.

"Tom," I said, "is there anything in this world that's more important than friendship?"

"Jee-zuz! I knew it! I just knew it! It's so absurd. You've

accomplished so much in Spanish. There's no reason for you to cheat."

"Cheat? Who said anything about cheating? I'm just going to help a good friend who's in a jam."

"By stealing the final exam?"

"Al, do you know for a fact that the test you have is actually the Spanish final?" I asked.

Al played the game. "Well, of course I'm not one hundred percent sure." He punched my arm.

"So, it's possible that the paper you have is *not* the exam," I said.

"Sure!"

"It could be one of several exams being considered by the department."

"Absolutely!"

"It could even be an old exam from last year or the year before."

"Fuckin' A!"

"See what I mean, Tom? This isn't really cheating. It's no different than going through an exam file. You've done that yourself. Are you a cheater when you study a few old tests at the fraternity?"

"It's not the same and you know it!"

"Tom, we just can't be sure that Al has the real exam. It's possible old Ramirez made the whole thing up to earn a few extra pesos. And even if this is the exam, there's every chance the department will discover what's happened and they'll make up a new one."

"This is the most ridiculous pack of horse manure I've ever heard!" Tom said. He stood up and stretched the kinks from his back. "Mitch and Al are plenty bad, but you are by far the sickest one of the bunch." He began walking away from us.

His mention of Mitch's name gave me a new idea that I couldn't resist throwing at him. "Tom, if it makes you feel any better, we'll eat the exam when we're done with it!"

25

•••

It was a memorable evening, filled with poignant ingredients that time has batter-dipped, deep-fried, and still occasionally serves to me without appreciable loss of crispness or flavor. It was our very own Last Supper. It marked the last time that all of us were together before each went to his respective crucifixion. It was a brief, pleasant interlude just before the shit hit the fan, and like the original Last Supper, it even had a betrayal.

Before I describe the dinner and the incredible logistics involved in its preparation, I must say a few words about Al Carter. Al was not the star. I'm not even sure he played a supporting role. If awards were to be given, he would probably have won for musical score or maybe special effects.

It was only two days before the Spanish final, and Al was really sweating it. I had spent a lot of time trying to help, but it just didn't come that easy for him, and he still worried that the test might be a red herring. Lately he had become increasingly paranoid over his pen deal. His inventory was still extremely high, and he was afraid the administration might be onto him. He had asked the factory salesman to help him by taking back a few thousand pens. The salesman refused, and when Al persisted, there were some veiled threats. Actually, the salesman had asked if Al was willing to return his Miami trip.

The mood had gotten ugly, and it put additional pressure on Al to study his Spanish. If he failed and had to stay an extra semester, there was the distinct possibility he might be arrested. He had become a desperate man. He had to pass the test with a high C.

Throughout most of the meal, Al sat alone at the far end of the table, reciting the long list of Spanish dictation. Occasionally he referred to his copy of the test that lay on his lap, but most of the exam had been memorized.

Because Al really had no idea what each individual word meant, the sentences had no expression and came out in a monotone. Spanish is a lot like Latin, so it sounded exactly like the Gregorian chant. Al sang the words in a soft, mellow monotone. "Me asusta la idea de pasar seis semanas de verano en Sevilla." And every time he chanted, it was difficult to refrain from singing Amen.

It didn't really matter that the translation was "The idea of spending six weeks of summer in Seville frightened me." For all I know, that might be exactly what they are saying when they chant in Latin.

Al Carter not only supplied the background for our dinner; he *was* the background. His continuous chanting created the mood. It was like a good sound track. You hardly realized it was there, because it blended so well with the action. During a lull in the conversation, which was rare, you could hear old Al going through his rituals. It reminded me of a Catholic hospital during vespers.

Except for a few worthless words he had with Tom, Al said absolutely nothing. But he did chant a great deal and was in the background the whole time.

Our fine dinner party kicked off Senior Weekend. Twelve people attended the extravaganza in our apartment. It was a unique meal, with Mitch having stolen most of what was served including thirty-six lobster tails and nine dozen shrimp. He stole the vegetables, the condiments, and two cherry-topped cheese cakes. He stole many bottles of vintage French wine and two magnums of Piper Heidsieck champagne as well as an elegant pair of bronze candlesticks and a great assortment of mixed nuts, although I would have preferred some pistachios and I told him so. He made four separate trips to harvest a crop like this. The project was so massive that the infamous blue raincoat was inadequate. Lobster tails were jammed into his underpants and under his T-shirt. Raw shrimp were forced down into his socks. Every pocket, sleeve, and cuff was stuffed with something edible. And every time he emerged from Save-a-Penny, he smelled more and more like Fisherman's Wharf.

The dinner was important to Mitch for two reasons. Behind that rocklike façade, I'm sure he realized a segment of his life was about to end, and this was his way to say good-bye. The dinner was also an anniversary present for his parents, who drove from Williamsport to celebrate the happy occasion with their wonderful, loving son. Naturally, they never suspected how Mitch got the food or the expensive Cuban cigars, neatly packaged individually in white metal cylinders, or the two exquisite silver wine goblets that Mitch gave them. "Dear Mom and Dad, This is my small way of repaying you both for all the happiness you have given me. Your loving son, Mitchel Howard Carpenter."

I thought it a bit much signing his full name like that. Just "Mitch" would have been sufficient. But, it was a lovely thought, and the fact that everything had been stolen did not remove any of the luster from that emotional moment.

Gladys Carpenter, who sat directly across from me, said, "What do you think of our Mitch, Arthur?" She was a lovely woman, and had she been able to read my mind, she would have been heartbroken.

I couldn't look at her. I chose instead to stare directly at Mitch, who at that moment was standing behind his mother, preparing to fill her glass with champagne. "Mrs. Carpenter," I said, trying desperately to hold back the laughter, "you can really be proud of your son. He's our good friend, and he's a credit to you and Mr. Carpenter." Upon mouthing this absurdity, I nudged Carol while Mitch, satisfied with my reply, went busily around the table with his Piper Heidsieck.

"Did he really steal everything?" Carol whispered.

"Everything except the soda. That's his rule. He always pays for the soda. He's a man of principles, although I must say the principles are always subject to change."

"Hey, you two lovebirds, save that love talk for later." It came from the sneering mouth of J.P. Zuckerman, and when he said it, he stared at Carol—my Carol, and of course, I fumed.

I had only seen him a few times since Harrisburg. He had been invited to the dinner over my objections. "Let bygones be bygones," Mitch had said. "Besides, he'll add some color." Mitch was right, but black is not the kind of color that goes over big at a dinner party. As always, J.P.'s presence began to inhibit me. This time I was determined not to let him get me down. It was supposed to be a happy time, and I felt I must mount a verbal attack to keep him from getting to me.

As you must know by now, the normal way to attack was to go after Mom, but because of my history with J.P., I made an exception. "Tell me, J.P., how is your dad?" It drew a laugh from the guests, which the Carpenters didn't quite understand.

"Dad is just fine, Arthur," said J.P., his mouth frozen in a comedy mask. He continued to stare at Carol, and it continued to piss me off.

"Is he back from Pittsburgh?"

"He's back, Arthur."

"I understand he was involved in some sort of car accident out there." This brought more laughs from the guys and more quizzical looks from Mr. and Mrs. Carpenter.

"Yes, but he's much better now. He's made a complete recovery. As good as new."

I had to stay on the offensive. "I'm glad. There was a rumor going around that—well, that your father was dead, and frankly, I was a little bit concerned." This time the laughter was deafening, and Mitch's poor parents were shocked.

"Art, what is this?" Carol whispered. "Will you stop it?" She pulled at my sleeve and Mitch was now frantically shaking his head at me.

"Don't worry about it," I said quietly to her. "I'll explain it to you later."

"I have no idea how a story like that got around. He's very much alive," J.P. said.

"You're sure he's not dead?"

"Quite sure, Arthur," and not once did his grotesque expression change.

Mitch was now behind me, reaching over to fill my glass. "Will you cut this shit!" he whispered.

"But look who I'm talking to. He's an animal," I said.

"My parents, dammit. My parents don't understand it. Now knock it off!"

"Okay, okay. Don't worry about it." But I couldn't resist a parting shot at this despicable creature who had killed his father, in spite of what he was now saying. "I'm really glad he's not dead. I've been meaning to ask you before about it, but it always seems to slip my mind." Before Mitch was able to reprimand me, I said, "I'm done. I promise you." And, of course, the guys were laughing.

I was finished, but I had the feeling that J.P. wasn't. There was just no way to embarrass him, and he always had the ammunition to come back and cause me a great deal of pain. I was most vulnerable when Carol was next to me, and J.P. knew it.

He had never taken his eyes off her during our conversation. He started to bear down on her when he said, "It's nice to have you here, Carol. Did you have a pleasant trip?"

"Yes, it was very nice, thank you."

It wasn't right that I should have to listen to this, and my flesh crawled accordingly. He was doing some light skirmishing.

"How do you like our campus?"

"Very much," she said.

I was trying desperately to be nonchalant. I leaned toward the Carpenters, appearing to be unconcerned with J.P.'s talk. I tried to involve myself in their conversation, but I heard only J.P.'s voice. He discussed his plans for the summer. While his own date listened politely, he told Carol about the chain of Zuckerman Theaters that he would be running. This led to a discussion of Harrisburg. It was all meaningless chatter, but I was still apprehensive and was afraid to turn him off.

Then, without warning, he suddenly closed in. "By the way, Carol, where are you staying?"

Bingo! There was no nerve in my body that was more exposed than the one J.P. had just touched. He was a prick— there was no doubt about it. But dammit, he was a smart, intuitive prick, and that is the worst kind. He had that uncanny ability to quickly determine how best to get to me.

For a long time I had agonized over where Carol would stay. There were several options: A motel, my apartment, the dormitory. The situation clearly called for a decision, so it was predictable that I would vacillate. It was likely that my decision would be "no decision." My choice implied a commitment. And as hard as an ordinary decision might be for me, a decision coupled with a commitment was even harder.

What's the big deal? Where is the great commitment? A motel committed me to going all the way with Carol. The dormitory committed me to not going all the way. And if Carol stayed at my apartment, I would have to ask my roommates to move out. It's not that they wouldn't have done it. Fact is, they both volunteered to leave, but I refused their offer. Asking them to leave would have been a positive decision and a grave commitment. And worst of all, they would have known what we did.

You find this a little hard to believe, don't you? But behind your goddamn smugness you have fourteen years of retrospect wrapped comfortably around your shoulders. I know the whole thing was absurd, but—that's the way it was. In those days, even the ass-men couldn't talk about it if it was with women they loved. In other words, the ass-man cometh, but not with his girlfriend. You could make love only with someone you didn't love, and if it happened with a girlfriend, you made damn sure nobody knew about it. You wouldn't want your girlfriend to be known as a whore.

Speaking of whores, it was Daisy Boyle who inadvertently saved me. She had not been an invited guest, but had come as J.P.'s date. Mitch didn't know about it before that evening, so when she appeared at the door on J.P.'s arm, there was not much that could be done about it.

"But my parents," Mitch had said to J.P. "This is an insult to my parents."

"Daisy won't bother your parents, unless of course, your father is looking for something." Before Mitch could start ranting, J.P. said, "Only kidding, Mitch." J.P. knew when to back off.

Most of the guests had already arrived, and Mitch didn't want to make a scene. "Okay, she can stay, but tell her to keep her mouth shut. Don't embarrass me!"

So there sat Daisy, reeking of pungent perfume, and of course she was wearing her grinning foxes. I was somewhat in awe of her. With the possible exception of Mr. Carpenter, she had screwed every male at the table at least once. When Carol was unable to answer J.P.'s question and I had been stricken dumb, Daisy said, "Oh, Carol, why don't you stay with me?" Everyone laughed except Mitch's confused parents.

"No thanks, Daisy. I've made other arrangements," Carol said.

It seemed like all other conversation stopped and everyone was looking at me. I gulped my wine and pretended to be the invisible man.

"You really shouldn't drink so much, Arthur. You know what happens to you when you've had one too many." Daisy said it in her best slattern's voice, and this time even the parents laughed.

Carol didn't, and neither did I. But the short exchange got everyone's mind off the original question, and by the time J.P. had remembered, Mitch had finished pouring the champagne.

"Art, you're good at this. You make the toast," Mitch said.

"Only if Tom will join us," I said.

"Where is Tom?" asked Mrs. Carpenter.

"He's in the bedroom studying for his finals," Mitch said.

"Doesn't he even break for dinner?" Mr. Carpenter asked.

"He hasn't been feeling well. An upset stomach or something," I said. I didn't have the heart to tell him that the dinner was being boycotted because his beloved son had stolen everything from soup to nuts. I just couldn't say that Tom chose to stay in his room rather than dine with a thief like Mitch, a prick like J.P., a whore like Daisy, and cheats like Al and me.

"Charles, why don't you see if you can persuade Tom to join us?" I said. "You're about the only one he's not pissed off at." I had spoken quietly. I didn't want the Carpenters to hear.

But Wickers was incapable of answering quietly. His piercing words always seemed to rise above any conversation. "You're not entirely correct, Ahthuh. Don't you remembah? I was the one who thought Tom committed suicide."

Mitch's parents were looking our way again. Most of the evening's conversation was quite confusing to them.

"Oh, I don't think Tom would hold a grudge over something as minor as that. So what if you thought he'd killed himself? It's not such a terrible mistake. Mitch and I thought he was dead too, you know."

"Hmm. Maybe youah right, Ahthuh."

"Sure, I'm right. You know Tom. He's too nice a guy to stay angry. He's so pissed off at us, he probably won't even remember he's pissed off at you."

"I'll get him," Wickers said, rising to go to the bedroom. "Unless, of course, he's dead." He threw his head back and cackled. I've been told I have a weird sense of humor, and although people never say it to my face, I'm certain they think I'm pretty strange. But I couldn't hold a candle to Chahles M. Wickahs in that department.

With Wickers gone on his mission, I felt obligated to say a few words to his date. I think her name was Sybil, and except that she tended to stare a great deal and needed some orthodontal work, I remember nothing about her. She was as nondescript as a person could be. After that evening, I never saw her again, and until this moment, I have never even thought of her.

"Are you enjoying yourself?" I asked, flashing my amiable smile. I wasn't sure if her name was Sybil, and there was no point in taking a chance.

"After a fashion," said whatshername. "You're Arthur, aren't you?"

"Yes, I am. I guess it's not easy meeting so many new people and remembering everyone's name." God, I hated small talk.

She said, "Charles has spoken about you."

"Oh, really?" It was so painful for me.

She nodded and stared.

"I hope he said some nice things about me."

"No, not really."

And that concluded my first and only conversation with Sybil. Wickers had returned with Tom behind him. "He's agreed to join us for the toast and spend the rest of the evening with us," Wickers said triumphantly.

"How did you manage that?" I whispered.

"He'll drink the toast with soda," said Wickers, and in a very loud voice, he explained to Sybil, "I forgot to tell you, soda is the only thing that Mitchel doesn't steal."

It was like watching a Ping-Pong match the way Mitch's

parents kept craning their heads back and forth. They were hearing some pretty preposterous stuff.

When things had quieted down, I stood up to give the toast. Everyone looked up at me except Al, who was now chanting about a train arriving over three hours late in Guadalajara. Out of respect for Mr. and Mrs. Carpenter, I felt he should stop, at least while I was toasting them.

"Al?" I said.

He was oblivious and continued his chanting, this time about a seafood dish that was extremely popular in the restaurants of Barcelona.

"Al!" I said in a much louder voice.

"¿Sí?"

"Al, first of all, it's *los* restaurantes."

"What did I say?"

"You said, *las* restaurantes."

"Gracias, Art," and he began chanting again, this time about the high cost of groceries in Madrid.

"Al, do you think you could hold up on that for a minute or two? We're going to toast the Carpenters."

"Oh, sure, Art. I'm sorry." He placed a cigarette in the corner of his mouth and let it dangle while he searched for a light. He noticed that Tom had joined the group. "Tom, old buddy. Good to see you out of hibernation." Then he pointed to the unlit cigarette. "How 'bout a match?"

"I don't smoke," Tom said curtly.

"Yeah, that's right. It figures you wouldn't. Well, let me give you a match—my shit and your mother's meat loaf."

It brought a big laugh from everyone at that end of the table. "Jee-zuz," said Tom to anyone who would listen, "I have a sense of humor. It's not that I don't have a sense of humor. I just can't see what's so funny about that stuff. Art, can you honestly say that's funny?"

Although the others broke up, I managed to control my own laughter, and I shook my head.

When the latest round of laughter subsided, I began. "I'd like to propose a toast to Mr. and Mrs. Carpenter, who are celebrating their twenty-fifth wedding anniversary today. We're honored that they're sharing their happy occasion with our little group. We wish you many years of continued happiness. Mitch is lucky to have parents like you. And you have every reason to be extremely proud of your wonderful son—our good friend Mitchel."

I looked over at Mitch with something less than the loving looks now focused on him by his parents and his date, Miss Glenda Fenstemacher, a tall, pretty girl who loved to eat and drink.

He looked back and I could feel the tension mounting. Like most people, he exaggerated my dangerousness. I never even considered exposing his terrible secret, but that was his greatest fear at that moment. As he glared at me, he seemed to be saying, "If you embarrass me in front of my parents, I'll kick your fuckin' head in." I hadn't planned to proceed any further, but Mitch's looks spirited me on.

"Let's not forget that it is Mitch who almost single-handedly made this evening possible. And although some of us may take issue with his methods," and I looked directly at Tom, "I'm sure we'll all agree—Mitch gets the job done. When you make an omelette, you have to break a few eggs. Right, Tom?" I threw my best Al Carter punch, which landed on Tom's shoulder.

Everyone laughed except Tom and Mitch. Wickers went completely out of control in the loudest cackling fit I had ever heard. His eyes rolled high up into his forehead and his chair tilted backwards, spilling him over the back and onto the floor. No one moved to help him, but in only a second or two he was back in view, sitting on the chair again and giggling louder than ever. I should have been used to his insanity, but I was still amazed by this latest display. My remarks, at best, were moderately funny, and I was not prepared for such a reaction, even from Charles M. Wickers. Maybe I was really an extremely funny person—funnier than I ever had imagined—and only Wickers was sharp enough to catch the humor. I would like to have believed that, but I'm afraid it was just another example of Wickers being tuned to a different station.

When he seemed to regain control, I calmly said, "Charles, are you all right?"

He wiped the tears from his face. "Oh, Gahd, Ahthuh. I nevah laughed so hahd in my life."

"I know, Charles. I could see you really broke up. Was it really that funny?"

"It's the funniest thing I evah remembah."

I looked into his eyes and tried to determine just what went on inside that crazed mind. Then I remembered my earlier pledge to listen to his nonsense without probing. I accepted his answer and proceeded with the toast. "I know everyone will agree that tonight Mitch made the finest omelette in history. So let's drink to the three Carpenters and wish them continued success and happiness."

Before the evening was over, most everyone at the table had given a toast of some kind. One notable exception was Al Carter, who, after my opening round, returned to his chanting and kept pretty much to himself. Even when J.P. lifted his glass to Al and in an overly dramatic voice said, "May your enterprise prosper," an obvious Shakespearean reference to the Spanish final, Al barely broke stride. He merely nodded to J.P., who was impressed with any kind of foul play, and sang on about the heavy Moorish influence in many areas of contemporary Spanish life.

The other person who took no part in the festivities was Mitch's date, Glenda Fenstemacher. At about the same time that J.P. was giving his toast, Glenda became nauseated. Although J.P. could turn anyone's stomach, I'm certain there was no cause-effect relationship. It was a combination of too much food and drink, and the fast pace of the evening had taken its toll on her. She had whispered to Mitch that she wasn't feeling well, and he told her not to embarrass him in front of his parents. I give Glenda a lot of credit for the way she handled herself. After three or four toasts, when at last she could no longer control her urge to purge, she politely excused herself. Then she calmly walked to the bathroom, where she spent the balance of the evening vomiting, gargling with Green Mint, and reading Eustace Chesser's *Love Without Fear*.

And again, I must say it was to Glenda Fenstemacher's eternal credit that during her illness she was never a burden to anyone. She cheerfully accepted her sad lot and caused no pain for Mitch and his parents. When one of the other guests needed the bathroom facilities, she took her book and went to the bedroom. She could have given the brothers of Delta Pi Beta a few lessons on general vomiting etiquette. She was neat and quiet, and except for the periodic flushings, no one would have suspected that Glenda had taken up residence in the bathroom. As far as I was concerned, the flushing provided a nice counterpoint to Al's chanting and kept the momentum going for the entire evening.

When the champagne and the wine kicked, we started on the beer. By now, the presence of Mitch's parents no longer inhibited us. By the end of the evening, everyone, including the folks, was really bombed. The fine party had degenerated into a fraternity-style drinking party. The silver goblets of wine were replaced by paper cups of beer. Over my protests, everyone sang "The Muffin Man," a disgusting little ditty that was typical of my Keystone days.

It was sung to the tune of "Jingle Bells," and Mitch started, "Does Art know, does Art know, does Art know his name? Does Art know the Muffin Man who lives on Brewery Lane?"

I reluctantly placed a beer cup on top of my head and sang, "Yes, I know, yes, I know, yes, I know his name. Yes, I know the Muffin Man who lives on Brewery Lane . . ." Then I sang a verse using Tom's name.

The mindless tune made its way around the table until everyone had sung a verse. After each solo, the singer chug-a-lugged the contents of the cup. Occasionally a cup would fall off someone's head, drenching him with beer. This was occasion for raucous laughter.

When the song had run its course, Mr. Carpenter stood and gave the final toast of the evening. "I propose this toast to all of you guys and your gals. You're a swell bunch of youngsters, and Gladys and I are both right proud of all of you. Here's to you kids, the Class of Nineteen Hundred Sixty One—you're the cream of the crop."

We laughed and shouted and then broke into the spontaneous singing of the Keystone Fight Song. Even Al lifted his head from his papers to join in. And Glenda quickly brushed her teeth with her finger and stumbled out of the bathroom for this grand finale.

With my permission, Mitch had credited his account for a portion of the dinner's cost. It made me sort of a co-host for the party, so now I was performing one of my official duties—saying good-bye. Mitch and I stood at the doorway as the curtain began to close on our college days.

Wickers and Sybil were the first to leave. He pumped Mitch's hand and looked at the remains of the massive dinner that had been lifted from the aisles of the Save-a-Penny. In the most picturesque words I ever heard, he said, "Mitchel, this time you really raped the harvest." Then he turned to me, and his eyes reddened. I was shocked to hear his voice cracking when he said, "Ahtie, you've made this a good yea-ah for me. Thank you." He shook my hand and he was genuinely sad to be saying good-bye.

I'm not particularly proud to say that his unexpected warmth made me uncomfortable. He was not in his otherworld when he spoke, and he wasn't drunk. There was real feeling. I didn't know how I helped him have a good year and I was uneasy. I wasn't pleased with myself at that moment.

"Good luck, Charles. I'll see you around," I said, cursing myself for choking.

"We'll keep in touch, won't we?" he asked.

"Of course, we will. Graduation doesn't mean the end of friendship."

"Good, Ahtie. I know you mean that. Good-bye."

He walked through the doorway and our strange friendship ended.

"Good-bye, Arthur!" Mrs. Carpenter said, extending her hand to me. I took it and we kissed. "Thank you for the lovely evening." She too was fighting a losing battle with the tears.

"I'm glad you had a good time, but it was really Mitch who—"

"Never mind about Mitchel. We're his parents. He's stuck with us. But you're not, Art. And that's why we appreciate your sweetness."

The choking that left with Wickers was back.

"You know, Mitch talks about you a lot. He's really quite fond of you. And from what he says, everyone feels the same way."

I was no longer able to answer, so I didn't try.

"What are your plans?" she asked.

"My plans?" Her question caught me off guard. At first I thought she was asking me about my plans with Carol for the remainder of the evening. Carol was still very much on my mind, and a few hours in J.P.'s company had left me paranoid on that matter.

"What will you do after graduation?"

I couldn't even bring myself to give the standard "Nothing concrete—but I have a few irons in the fire" reply. Her talk had stripped all the bullshit from me and I was scared.

"Mrs. Carpenter, I really don't know." They were the first honest words I had spoken in a long time.

"Well, you don't have anything to worry about. You can do

anything you want. And I mean anything. You have what it takes."

"Thank you." I didn't know what it took, but I was certain I didn't have it.

"Mitch is a problem. He wants to go to medical school more than anything else in the world. But I'm beginning to think it's not in the cards."

I flashed a picture of the cards tumbling out an open window. "Don't give up!" I said. "Something will turn up."

"I hope so." She looked away from me and she seemed to grow weary and sad. But just as quickly she pulled herself together and her effervescence returned. "Well—you know where Williamsport is. Let's keep in touch."

"Don't worry, Mrs. Carpenter, I'll be visiting you. I'll be there so often, you'll get sick of me."

She and her husband finished their good-byes and stepped into the hall. I never saw either of them again.

"Arthur," said J.P.

"J.P.," I replied.

"I guess this is it," said J.P.

"Uh—yeah, it appears that it is." I didn't look at him.

"Good luck to you." He smiled and his goddamn eyes fell on Carol.

"Arthur, I'd like to think we had a decent rapport between us this year."

"Uh—yeah."

"I hope that we may continue after graduation as something more than acquaintances."

"What did you have in mind, J.P.?"

"Friends, Arthur. Make new friends, but keep the old. One is silver—"

"And the other is gold." And to the oldest, goldest prick I ever knew, I said, "See you in Harrisburg, J.P."

"Me too, Arthur?" asked Daisy.

"I'll see you both in Harrisburg. You can count on that."

They left our apartment. I never saw either of them again.

"I'm nervous, Art. What if it isn't the test?" Al said.

"Don't sweat it!" I said. "I'm sure it's the test."

"You jay-ohin' me, man? Huh? You really believe that? Huh, man? You're not shittin' me, are you? Huh?"

"What's the first sentence in the exam?" I asked.

From memory he recited, "Me asusta la idea—"

"Okay, take it from me, Pidal is going to stand up and say, Estudiantes, atención!—Dictado—numero uno—Me asusta la idea, etcetera, etcetera. And when you hear those words, Al baby, and believe me, you'll hear them, you'll want to stand up and cheer."

"Thanks, Art. I hope you're right. Hey, Art, I won't be sitting with you at the exam. Too suspicious, don't you think? So, in case we don't see each other, I'll say good-bye now."

"Okay, Al. Lots of luck." I shook his hand. "I'll see you this summer."

He folded his papers and stuffed them into his back pants pocket. He walked into the hallway, but before he got too far away, he pulled out the paper and started chanting again. I saw him at the Spanish final two days later, but we didn't talk. And after that, I never saw him again.

26

• •

The three crises began on Saturday when Al Carter left our apartment at the stroke of midnight. The end came some thirty-six hours later with the arrival of the U.S. mail at high noon. The crises involved Carol, Al, and Mitch, in that order. I played a peripheral role in all three. You might say I was the catalyst in the proceedings, taking no real active part—a shadowy figure just passively witnessing and being carried in any direction the currents happened to flow.

Of the three crises, I would characterize one as a seemingly hopeless case that miraculously turned into a stunning victory. The second was a seemingly great triumph that became one of the biggest disasters since Charles Van Doren was caught cheating. The third was a tie—no contest—a stalemate. And it was on that most unmemorable record of one win, one loss, one tie that I wrapped up my lackluster college career—four long years that were summed up in the Keystone Yearbook with the words "picture not available."

Mitch motioned me toward the bedroom so Carol wouldn't hear. "Don't be an asshole!" he whispered. "Just give us the word and we'll move out. Right, Tom?"

Tom was sitting on the edge of the bed, removing his shoes and socks. He looked out at me through the doorway. "Just say the word and we leave!"

"It's not necessary. I told you guys that before. Now would you get off my back!"

But Mitch was persistent. In spite of what I said, he was still sure that I really wanted them to leave. Perhaps he was right, but I was Pennsylvania's leading exponent of not thinking. And since I had forced myself not to think about it, I really didn't know what I wanted.

"Suppose Tom and I sleep in the living room. Then you and Carol can uhhh—" He threw his head backward toward the bedroom.

"Don't worry about us! I appreciate your concern, but really—we're fine. I'll see you guys tomorrow."

"Okay," Tom said. "Suit yourself."

"I still say you're an asshole," Mitch said, "I just want you to know that."

"Your remarks are duly noted. Thank you for sharing your thoughts with me." I walked back into the living room and sat down next to Carol. I heard them arguing in the bedroom. Most of the words were muffled, but I did hear Tom say that something was none of Mitch's business. I assumed they were talking about me and most likely my sleeping arrangements. The word "asshole" popped up two more times, but then, after a few minutes, the conversation ended. Now Carol and I were alone.

She was sitting on the couch, her legs drawn up beneath her, and on her lap she held a tattered throw pillow, too tightly, it seemed. Often I had seen her in this position, and thought the pillow was strategically placed as a first-line defense against me. I thought of asking her about it but could never quite get the words out. It was much too delicate a subject. Unfortunately, most areas of interest were too delicate or too sacred to talk about, so the important stuff remained inside me, causing immeasurable damage to my working parts, I'm sure.

· 171 ·

As I crossed the living room, a serious thought surfaced. Where would she spend the night? It was imperative that it be discussed—immediately. Here I was, near the journey's end with my "Virgin Mary," no room at the inn, and all I could say to her was, "Carol, you really shouldn't sit like that."

"Why?"

"You'll cut off the blood circulation in your legs."

I'm sure she was expecting a great deal more, and she certainly was entitled to it. I concentrated on the lodging matter. I'm sure even Joseph must have discussed it with Mary, although he was a shadowy figure too, and for all I know, he also may have been unable to communicate. But I just couldn't get the words out. I chose to avoid the issue entirely by using diversionary tactics. I sat down next to her on the couch, and without saying another word, I turned the radio on, switched off the floor lamp, and began to make out. "Making out" was all sexual activity ranging from kissing on the lips to anything short of going all the way. Today it's called foreplay, but there's one big difference. It's only the preliminary contest, a warm-up for the main event which, barring unforeseen difficulties, usually follows. Making out *was* the main event, often developing into a three- or four-hour marathon, and in the process, superhuman endurance records were set.

I had proceeded to "feeling her up" outside the clothes— no further than that, when suddenly she pulled away and said, "Art, there's something I must ask you." This statement has always been the second most frightening phrase in the world for me. And because of what I was doing at the time, her words became an instant ball-breaker. I sat there stunned and terrified.

"What is it?" I finally managed to whisper, and I trembled in anticipation.

She sat quietly for a few seconds and the suspense mounted. Finally she said, "Where am I staying tonight?"

"This is a hell of a time to ask a question like that."

"You're right. I should have asked you hours ago. Of course, if you had told me the arrangements, I wouldn't have asked you at all."

"Well," I said, "we have any number of options open to us."

She had that knowing look. "In other words, you didn't make any arrangements."

"No, that's not true."

"Then tell me."

"Well, I, uh—thought it would be nice if you, uh—stayed right here."

"Here, in the apartment?"

"Yes."

"With you?"

"Of course with me. Certainly not with those two creeps in the bedroom." She smiled and seemed to be genuinely pleased that I would not be sending her away. "It's okay with you?" I asked.

"Sure! It's what I wanted."

I was puzzled. "If that's what you wanted all the time, then why didn't you say something?"

"I was afraid."

"Afraid? What in hell were you afraid of?"

"You."

"Me?" I really was amazed. I just couldn't believe that anyone, least of all Carol, could be afraid of me. "Don't be afraid to talk to me! My God, if we can't communicate with each other, we'll have no relationship at all." I winced when I said it. There was no one in the entire world less able to communicate than good old Arthur.

"When did you decide I would be staying here?" she asked.

I could feel her love. "I don't know. I really didn't think about it all that much. I didn't want to make a big deal out of it." It was said so nonchalantly that I found myself slipping into the same bullshit act I played with the guys. And it bothered me. Carol was not one of the guys, and she deserved better. I was accepting her admiration under false pretenses, and short-changing her over and over again. And it was only fitting that the Platters were singing "The Great Pretender."

"What are you thinking, Art?"

"I'm thinking that it's time to be honest. I just said I hardly thought of where you'd be staying. Well, that's a goddamn lie. In the last week I must have run it through my mind at least a thousand times. I was even thinking about it when you asked me. You were right—I hadn't made any arrangements. And if you hadn't brought it up, I'd probably still be sitting here, choking on it."

"Why, Art?"

"Probably because *I* was afraid."

"Of me?"

"Of you, yes. Of everything, actually. I'm pretty much afraid of everything. What would they call a phobia like that—paranoia?"

"I don't believe it," she said, shaking her head. "Nobody would believe it. Not you."

"I'm afraid it's true. I just happen to be a very good actor, so I do manage to fool most of the people most of the time."

"You fooled me. I always thought you were bursting with confidence."

"It's what I do best—this confidence bit. That's what I've been trying to tell you. I'm really a confidence man."

"That's funny."

"No, not really. I fool most of the people—not all of them."

"Who don't you fool?"

"J.P. for one. He can see right through me. He knows I'm a fraud."

"You're wrong, Art. First of all, you're not a fraud. Secondly, J.P. doesn't know it."

"You're nuts, you know. In your own way, you're as crazy as I am—crazier, even. I never thought you were insane before—but you are definitely a very sick woman."

"Would you like to know what J.P. said to me tonight?" she asked.

I braced myself. "What did the goddamn bastard say?"

"The goddamn bastard said you were the sharpest, cleverest guy he's ever met."

"You're putting me on."

"I'm not. It's just hard to believe what you've told me."

"Are you disappointed in me?" I asked.

"Are you disappointed in yourself?"

"Once—just once," I said as I took her hands, "would you not answer a question with a question?"

"Okay," she said finally, "I guess I'm a little disappointed."

"Thank you for not trying to con the conner. I'm the master of deceit—not you. Now, one more question for you, my dear, and I would like an answer that is free of mierda." I often lapsed into Spanish words and phrases, but I quickly remembered that Carol's foreign language was French. "Shit," I explained. "Mierda is Spanish for shit. Now I want an honest answer."

"Okay. No mierda."

"Bien—I've revealed to you that I am only human, and in many respects, subhuman. You have revealed your disappointment in me. Now—and I want the truth, and no questions, please. Does it mean you won't love me as much?" I did not have my usual compulsion to look away, and I considered that a hopeful sign.

It seemed to be my night for stirring emotions. She put her hands on my face. Her eyes were watery, but her voice was clear. "I think it means that I love you a lot more."

I kissed her, and we held each other—more tightly than ever before. Then she said, "Let's talk some more!" And for the next two hours, the old barriers began to fall away.

"No," I said. "It's certainly not that I want to go into my father's business. God knows, I don't want that. Trouble is, God also knows I don't want anything else. I just don't know what the hell I want. I seem to be floating in that direction. It seems to be the easiest way out."

"Why don't you try something else?"

"What, for instance?"

"Anything you want. Certainly in your interviews there must have been—"

"There were no interviews. I have no job offers."

"I'm not sure I understand."

"Of course you don't. How could you? I don't understand it myself. I'm handling my future exactly how I handle everything else. No planning! It's just like finding you a place to stay tonight. I'm a glider plane. Someone tows me into the air, and I ride the currents wherever they take me. I'm really quite powerless—just content to float as long as I can. And it just seems that the currents are moving toward my father's business."

"Mierda!—Am I pronouncing it right? Your analogy is mierda. A glider pilot isn't helpless. Sure, he uses the air currents, but he can still fly in any direction. He can soar or dive or do anything he wants."

"Okay, let's try a different analogy. I'm floating in a huge bathtub. Not swimming, mind you. Just floating. Not having the greatest time in the world, but not suffering, either. Occasionally I suds myself so I'm reasonably clean. Then suddenly, someone pulls the drain plug, and deep down in that gurgling hole is—guess what? Right! My father's business. The bathtub is gently tilted. So as the water drains, I'm drawn toward the hole. Oh, I guess I might escape by climbing up and over the side of the tub. But I don't. It's such a goddamn big tub and the walls are steep and slippery. And who knows what's outside the tub? Maybe a bigger tub. And I'm just not a climber. As I lie there and lazily watch the water draining, I hear the word 'Arthur' come belching up from the hole. It's quite inescapable. But I guess it's really not that terrible. It's not a whirlpool or a tidal wave. Just a steady, gentle tug, sucking me in. Now, do you like that analogy better?"

Tears were rolling down her cheeks. "I hated it," she said, wiping her eyes. "Forget your silly stories and fears and answer this question—Is this what you want?"

"No, not really."

"Then don't do it. It's as simple as that."

"What will I do?"

"Anything you want. Buy a newspaper and go through the want ads. I'll help you. And if we don't find something, then go to graduate school or enlist or travel. It doesn't matter. The only thing that matters is that you get the hell out of that tub, because it's really not a tub at all—it's a box and you've built it for yourself. And the longer you stay, the harder it is to get out."

I had never discussed this with anyone before. I really wasn't being forced into the business, and I enthusiastically agreed to Carol's plan concerning my future. And it was only fitting that the Silhouettes were singing "Get a Job."

By this time my enthusiasm had considerably risen for Carol too. The talking had been great, but now I had the uncontrollable desire to get back to making out. So, armed with love and passion, I mounted an attack. I placed one hand inside her shirt and was frantically pulling at her bra straps while the other hand moved its way downward. We had played the scene hundreds of times before, so the plot was familiar. But this time feelings were infinitely more intense. That's why it felt like a knife in my chest when she said, "Arthur, there's something I must tell you!" These are the *most* terrifying words in the English language.

"What is it?" I gasped, and a prominent vein in my forehead throbbed.

"I think we've done this enough."

"My God, we just started!" I lunged for my watch on the coffee table to prove my point.

"No, I don't mean that. I mean this whole thing that we do all the time. It doesn't make any sense to me."

"I thought you liked it. I really did."

"Of course I like it, but—it just doesn't make any sense. We never complete what we start." Then, in what I thought was a complete change of subject she said, "Do you love Daisy?"

"Daisy? Are you nuts? Of course not."

"Yet, you drive two hours to make love with her."

"Oh, God! That's different. Certainly you're not jealous of Daisy—"

"Yes, I'm jealous of her. I know you're not in love with her, but you do make love with her. You say you love me—"

"I do love you."

"But you don't make love with me, and I traveled over three hours to be with you. This is what doesn't make any sense to me."

"But I thought that, uhhhhh . . ."

"That I didn't want that? Well, maybe at first I didn't, but we've been going steady a long time. We do everything that two people can do together, except for one thing—the most important thing. That's what's ridiculous. If we're in love, why can't we make love?"

"I don't know. I really don't know." For the first time in my life, I really thought about it. "There's only one problem," I said.

"You're not prepared. No prophylactics, right?"

"How did you know?" I asked.

"It kind of figures. I'm getting to know my customer pretty well." Her lips moved quickly and she seemed to be counting to herself. Then she smiled and said, "I think we're safe."

"Of course we are. Don't worry about Mitch and Tom. They won't bother us."

"That's not what I meant, Art."

"I know. But isn't there something wrong with this picture? You're the one that should be afraid—not me. I should be convincing you."

"Would you like to know what that is?" she asked.

"I think I know what it is," I said, "but you could have said something too—a long time ago."

"It's a conspiracy of silence. I'm not immune to it either."

We hadn't run out of things to say. At that moment it just seemed we had talked enough. The effects of the alcohol had long worn off, but the remainder of the evening still had that magical quality, a dreamlike state that is hard to reach without drugs. We lay quietly together on the couch, not touching— just looking, and more important, actually seeing each other for the first time. I don't know how long we were suspended this way, but I didn't have my usual impulse to look away or break the illusion in any other way. Neither of us said "I love you" or "I want you" or "I need you." There were no eternal pledges or promises. But we did feel a lot of love for each other, and somehow we communicated that feeling without words.

Then I said, "Carol, I have a great idea!" I sat up and began unbuttoning my shirt, and I never stopped looking directly into her eyes.

"What is it?" She also sat, stared, and unbuttoned her shirt, which for some reason was called a blouse.

"Let's put on a show!"

We quickly removed the rest of the clothes that prevented the show from going on. At last we held each other, finally free of all the encumbrances that had held us back too long. And it was only fitting that the Platters were singing "You've Got the Magic Touch."

Who thinks the sex scene was a cop-out? Well, I'm real sorry, but I can't change it. What did you expect—another Candy Barr flick? No way! So what if the camera pans away and fades out while we make love? That was precisely how it was done in those days. They didn't focus on a bunch of moving organs, a scene that looks more like what happens under the car hood when the ignition is turned on. Our first time was more than pistons, gears, and double overhead camshafts.

There are a few other reasons why I wouldn't want to elaborately detail that particular sex act. Both of us were awkward and somewhat unsure of ourselves. The earth didn't move and bells didn't ring. Of the 3,120 times we've made love since, all but three were better, as far as purely physical satisfaction is concerned. If it really were essential, I'd give the intimate details of more recent episodes. But as far as intense feelings are concerned, I have never felt more love or tenderness toward anyone, and the entire experience remains as vivid now as it was fourteen years ago.

One more thing. Before I go on to Al's crisis, I must remind you of something. I said there would be one win, one loss, and one tie. If you're keeping score, you may think this was the win. You're wrong! This was the tie. There is no doubt that great strides were made. In fact, if the scene had ended at 6:00 A.M., it would have been a win—a big win. But shortly past this hour, after comfortably sleeping in Carol's arms, I awoke. The sun was rising and I feared Tom or Mitch would stumble into the living room and find us together. To this day I can't say why this should have bothered me. They wouldn't have cared; Carol wouldn't have cared; I shouldn't have cared either. But in spite of my emergence as a viable human being, a bit of the old asshole ways still remained. I covered her and kissed her while she slept. Then I walked into the bedroom, fell into bed, and slept alone.

27

●●●

Al Carter was not religious. If anything, he was anti-religious. Take the way he criticized Tom for going to church every Sunday. "I'm-oh tell you sumpun', muh man," he said, lapsing into his black Philly dialect. "Dat muh-fuckin' stuff ain't nuthun' but a pack a sheeyit!"

Tom reacted in a predictable manner. "Blasphemer! Antichrist!" he shouted at Al, who, delighted with the reaction, gleefully strutted about the room. "Jee-zuz, don't you believe in God?"

"What's with this God bit? Sure I believe, muh man. But I have an agreement with the Big Guy. He don't bother me and I don't bother him. He do his work, I do mine."

Once Al was at our place when Mitch was having one of his more intimate discussions with the Lord. The whole scene really broke Al up.

"What's with Mr. Shit-for-Brains?" Al asked me. While in the bedroom, Mitch asked Yahweh why He allowed even the schools of chiropractic to reject him.

"I guess he's praying," I said.

"For what?" he asked.

"For help."

"You jay-ohin' me, man? If he wants to go to medical school, why don't he study? God don't give a shit about him." We heard glass shatter on the bedroom wall. I assumed it was Mitch and not the Lord who threw it. "No, sir. God never helps nobody. You gotta help yourself!"

"Don't you ever pray?" I asked.

"Only two or three times in my whole life," he said after racking his brain. "Once I prayed when my grandmother was real sick."

"And what happened?" I asked.

"She died."

"Hmmm," I said. I could have gone with the standard, "Oh, I'm so sorry," but in all honesty, I was not sorry, having never known the woman. Besides, she may have been dead for fifteen years, so a belated condolence would have been quite out of order. I decided it was best to say nothing concerning his grandmother's demise.

"You said you prayed a few times," I said.

"Yes, I remember praying when my grandfather was very sick. I think he had pneumonia or something like that. The doctor called my parents and told them it was pretty serious—so I prayed."

"And what happened?"

"He died."

I had said nothing about his grandmother, so I couldn't very well express my sympathy for gramps. Besides, I didn't think he was really looking for sympathy. "Any other times?" I asked.

He stopped cracking his gum and discontinued all of his other movements. After a few seconds he began nodding and said, "Rags."

"What?"

"I once had a little dog by the name of Rags." Al went on to describe the tiny rat terrier that had been his companion when he was twelve years old. From his sad expression and his cracking voice, I instantly knew that poor Rags had met the same fate as Al's grandparents.

"Rags was run over by the P.T.C."

"By what?"

"P.T.C.—the public bus company in Philly."

"Well, what does it mean?"

"It stands for Pennsylvania—no, wait a minute. I think it's Philadelphia Transit—or is it Transportation? Goddamn it! Who gives a shit?"

"Just curious," I said. "Go on with the story."

"The vet said Rags was hurt pretty bad, so I prayed."

"And he died," I said.

"She—Rags was a female. Yeah, she died. How did you know?"

"It figures. You have a piss-poor batting average."

"That's why I gave up on that religion bit. It was a losing proposition."

"Al, I'm really sorry to hear about Rags. But maybe you shouldn't wait for a crisis. Why don't you try daily or weekly prayers?"

"Hey, man, I don't want to fuck myself up with all that preventive medicine—it's no good for the system. Besides, I'm completely out of that now. I don't need Him at all—even in a crisis."

Al had studied all night. He knew his material well enough to get that high C. But there was one possibility that kept nagging at him. By 8:00 A.M., when he was washing down his fourth No-Doze with his twentieth cup of coffee, he was no longer able to subjugate the thought, and it suddenly bolted to the surface and broke water. WHAT IF THIS IS NOT THE TEST? So for the first time since Rags met the P.T.C. bus, Al Carter turned to the Lord.

"Let it be the test, God. Don't let me down. I don't ask for that much, Lord. Four times in twenty-two years. That's not being a pest. I'm not the best person in the world. You know it, God. But don't I deserve to win once in a while? I'm zero for three. Don't make me zero for four. Let it be the test!"

It was a beautiful sunny morning, and I sat on a bench in front of the Pierce Building, smoking, drinking coffee, and happily reflecting on my weekend with Carol. It had been real good, and for the first time I didn't have the down feeling that comes from holding things in. Saturday night had been a complete experience for me, and I replayed the entire sequence over and over again, savoring it more each time. Of course, I managed to block out my hasty exit from the couch. Sunday had been good, too. The doors that had opened for us the night before remained open. Before I drove her to the bus, we went through the want ads in *The New York Times* and circled five interesting possibilities. I agreed to call for interviews during the week. It was the first positive step I had taken regarding my future, and I remained buoyant even after she left.

I saw Al walking toward me and I paused in my delicious daydreaming to greet him. "God," he said, "I studied hard. I'm not shittin' You. I put lotsa time and money into it, God. Just let it be the test! I beg of You! Me asusta la idea de pasar seis semanas de verano en Sevilla. Got it?" His glassy eyes, bloodshot from lack of sleep, passed over me without seeing. He walked by me and climbed the steps.

I jumped off the bench, knocking the coffee to the ground. He was a pathetic sight and I stifled a laugh. "Hey, Al," I called out as he neared the entrance to the building. There was no sign that he heard. "Hey, Señor Carter!" I screamed, much louder than before.

This time my words must have penetrated through his Spanish-English garble. He stopped a few feet from the door and slowly turned. He was an apparition standing up there, an eerie harbinger of bad things to come. His hair, which was normally greased back in place, blew wildly in a sudden gust of wind. His red eyes raced back and forth, vainly trying to locate the source of interruption. I could read his lips, which mouthed the familiar first line of the Spanish test. It was no longer funny. He was a tragic figure standing up there, seemingly possessed and well on his way to self-destruction. I resisted the impulse to call out again and was happy he hadn't seen me. He searched for only a second or two more. Then he began mumbling again. He turned and disappeared inside the building.

"Ah, Señor Arturo, buenos días." It was Pidal, and he was strutting toward me, merrily swinging his attaché case. It was like old times and I hated him again. "I trust you have burned plenty of midnight oil studying hard for this exam." He knew I didn't have to study. This was his little joke and he winked at me. He looked at his watch. "Shall we be going?" He motioned gracefully toward the entrance, indicating he would like to walk with me. I nodded and began moving toward the building.

"Tell me, Arthur. What are your plans after graduation?"

I plodded on without looking up. I wanted to answer "mierda," but I was just a bit shaky. "Nada concreto, pero tengo algunas posibilidades." Translation: Nothing concrete, but I have a few irons in the fire.

I was startled to see him looking at me with great admiration. Jesus, I thought, I'm just not prepared for all these people liking me. Least of all Pidal.

"Señor Arturo, usted es el mejor estudiante de español. Y no es mierda." Translation: Mister Arthur, you are the greatest Spanish student. And that's no shit.

I couldn't hold back a smile, and upon seeing it, he gave me such an affectionate look that I feared he was about to embrace me right there on the steps of Pierce. But he settled on throwing his arm around my shoulder, and in this unorthodox manner, we marched up the steps.

It was now my time to pray. "Please, God," I whispered, "don't let anybody see us like this."

• • •

"I just can't wait any longer," Mitch said. I know it's coming today—but I gotta get going."

Tom looked up from his book. "What's coming today?" he asked.

"My acceptance. I can feel it in my bones. Some school out there wants me and today is the big day. How about bringing the mail in for me!"

"Sure! Where you off to?" Tom asked, but Mitch was already halfway into his blue raincoat in spite of the sunny, eighty-degree weather. "Never mind! I see where you're going."

"Have to pick up a few things at the market. Just lay the letter on the coffee table, Tom. Do you need anything?"

"You know I don't approve. I won't have any part of your—"

"Sure, fella. Just put the mail on the table. Okay?" And at the precise moment that Al sat in Pierce Hall anxiously awaiting Pidal's opening line, Mitch left our apartment for what would be his last trip to Save-a-Penny.

28

• •

The auditorium in Pierce Hall is funnel-shaped. The lecturer stands at the base of the funnel, and the seats, which completely surround the podium, rise upward at a frightening angle. I have had uncomfortable sensations when I sat near the top of the funnel. When walking down to the bottom, with no handrails to steady myself, I have been shaky. This was one reason that I sat in the bottom row. The other was that Al had positioned himself almost at the top, and I wanted to be as far away from him as possible. I had already given him enough help on this test, and I didn't want to take the chance of being associated with him.

Pidal sat on the edge of the table. He leaned over on one hand in the familiar tilted position as he scanned the four hundred faces that surrounded him. Pidal was very much in charge of the situation. Having all of his students together gave him an enormous sense of power. Had he known, however, that twenty-five percent of the people in the hall had conspired to cheat him, he might have been less calm. He inhaled his cigarette, looked at his watch, and occasionally nodded to one of his students who might have said "Buenos dias, Señor Pidal."

There's always nervous tension just before a final exam. But there seemed to be a lot more this time—perhaps because one hundred students were keying themselves on Pidal's first sentence. No one was more attached to the opening line than Al Carter, who, drained of his last ounce of energy, sat motionless, staring down at Pidal. Al had retired his case, and it was now completely in the Lord's hands. Occasionally his lips would move very slowly and out came the words, "Me asusta la idea," but there was no more mention of God.

Señor Pidal looked at his watch. He ground his cigarette into the sole of his shoe and lifted himself off the table. He slowly walked to the podium. He tapped the microphone. It was live. "Estudiantes, ¡atención! Dictado—numero uno—" One hundred students held their breath. "Me asusta la idea de pasar seis semanas de verano en Sevilla."

The great sigh of relief started up near the top of the funnel and fanned out in all directions. In waves it rolled around the room, cascading up and down the steep aisles until Pidal shouted "¡Silencio, por favor!" Translation: Silence, please!

Al Carter smiled and looked upward. "Thank you, muh man," he said and he quickly wrote down the words, completing entire sentences before they were even dictated.

Mitch didn't see the two men when he walked inside the Save-a-Penny. He would have proceeded more cautiously had he known they were there. But it was part of their job to be inconspicuous. They didn't speak, but when Mitch wheeled the shopping cart into the produce department, they glanced at each other and nodded. Then they slowly followed, keeping a respectable distance behind the alleged thief.

Mitch fondled a cantaloupe. It was not up to his standards and he rejected it. He picked up another, and after caressing, squeezing, and shaking it, he gently placed the melon in the cart.

When Mitch dipped down into the tangerines, came up with three, and tossed them into the cart, the men looked at each other and shrugged their shoulders. But they continued to follow him.

When Mitch picked out four large ears of corn and placed them neatly into the cart, the one man became impatient. He motioned his partner to step back, and they met behind a giant skyscraper of Metrecal. "This must be the wrong guy. We're wasting our time," he said.

"Just be patient," said the other. "He's the one, all right. Don't give up so easily!" And while they talked, they never saw Mitch put six limes and three lemons into his raincoat. When they emerged from behind the Metrecal, the suspect was far down the aisle, heading toward the soda department.

Mitch reached for two quarts of Seven-Up, and in accordance with his one unbreakable rule, he placed the bottles in the cart. Then he lifted a bottle of Coke from a lower shelf and gave the cart a good lead over the raincoat.

The two men hurriedly walked past Mitch, turned the corner, and met behind a giant pile of Lestoil, the liquid detergent as modern as today.

"Goddamn it! I'm beginning to feel like an asshole. This kid's no crook!"

"Christ, man. Just give him a little more rope and he'll hang himself." And while they argued, Mitch put four tiny cans of Bloody Mary mix into his raincoat.

Now Mitch turned the corner and headed for meats and poultry, the long counter across the rear of the store, perpendicular to the other aisles. When he was within a few feet of his antagonists, they quickly turned away and stumbled down the long line of detergents. They stopped finally at Mr. Clean, feigning interest in the picture of the smiling bald giant, who claimed he could get rid of dirt and grime and grease in just a minute.

As Mitch examined the steaks and chops, the men decided to get a better view of the action. They doubled back to the Lestoil, turned, and walked to a door on the far end of the meat counter. Seconds later they were watching the suspect through a range of one-way mirrors, placed directly behind the standing ribs. In the time it took them to get from Mr. Clean to the window, Mitch, incredible luck still on his side, harvested three baby lamb chops, six links of country sausage, a pound of boiled ham, and a foot of aged pepperoni.

Mitch inspected a sirloin but was not satisfied. He shook his head in obvious disappointment and rang the bell for service.

"Hi!" said the counterman, wiping some blood on his apron. "Hot enough for you today?"

Mitch felt just a bit self-conscious in the heavy blue raincoat, but he realized it was just something that countermen said from time to time. "The weather is just fine, but I can't say the same for your selection today."

"Well, we can sure take care of that for you. After all, we at Save-a-Penny are here to please. What's your pleasure?"

"I'd like a couple of sirloins—about this thick." Mitch separated his thumb and forefinger about an inch and three-quarters and held up his hand to the counterman.

"No problem at all. Did you say you wanted two steaks?"

"Make it three."

"Have 'em for you in a minute." The man left to cut the special steaks.

Mitch picked up a small Cornish hen. Cart or pocket? It was a toss-up. He held it for a few seconds in the palm of his right hand and he pondered his choice. He looked from side to side to see if anyone was watching. The men strained behind the glass. Mitch laid the bird into the cart.

"Shit!" said the men and for the first time they began to feel that the anonymous tip they had received was a hoax.

While the men argued, Mitch suddenly remembered something and scooted down the detergent aisle. He was well out of their range when he put the small box of S.O.S. in his pocket, then sauntered back to the meat counter.

"You'll never eat better steaks than these, my friend," said the counterman, holding out three fine pieces of meat for Mitch's approval.

Fuckin' A, Mitch thought, and he salivated. "You did a real good job, fella," he said.

The counterman neatly wrapped the meat in brown paper. Then he weighed the package and wrote the price with a black crayon. "Thank you for shopping Save-a-Penny." He smiled and handed it over to Mitch.

Mitch laid the steaks in the upper section of the cart. He began rolling again, this time parallel to the meat counter. The two men cursed each other, but behind the glass they kept pace with Mitch. "Biggest waste of time I ever—" said the one, but he stopped short as the other grabbed his arm and excitedly pointed out through the glass.

Mitch had been waiting for the counterman to leave. When he assumed he was no longer being watched, he quickly picked up the expensive steaks and shoved them into his raincoat.

The two men smiled and shook hands. They congratulated each other and exulted in their great victory. Mitch took a left turn into breakfast foods and while still in view of his unseen observers, he further delighted them by lifting up the Cornish hen and jamming the small bird into his raincoat pocket.

It was a day for unseen observers. At the Save-a-Penny they continued to follow Mitch, who further incriminated himself with every additional raincoat deposit. And in Pierce Hall, Al had been placed under surveillance too. A proctor had reported to Pidal that "something strange" was going on up near the top of the funnel. He had observed that throughout the exam a student had been talking constantly, jerking back and forth in his seat, and was acting in a suspicious manner. Furthermore, he seemed to be giving signals to unidentified persons seated around him by snapping his fingers and clapping his hands in a code that had not yet been broken.

"Do you have his name?" Pidal asked, and his voice quivered with excitement.

"No, señor, maybe you would recognize him," said the

proctor, and he explained to his master just where the strange suspect was sitting.

Pidal squinted and shielded his eyes with his hand as he searched the upper rows of the funnel. When at last his scrutiny focused on the alleged cheat, he said, "¡Vaya—es Señor Carter!" Translation: Well now—it's Mr. Carter.

"Do you know him, sir?" asked the proctor.

"Por supuesto—este hombre loco se encuentra en mi clase. Es tonto estúpido. No sabe su fondillo de un hueco en la tierra." Translation: Of course—this lunatic is in my class. He's a stupid fool. He doesn't know his ass from a hole in the ground.

The proctor thought Pidal was trying to be funny, so he dutifully responded by laughing. Pidal dropped his hand from his forehead and wheeled around to face the startled assistant. "You laugh?" he squealed. "You think it's funny that someone cheats Pidal?"

"No, sir. I only thought that—"

"This imbecile is cheating me," he shouted. "And that's not funny."

"Well, we're really not sure if he's—"

"Well, I'm sure!" he screamed.

Pidal was ranting and his eyes flashed wildly at the proctor. He began searching his suit jacket and finally withdrew a gold pillbox from his breast pocket. He popped several capsules into his mouth and washed them down with a hastily poured glass of water. Seconds later, in a slightly calmer voice, he said, "You listen to me! I hate fools and cheats. Albert Carter is both. No question about it. Now I want you to watch him closely. Before this examination is over, I want you to get the goods on him. ¿Comprende usted lo que estoy diciendo?" Translation: Do you understand what I'm saying?

"Sí, señor!"

"Nadie engaña Don Ramón Menéndez Pidal." Translation: No one cheats Don Ramón Menéndez Pidal.

He didn't know that along with Al Carter some ninety-nine

others were also cheating him at that moment. And this figure didn't include the large group of regular cheaters who, unaware that a test had been stolen, were just slugging away using conventional methods. Some copied from their neighbors, while others, who had written answers on shirtcuffs, handkerchiefs, watches, and the soles of their shoes, occasionally referred to their notes. And of course, Pidal didn't know that his dearest friend, Ramirez Carrega, had also cheated him by stealing the exam and selling it to the likes of Albert Carter.

While Pidal gazed upward and clasped his hands till the knuckles turned white, his henchmen fanned out and around the upper levels of the funnel. They surrounded the suspect and observed him from several vantage points. In order to remain inconspicuous, they slithered up and down the steep aisles and across the precarious catwalks. The proctors need not have tried so hard to pass unnoticed. By this time, Al was completely oblivious to all outside stimuli and was totally absorbed in his own world.

"Señor Carter!" The proctor had called out Al's name for the third time, and still there was no indication he had been heard. Al shifted in his seat, but he didn't look up. The proctor was becoming impatient, and he leaned into the row, disregarding the students in the two outer seats. He tapped Al on the shoulder.

"What is it?" Al asked, looking up in surprise.

"Señor Carter, may we see you for a minute?"

"Watchoo want?"

"Would you stand up, Señor Carter, and move out to the aisle? We don't want to disturb the other students."

"I'm-oh stand up, muh man, when you tell me what's going on." Al was still cool, but he was thinking of Ramirez Carrega and the stolen test.

"Have it your way, señor. We have reason to believe you are cheating on this exam."

Al's face turned the same color as the knuckles of Señor

Pidal, who anxiously watched the proceedings from the base of the funnel. Al gasped and tried to compose himself. He stood up and moved toward the two proctors. In his nervous scramble he trampled the feet of the other students. Despite his momentary panic, he tried to bluff them. "It's a lie! You're lying and you know it!" Some rotten bastard must have turned me in, he thought to himself. Someone found out about the test and was pissed 'cause he wasn't in on it.

"We've been watching you for the past twenty minutes, señor. You've been asking for and giving answers. We know about your code."

"My code?" Al was puzzled.

"You've worked out a system. You pass out answers by snapping your fingers and clapping your hands."

The acoustics in the funnel are quite good, and at least one-third of the people in the room heard Al's laugh. He was now standing in the aisle with the proctors, and he was relieved to discover that they really didn't know the truth. They were wrong in their accusations and he was innocent. Their conclusion was correct. Sure he had been cheating, but that was different. They had no evidence.

"We'd like you to come down with us."

"You jay-ohin' me, man?" The question was spoken loud enough to be heard by over half the people in the auditorium. His mind was spinning. The irony of it! His plan had worked perfectly, but here he was, accused of cheating, and he was very much in trouble.

"Let's discuss this with Señor Pidal!"

They were arresting officers who had read him his rights and were now about to take him to court. They reached out to grab his arms and he instinctively pulled back. In a voice that was heard by all of the people in the funnel, he shouted, "You guys are out of your fuckin' minds!"

As they led him down the incline to the kangaroo court of Señor Pidal, Al's spirits sank in direct proportion to the altitude. Al's crisis unfolded only a few feet away from me. I was frightened too, but I tried to view the scene as a detached observer.

Pidal's face radiated. "Ah, Señor Carter," he said, "what seems to be the problem?"

"The problem is that these guys think I was cheating."

"And were you?"

"Sheeeyit! I never cheated in anything."

I laughed.

"Well, why would my associates say you were cheating?"

"They're liars, Señor Pidal. They're a bunch of damned liars."

"Really, señor? That makes no sense."

I nodded.

"Not to me either, but for some reason, these cats are trying to put the screws to me."

"I'm a reasonable man, Señor Carter, and I want to be fair. No one will say Don Pidal is unfair. For the moment, I'll assume you're not guilty and that a mistake has been made. Isn't that being fair?" Al nodded and Pidal continued. "Could it be that you gave them reason to suspect you might be cheating? Perhaps a movement that might be misinterpreted?"

"I didn't cheat. They're liars," Al said defiantly.

"Excuse me, Señor Pidal," said the proctor, "but this man has been talking throughout the exam. We stood only a few feet away and heard him asking questions. He also snapped his fingers and clapped his hands in some sort of secret code."

"Señor Carter?" said Pidal. "What about this?"

"It's my way. It's the way I am all the time. I'm nervous and jumpy and that's the way I let out steam. Knowadamean?" To demonstrate, he snapped and clapped, and to the amazement of everyone, he lifted his arms to shoulder height and did a quick mummer's strut. Some of the students had finished the exam, and as they proceeded downward, they watched this bizarre confrontation.

"That's not necessary!" said Pidal, and I scored the round for Al.

"They're lying. I don't know why they're lying, but they're lying. They have absolutely no proof. No, sir. No proof, whatsoever."

I nodded.

"Señor Carter, you acted suspiciously. My assistants apprehended you for that reason. You have no proof that you weren't cheating."

Al shifted into his indignant act. "Hey, man, we ain't livin' in Spain. This is the old U.S. of A. It's *innocent* till proven *guilty*. You got it ass-backwards. Knowadamean?"

I smiled.

Al was a good talker but often he just didn't know when to stop. "Señor Pidal, I've never cheated in my life. But if you want proof of my innocence, why don't you check the tests of all the people that sat near me?"

I followed the gazes of Pidal, Al, and the two proctors up to the section of the funnel where Al had been sitting. The area was now entirely deserted.

"As you can see, Señor Carter, that would be quite impossible. It seems everyone is finished."

"That sounds like a real good idea. If you're done with me, señor, I would like to finish the test too." Al smiled and extended his hand toward Pidal. "May I have my exam back—por favor?"

Pidal held the exam up to his lips and whistled "La Cucaracha" into the partially opened pages. He was sitting on the edge of the table, motionless, when suddenly his eyes opened wide. He placed the exam on the lectern. "Mi amigo, you have given me an excellent idea. I don't have to check out your work against someone else's. All I have to do is compare your work against—" And he paused while he opened the booklet. "—your own work. Your own *previous* work, that is."

He was totally aware of Al's mediocre records as he flipped through the pages. He knew it was not Al Carter's work. In a bitchy, sarcastic voice he said, "This is good work. No, pardon me—this is excellent work."

"Gracias," Al said.

"Don't thank me, you fool! I'm not complimenting you! This obviously is not your work!"

"Hey, wait a minute! You have no proof!"

"No proof?" Pidal was screaming. "You have sat in my class this entire semester and have been nothing but an unmitigated ass, a fool—¡ESTÚPIDO!" And in a piercingly good imitation of Al, he said, "Knowadamean?"

"So, I'm to be condemned for my expertise," Al said.

"Lying swineherd, you have no expertise! There's only one student in this class who is capable of doing this work."

I panicked.

Pidal shot a quick glance at me. He noted where I was sitting, then dismissed a fleeting thought. He shrugged his shoulders at me as if to say, "I'm terribly sorry, Señor Arturo. Excuse me, por favor."

I was out of danger—at least for the moment. But things were getting too hot, and I decided to flee a ship that might be sinking. I had finished the exam, and although still curious, I felt I would be a lot safer in another part of town.

"So, it's proof you want? Fine—I'll give it to you. Let's start with the very first sentence. Read it!" Pidal handed the booklet to Al, who proudly recited with excellent articulation. After all, he had read it close to one thousand times before.

"Now translate it!" said Pidal.

"Pardon?"

"I said translate it!"

"But this was just dictation. You didn't ask us to translate this part of the test."

"But I'm asking you now—translate it!"

"No! I won't. That wasn't part of the test. You have no proof! I knew what was in the test. I'm not required to know anything else. Now, if it's all the same to you, I'd like to finish."

It was a brazen attempt on Al's part, but Pidal had another idea. "You might be right. Maybe I can't prove you're guilty. But I know you're a cheat. And you know you're a cheat. And

I'm going to the Dean of the college and I will insist he post-pone your graduation until this matter is settled to my satisfaction."

Pidal had pushed the right button this time. He had hit on Al's greatest fear. And as I walked toward the podium, I could see Al was reeling, terribly shaken by Pidal's threat.

It's possible Pidal was only bluffing. Even if he had fol-lowed through, the Dean would probably have had no part of the flimsy case. But there's really no point in speculating. The reality was that Al had a second attack of diarrhetic mouth, and this time it was fatal.

In the immortal words of Neville Chamberlain and Tom Nelson, Al said, "Can't we compromise?"

"¿Señor?"

"I'll take the test over again. Right now! That will prove it one way or the other."

I arrived at this moment and laid my test on the table.

Although Pidal was running Al's suggestion through his mind, he felt obliged to talk to me. "Ah, Señor Arturo—buena suerte." Translation: good luck. We expect big things from you.

"¡Gracias!" I said, taking his outstretched hand.

"You'll have to excuse me. I have this minor problem here," he said.

"Of course, señor. Adiós!" I looked at Al, who was com-posed again, and he seemed to be saying, "Don't worry, Art." I turned and walked toward the door.

"Señor Carter," Pidal said curtly. "I agree to your plan. If you will sit down, we'll start over again."

Al, desperately trying to conceal his famous shit-eating grin, took a seat in the front row while Pidal searched his attaché case for the test.

It was déjà vu as Al awaited the opening line. But this time there was no anxiety—just a serene sense of confidence. He had actually written half the sentence in his booklet before

Pidal had even begun. And it was still another few seconds after that before he realized Pidal had switched tests.

I was at the door with my back to them when I heard the trapdoor being sprung. And while Al was scribbling about vacations in Seville, Pidal, gleefully reading an old test, spoke about the sinking of the Spanish Armada in the English Channel.

Before closing the door on the sorry scene, I spun around for one last look, hoping I would not be turned into a pillar of salt. Al was no longer writing, snapping, clapping, or mumbling. In a catatonic state, he was staring—at nothing in particular. Then I looked at Pidal. He had not been this ecstatic since my own downfall. I looked around the funnel and it was filled again—this time with hundreds of screaming partisans of Pidal. And I heard shouts and echoes of "¡Viva Pidal!" and "¡Olé!" And a band of mariachis paraded up and down the steep aisles as they serenaded the triumphant professor.

I shut the door and slowly began walking. I picked up the pace and soon I was running—faster than I had ever run before.

29

●●●

"Where's Mitch?" I was out of breath when I reached the apartment. I wanted very much to tell someone the story—but not Tom. I was not in the mood for one of his I-told-you-so sermons.

Tom looked up from his book. "He's 'shopping.' " His voice was sarcastic. "How did everything go with Pidal today?"

"Just fine. I'll see you later."

Before I could dash out the door, Tom handed me an envelope. "Give this to Mitch! He was anxious to get it. Another rejection, I'm sure. You know, Art—one of these days they're going to get Mitch. This stealing is really getting out of hand!"

"Sure, Tom." I put the envelope in my pocket and raced on to the Save-a-Penny.

Mitch heard them before he saw them. He was in gourmet foods, reaching for a bottle of macadamia nuts when he heard a man in the next aisle say, "Just wait till he gets out of the store. Then we'll grab him."

For a long time Mitch had no longer considered the possibility of being caught. It couldn't or wouldn't happen to him, so it really wasn't productive to worry about it. Stealing had become second nature to him now, like breathing out and breathing in, as the song goes. So when the words drifted over the racks of sesame oil and rattlesnake meat, Mitch thought they might be talking about a shoplifter in the store. Since he wasn't a shoplifter, they certainly weren't talking about him. He put the nuts into his raincoat and continued down the aisle.

He had just harvested some Swiss chocolates filled with various liqueurs, and he was eyeing a can of back-fin crabmeat when he felt their presence. He didn't look up immediately, but somehow he knew they were watching him—a shoplifter, crook, petty thief, and ungrateful bum who was about to bring heaps of disgrace on his poor parents who had struggled all their lives so he could have some of the better things in life. Amen.

They were standing at the end of the aisle, nonchalantly poking at some rare blends of tea and trying desperately to be cool. Mitch was positive they were after him. Now it was Mitch's turn to try to be cool. He grasped the crabmeat, pretended to read the label, and placed it in the cart. To further prove his innocence, he hastily began grabbing items—any items—off the shelves. He threw them into the cart, hoping the men might be dissuaded.

Slowly he moved away from them. His cart was now half filled with rare, expensive foods from the four corners of the earth. Several times he turned back and stared at them to be sure they were keeping far away. He was terrified, but despite his panic, he was still able to formulate a plan. He wasn't sure if it was a workable plan, but it was certainly worth a try. And the success of the plan depended on his keeping a maximum distance between him and the men.

Mitch continued moving slowly. But when he reached the end of gourmet foods and rolled around the corner into the head of the stretch, his speed increased. When he was about five feet down the aisle, he broke into a rapid trot, reached into the left pocket of his coat, withdrew the sirloins, and flung them high into the top row of Kellogg's Corn Flakes. Lemons and limes went soaring through the store. A pepperoni flew over four aisles, landing in the fresh baked goods, while the boiled ham and sausage links came to rest, unfortunately, in the kosher food department.

Mitch tore down the aisle like a giant, crippled airplane on a frantic mayday flight, jettisoning its entire cargo to avoid a disastrous crash. And with each helter-skelter toss, he gave an anguished cry, beseeching the Lord for help. When finally he reached down into the lining at the base of his coat and retrieved his beloved lobster tails, he was near hysteria, pleading with God for a deal. He was ready to repent.

I had just arrived at the Save-a-Penny, and I suspected something was wrong when a baby lamb chop sailed some three feet over my head and crash-landed into the artichokes. A box of expensive Swiss chocolates stood next to a box of Modess. As I walked through the store, I noticed the strange juxtaposition of many other foodstuffs, as if a tornado had twisted its way up and down the aisles. When I found a lobster tail reposing amongst the avocados, I knew Mitch was involved. Seconds later, when I heard the familiar sobbing prayers and the word "parents" popping out repeatedly, my fears were confirmed.

I quickly turned the corner and saw Mitch halfway down the last aisle in the store. He stood quietly in front of the cat-food. Down at the far end, the two men, totally surprised by Mitch's food-disposal plan, also were motionless. They had been patient with their prey, but now it appeared they may have blundered by waiting too long.

Mitch put his hand into the raincoat. The only remaining item was the Cornish hen. He began pulling it out, but it wouldn't fit through the pocket. He yanked desperately at the bird, but it was hopelessly lodged. The men realized they still had a chance. They closed in on Mitch, who still had his hand in the cookie jar.

Less than a half hour before, I had helplessly watched a

friend fall to the wolves. Now it appeared the scene might be repeated. As I moved toward Mitch, I said, "Rip it!"

He looked up at me. He didn't understand.

"The pocket—rip the fucking pocket!" I screamed.

He gave a hard yank at the material, and the coat that had set the all-time record for housing stolen food was torn apart. Mitch bent down to retrieve the Cornish hen, which had fallen to the floor. He held it in the palm of his hand and was preparing to shot-put it over the towering wall of Purina Cat Chow, when the men arrived.

"Hold it right there! You're under arrest!"

"Arrest?" I said. "Why are you arresting him?"

"For shoplifting."

"He hasn't stolen a thing. Just look at all that crap in the cart. Doesn't look like shoplifting to me."

"What about that chicken?"

"Chicken! That's no chicken. That's a Cornish hen. What makes you think he's stealing it? That's tonight's dinner and he's buying it. Right, Mitch?"

Until this time I wasn't sure if Mitch was still aware of what was happening. But apparently he understood. He nodded, tilted his hand, and the hen fell into the cart.

The men looked at each other and then at me. "You're a wise fuckin' bastard, aren't you?" said the one. I decided it was better not to answer even though I didn't think I was a wise fucking bastard. They shrugged their shoulders and walked past us. The confrontation was over and Mitch was free.

A few feet from where we were standing was a stool, probably forgotten by some forgetful clerk. Mitch staggered over and sat down. It had been traumatic for him, and now he held his head in his hands and sobbed. When he had sufficiently composed himself, I put my hand on his shoulder and said, "Mitch, let's get the hell out of here!"

"One minute, Art." Then he continued a conversation which

he had begun with the Lord while he was flying down the aisle. Out of respect I moved away and was amazed to discover that Purina also made Goat Chow and Monkey Chow.

I didn't intend to eavesdrop, but it was difficult not to hear. Mitch's voice just seemed to carry. In gratitude to God he had agreed never to steal or gamble again. Then there was the standard prayer that he should never embarrass his parents. But his closing remarks were a little different this time. "Thank you for sending me a wonderful friend like Arthur," he said. Of course, I was embarrassed.

As a postscript he added, "One more thing, God. If it's not too much to ask, I would appreciate some sign that you have heard all of this. Okay? Any sign will do. Whatever you like, God. I'll leave that completely up to you." Then Mitch wiped his eyes and stood.

"Ready to go?" I asked.

"Fuckin' A!"

As we approached the checkout counter, Mitch said, "Art, there are two things I must ask you."

"I'm listening."

"I still owe you some money on the debt. It's not that much, but I've agreed not to steal anymore."

"Yes, I heard."

"Will you let me off the hook?"

I thought about it. "Sure! Just forget it." There was really no point in pressing him for the money. It was a hopeless case. Besides, I just didn't care anymore. "You said there were two things you wanted to discuss."

"Yeah, I did," he said sheepishly. "It looks like I 'bought' a shitload of high-priced gourmet foods, and I, uhh—seem to have a slight problem."

"Okay, okay. I get the message." I was willing to pay a portion of the bill. I sighed and reached for my wallet. I still had Mitch's letter in my pocket. "This came for you today," I said, as I pulled out the envelope and handed it over to the ex-shoplifter.

While the checker computed the cost of our quail eggs, snails, caviar, and the like, Mitch opened his mail and excitedly read the amazing news.

"Thank you, God!" he screamed. "Thank you for my sign, oh Lord. Look, Art! I'm accepted! Can you believe it? I've been accepted into dental school."

It was hard to believe, but he handed the envelope to me and there it was—the official letter of acceptance from some obscure little dental school in South Dakota. I was positive no one had ever heard of the school, but nevertheless, it was a dental school. God, in His infinite wisdom, had given Mitch His sign, right there at the checkout counter of the Save-a-Penny Market. I was truly dazed by the astonishing news, and while Mitch sang, danced, and cried for joy in the front of the store, I stood at the register and paid the entire bill.

30

●●●

"Hello."

"Arthur?"

"Yes, Mother."

"It's Mother."

"Yes, Mother." I braced for the inevitable.

"Are you all right, Arthur?"

"Yes, Mother. I'm fine." I hoped that she would be reporting on a grave illness instead of the usual death.

"That's good, Arthur. How are the finals coming along?"

"Fine! Just fine, Mother."

"Arthur?"

Okay, get ready, fella. Here it comes. Brace yourself. Let's hear it for sickness. All those in favor of sickness, please signify by saying "aye."

"I'm afraid I have a bit of bad news."

Sounds terrific so far. Sounds real good. Note that she said bad—not sad. Big difference, you know. Bad means illness and not the untimely passing of someone. It's definitely sickness. Now let it be a neighbor or one of her friends or even a distant relative. Just keep it away from the immediate family and I'll be satisfied.

"It's Uncle Dave."

"Uncle Dave? What's wrong?" I asked the question, but I knew it had to be one of two choices. I hoped it was a heart attack. Cancer's a bitch, and maybe the attack was a mild one.

"He had a coronary this morning. He's in Intensive Care at Atherton General."

"How is he?"

"Well, you know about these things, Arthur. Any heart attack is serious."

Great! At least it was a mild one. Uncle Dave is one of the few guys I really like. He's not really my uncle. My parents' friends are called aunt and uncle. Uncle Dave is not only a close friend of theirs, but he's also my father's partner.

"Had he been sick?" This is a required question.

"We don't understand it. Dave hasn't been in a hospital since God knows when. Never had a heart attack before. Never even complained of a chest pain."

God help me, but it's almost funny. As much as I like Dave, I have to contain the laughter. Her rule is, If you've never had a heart attack before, you can't have one now.

"He'll be okay, Mother."

"Uncle Dave's no youngster, Arthur."

"Don't worry about him. He'll be up and around in no time."

She paused and I heard the gears shift. "How are the interviews coming along?"

I glanced down at the *Times* on my lap. I looked at the red circles Carol and I had drawn around the five possibilities. Believe it or not, I had already called two and made appointments. "Real good. I have an interview tomorrow morning at nine."

"Arthur?" She's launching a torpedo at me. "With Uncle Dave sick like this—you know, Dad really could use some help."

It's homing in at me. I must take evasive action. After all, I've finally done something in regard to my future. At least

I should make some attempt to follow through. "What are you saying, Mother?"

"I'm saying it would be nice if you came into the business."

Direct hit! Try to stay afloat! "Well, I don't know. I have all of these interviews."

"He needs you, Arthur."

"Why don't you let me think about it? I'll be home on Monday. I'll make a decision by then. Okay? Give my regards to Uncle Dave."

After we said good-bye, I stared at the phone and held it in my hand for a long time. Then I methodically rolled the *Times* into a compact ball. When it approximated the size of a grapefruit, I tossed a high arching shot across the room. It hit the wall, rimmed the wastepaper basket, and fell to the floor. Then I sat on the couch for a long time and stared.

I really should go to those interviews. Calling for the appointments was the hard part, and I've already done that. What the hell is the matter with me? Nothing is preventing me from keeping those appointments. There's absolutely nothing to lose and everything to gain. It would confirm *Carol's* faith in me. It would confirm *my* faith in me. It would even confirm my *parents'* faith in me. I certainly would benefit from all of that faith. And even if I do show up next Monday and say yes, it will only be a temporary thing. When Uncle Dave gets better, I'll be that much ahead of the game.

The decision was made. I rose and as I walked across the room, I whistled the Fight Song. But it was almost unrecognizable. I whistled it to a beat that matched my sluggish pace, and I transposed it into a minor key. It was a dirge. It was the death knell of my college career. The curtain was coming down. I picked up the paper ball and stared at it. Then I dropped it in the basket. I walked into the bedroom and closed the door behind me. It was only eight-thirty, but it was well past my bedtime.

The Fight Song was now nothing more than disagreeable static. I sat transfixed, resting my chin in the palm of my hand, staring at the snowstorm on my TV set, pondering the many roads not taken.

I lit the last Lucky in the pack and flipped the dial a few times by remote control. I finally settled on *Laura* and watched long enough to finish my smoke. Then I stubbed the cigarette in the mountain of pistachio shells and turned off the TV. I carried the empty soda bottle and the ashtray into the kitchen. I flipped off the lights. Now there was only one chore left before going to bed.

I returned to the card table and undid my last game of solitaire. I collected the cards and carried the deck across the family room. I unlocked the patio door and slid open the heavy glass. It had begun to snow, and an icy chill knifed through me. I looked out past the costly brick-lined patio that had cracked several times from mine settling, past the twenty rhododendron bushes that bloomed only for a few hours a year, down to the spot at the end of the property where I might build that tennis court in the spring, if spring ever came.

I looked at the developing blizzard. If it continued, everything in Atherton would be shut down by morning. I took a deep breath. Then I drew back my arm and sailed the pack out the door. The cards caught a wind that carried them high, held them motionless for a second, and then sprinkled them merrily around Atherton. I locked the door and joined Carol in bed.

32

••

The phone brought me only halfway out of my deep sleep. I was aware of the ringing, but couldn't move to silence it. I heard Carol's voice, but it was vague. I prayed the call was not for me.

"Art, wake up!" She nudged me gently and began massaging my neck.

"Not now," I mumbled into the pillow "I just don't feel like making love now. Not till I work this whole thing out. I just can't—"

"Art, you're wanted on the phone." She kissed my ear.

"¿Qué?" I said, trying to clear my mind. I yawned and stretched.

"It's your mother. She's on the phone."

"Oh, Jesus Christ! It must be about Uncle Dave. Something happened to Uncle Dave."

"Dave died two years ago, Art. C'mon, wake up!"

The last cobweb cleared. I squinted at the clock and bolted upward. "My God, it's only seven-thirty. It must be a major disaster this time." My heart was pounding as Carol handed me the phone. "Hello?"

"Arthur, how are you?"

"I'm just great. Mother, it's seven-thirty in the morning. What's wrong?" I tried desperately to steady my hand.

"Did you hear?"

"Hear what?" My head throbbed.

"Then you haven't read the paper."

It was really going to be a big one this time. I managed to lift my semiparalyzed hand and pointed to the folded copy of the Atherton Tribune on the bureau. Carol picked it up and tossed it to me. It was the biggest, blackest headline since J.F.K. was murdered. It was shocking—reading that news and having my mother give a simultaneous running commentary. "The Anthracite Commuter crashed last night!" she said. "Right after takeoff. Eighteen people were killed!"

"Y-y-yes, Mother." My teeth were chattering. "I'm looking at the paper now. What happened?"

"Nobody knows. It just crashed. I don't understand it. They've been running that flight for years—and they never had a problem before."

"Never even sick," I mumbled.

"What?"

"I said it doesn't make sense."

"It's a terrible thing for Atherton!" she said.

"For Atherton?"

"Certainly! It's a tremendous setback for the town. Don't you think so?"

"For the victims, for their families. But who gives a damn about Atherton?"

"Of course I meant the people. What's wrong with you, Arthur?"

"I'm just upset about this. I'm sorry."

"We're all upset over it. After all, any one of us could have been on that flight . . . How's everything?"

"Oh, just fine, Mother. I'll talk to you later."

I was still deeply engrossed in the screaming headlines. Reading about a plane crash, especially one so close to home, was genuinely fascinating, in a sick sort of way. I was now on my third cup of coffee. I had read the lead article several times and was now prepared to read every word of every associated story.

"This is the most terrifying thing I ever read!" I mumbled to Carol, who sat with me at the table. She couldn't see me, since I was hidden by the newspaper. "They have no idea what caused it. Scariest goddamn thing! . . . But do you want to know something? The press is one big pain in the ass!"

"What do you mean?"

"They love to really dramatize this kind of thing. The death toll isn't enough for them. They have to add all this other stuff."

"Like what?"

"A man that was supposed to take the commuter flight and changed at the last minute. Here's a guy who had booked another flight but changed to this one. A woman flying for the first time. They just go on and on."

"They know what sells papers."

"Only ghouls are interested in this. No sane person would get involved." I continued to pore through the paper.

"You seem to be pretty involved yourself. You're not insane, are you?"

I folded the paper and laid it on the table. "The whole thing is really bothering me!"

"Of course it bothers you. It's horrible!"

"Here's what really gets me. They mention what the plane missed or what it might have hit on another day. Who gives a damn? Here, I'll show you what I mean." I picked up the paper and began reading, " 'The commuter narrowly missed the Mountain Shopping Center north of Atherton.' It's like giving thanks that no innocent people on the ground were involved. The passengers knew it was dangerous—so they're expendable."

"Yeah," said Carol, "I know what you mean. The fact that eighteen people died on the plane is perfectly acceptable."

"But thank God no one on the ground was killed!" This time I slammed the paper down and knocked over the coffee cup. Then I supported my forehead with my hands and sat silently, rubbing my eyes occasionally.

Carol leaned over and touched my arm. "Art, must you go in this morning? You're really upset. Why don't you go lie down for a while?"

"No, if I stay any longer I'll start watching it on the morning news. I've had enough of this disaster for a while. I'll wait for *Time* or *Newsweek*. They'll get even more mileage out of it. Probably say how awful it was for poor Atherton."

I stood up and began walking toward the door. Carol followed me. We embraced, but I was somewhere else.

"Art, why don't you take a Librium? It will help you relax. Maybe then you can forget about the crash."

"No, I don't need a Librium. I'm okay now. It's completely out of my mind." I smiled and kissed her again.

"I'm glad," she said. "You just can't let these things get to you."

"No more talk about it, I swear. The whole thing is forgotten." I kissed her one more time and was out the door. I took ten steps toward the garage. Then I turned around and walked back to the house. Carol was still standing at the door when I opened it.

"Forget something?" she asked.

"Someday," I ranted, pointing my finger for emphasis, "someday there's going to be a mid-air collision of two Boeing 747's. And the entire fucking, flaming mess is going to fall on Yankee Stadium—during the World Series. Just let the press try to get out of that one!" And I was off to work.

Later in the day I sat at my desk in a stupor. One central theme continued to haunt me. I watch the plane take off. I hear the engine sputter. I watch it go into its plunge. Then this roaring mass of steel and humanity is falling right on me. When it's only a few feet above my head, I snap out of it and I go back to reading a lease or stapling together the pages of my latest sales report.

After the last terrifying sequence, I remembered Carol's suggestion. I opened my top desk drawer and reached for the bottle of Librium. After I had washed it down with some cold coffee, I lifted the phone and called Carol.

"It's me," I said.

"How are you doing?"

"Fine, just fine."

"Not so good, right?"

"No, not so good," I said.

"You can't shake that crash, can you?"

"I don't understand it, Carol. Why should I be so obsessed with this thing? There's always a plane crash to read about."

"Art, the plane didn't go down in Africa!"

"Yeah, I know. But we've had our share of mine disasters. I'm used to the big tragedy, but I was never this shaky. There's something about this crash, and I just can't put my finger on it."

"You were down to begin with. Last night was a bummer for you. The crash just made it worse."

Someone knocked at my office door. I had been facing the window, and I swung the chair around. My secretary held up a fresh cup of coffee and the evening paper. I pointed to my desk and whispered a thank you to her.

"Come home early! Maybe you'll be more relaxed here," Carol said.

"I'll try. I still have to clean up a few things here. But I won't be late. 'Bye, honey."

33

• •

"You were down to begin with. Last night was a bummer for you!" Carol's words still echoed in my mind. I sipped my coffee and looked at the new, frightening pictures of the wreckage. I read the statement from the President of Anthracite Airlines. He vowed that service between Atherton and Philadelphia would continue as usual. An FAA representative was already in Atherton to investigate the cause of the crash. There were pictures of the two-man crew, a school-board member, the vice-president of a local bank, and the former football coach of Atherton High. *"You were down to begin with. Last night was a bummer for you!"*

I thought of last night—of my dinner—of my dinner companion. The terror took me by surprise. My God! How was he going back to Philly? I'm sure he was driving back. Yes, of course he was driving. He had a car. He drove to the restaurant. What the hell is wrong with me? But when he called me yesterday, didn't he say he had a rented car? Jesus! Maybe he returned it at the airport. Shit! Didn't he say something about taking the puddle-jumper back to Philadelphia? My God, I just don't remember what the hell he said. My hand shot out to the phone and I began to dial Carol. But my eye was automatically drawn to the passenger list in the paper. I put the phone back on the receiver.

I placed my finger on Adams, J.S., and began working down the column. By Lombardo, A.W., I still had not found it. I moved quickly over the bottom half of the list, flying over names, completely disregarding what each line meant. Suddenly, the name shot out at me like a ghostly remnant from an old 3-D movie. Second from the last entree on the death list, and placed between Van Horn, R.L., and Wolfe, F.H., was WICKERS, C. M.

34

• •

Carol poked her head into the bedroom and saw that my record-breaking sleep had finally ended. I lay very still, looking up at the ceiling. I was again watching the commuter flight. It was floating, then falling, then disintegrating. And each time it came down, I heard the cry, "Oh Gahd, Ahthuh!" followed by that high-pitched cackle I had almost forgotten.

"Art? How are you doing?" she asked.

"Great!" I flipped over on my side so I would be facing away from her. I didn't want her to see my tears. I pulled the blanket tightly around my neck and did my best to disappear. But she had already seen my anguish. She walked around the bed and sat on the edge.

She placed her hand on my shoulder and said, "Don't shut me out! I know what you must be going through with this thing. But you'd be a lot better off if you let it out."

"I don't want to shut you out." I propped myself up on an elbow. "But I'm not sure what I'm going through. I'd like to let it out, but I really don't know what I'm holding in."

"Maybe if you talked about it . . ."

"I really don't know what to talk about. Maybe if I could discuss it with someone who really knew him."

"Like Mitch?"

I nodded.

"Then call him!"

"Oh, I don't know. I feel sort of strange doing that." The telephone had an intimidating power over me. It was easier to talk in person and even easier to write a letter. Of course, the easiest way was to do absolutely nothing.

She lifted the phone from the night table and handed it to me. "Call him, Art!"

"Carol, I can't. I don't have his number. He's in his new office, you know." I mused over my latest attempt. I still found it incredible that Mitch was not only a highly successful oral surgeon, but also an entrepreneur. He had just completed his own office building—an eight-story edifice that housed his own luxurious suite plus another thirty professional offices.

"I'll dial information for you."

She was forcing me to make the call. While she dialed the long series of numbers that I could never quite remember, I anticipated the conversation that would be taking place in a few minutes. How do you get into the meat of it? Hiya, Mitch. It's Art. Howyadoin'? How's Glenda? The family? The new building? The opening round is over—now the nitty-gritty. How about this—Did you read 'bout—no, wait—I guess you heard about that horrible plane crash in Atherton? That's one way to open it. Or I could start this way—Do you remember a guy by the name of Wickers? No, that's no good. Of course he remembers him. Maybe I could dispense with the entire conversation and start the way Charles himself would have done it. Hello, Mitch. Wickers is dead!

"Here," Carol said, and she handed the phone to me. "It's ringing."

"Good morning. Dr. Carpenter's office. One moment, please." Then nothing. One of the reasons why I hate the phone. In real life you're not put on hold, that maddening isolation where sight and sound never penetrate. As the seconds passed, I cursed myself for not calling person-to-person.

"I'm sorry to keep you waiting, sir. How may I help you?"

"I'd like to speak to Dr. Carpenter."

"One moment, please." On hold again.

Then after twenty seconds another female voice said, "Doctor's office, may I help you?"

"Yes. May I speak with Dr. Carpenter?"

"Do you wish to make an appointment with Doctor?"

"No, I want to talk to him."

"Are you currently a patient of Doctor's?"

"No, ma'am."

"Then, may I ask the nature of your call, sir?"

"It's personal."

"One moment, please. I'll see if I can locate Doctor."

I was placed on hold again and was becoming increasingly pissed off. I covered the phone and to Carol I said, "Doctor must be a very busy man."

"I'm sorry, sir. Doctor is in conference now. If you will kindly leave your name, I'll see that Doctor receives the message."

I'd had just about enough of both Doctor and Secretary at this point. "Is Doctor in surgery right now?" I asked.

"No, sir."

"Then here's what I want you to do if *you'll* be so kind." The pressure was rising. "You tell Doctor that Businessman is calling from Atherton and Doctor had better get his ass on the fucking phone—right now!"

On hold again. "Doctor is one big pain in the ass!" I said to Carol.

"Art? Is that you?" It was the familiar voice of the ex-thief.

"Yeah, it's me. Christ! You're hard to locate. What the hell were you doing?"

"Takin' a jump! What's doing in Atherton? You still raking it in hand over fist?"

"I'm making ends meet. Seems that you're the one who's really the big businessman."

"Fuckin' A! Hey, Art, are you looking for a situation?"

"No, Carol and I are doing fine."

"Dumb ass! I'm talking about business. If you have a few thousand laying around, we could throw up an office building. But I don't want to put you on the spot. You seem to have something else on your mind."

"Yeah, I—uhhh." I flashed on the plane, the newspaper headline, Wickers saying good-bye at the restaurant. "I— uhhhh—I'm afraid I have some bad news." So with all the choices I had, I elected to play the part of my mother. I told him about my dinner with Wickers. Then I detailed the crash, my reaction to it, and my horrible discovery.

"I'm really shocked!" Mitch said. "I just can't believe it!"

"I can't either. I liked Wickers."

"Yeah," said Mitch. "We had a lot of laughs with him." There was a long pause in the conversation. I was thinking about his absurd joke and the riotous Last Supper.

"Art, did you ever meet his family?"

"No, I didn't. They lived in Philadelphia, but I lost contact with him after graduation. I'd like to do something, but I just don't know what."

"Why don't you drive to Philly and pay your respects?"

"Oh, I don't know. Maybe if somebody would go with me." I am unable to make a condolence call by myself. "How about you? Would you come with me?"

"I'd like to, Art. I really would go with you, but I just can't get out of here so easily. If I weren't so damn far away—it's halfway across the country. If I were still in Pennsylvania it would be different."

"It's okay. I understand."

"I'll be in Philadelphia this summer—a convention. Maybe we can get together then. I'd want to visit his family."

"Sounds good. Okay, we'll get together when you're in town."

"Great! We'll play some gin, too. I'll teach you a lesson . . . Art, I really feel bad about Charles."

"I know you do. Take care."

"Good-bye, Art."

Carol was right. I did feel a little bit better. Now I wasn't quite so isolated in my mourning. Somehow Mitch's knowing made the burden a little easier to carry. Perhaps I should start making random calls. I would tell the tragic news to anyone. That would make it even easier for me. Hello, Mother? You remember Charles Wickers, don't you? I went to school with him. Would you believe he was on the plane yesterday? Isn't it awful? . . . I could tell my salesmen, my shippers, the girls in the office, people in the street. I guess everyone knows about the terrible plane crash. I lost a real close friend in that one—so close that until the night of his death I hadn't seen him in over fourteen years. Went to Keystone with him. I just can't believe it . . .

As I thought of the people I could call, I thought of Tom. Who could be more important than Tom? I'll call him. No, I'll go even one step further. "Carol," I said, "I'm going to New Jersey."

35

. . . .

I took my boots off at the door. I wouldn't dare dirty the luxurious Karastan that graced the staid outer office. I quickly removed my shiny yellow ski jacket. Somehow it was out of place in the old-line law offices of Burnfield, Scott, and Nelson. As I walked to the receptionist's desk I saw the huge photograph of Tom. It dominated the dark oak paneled wall. Emblazoned in red and bringing life to a drab room of grays and browns were the words, "Vote Tom Nelson—for Honest Government!"

"May I help you?" asked the smiling secretary.

"Yes. First by telling me what this is all about." I pointed to the sign.

"For sure! Mr. Nelson is running for Attorney General of New Jersey."

"Really? That's great! . . . I'd like to see Attorney General Nelson."

"Do you have an appointment, sir?"

"No, but I'm an old friend. I was passing through New Jersey. I just wanted to see Mr. Nelson for a minute or two."

"And what is your name, sir?"

"Just tell him Arthur from Atherton is here."

"One moment, Mr. Arthur." She spoke into the phone and then said, "Go right in, Mr. Arthur. Mr. Nelson's office is at the end of that hallway."

"Jee-zuz! How the hell are you, Art?" Tom leaned over his polished teak desk and shook my hand in the Delta Pi Beta grip. "Sit down, you old son-of-a gun!"

I sat in a finely upholstered easy chair and looked around his manicured office. The walls were filled with awards of all kinds, dating back to his days at Keystone. "You've come a long way since the Young Democrats. It looks like you're well on the way to becoming the new Robert Kennedy."

He smiled. "I don't know about that." He began tapping a large white pipe on the side of his wastepaper basket.

"C'mon, Tom! J.F.K. would be proud of you."

He dipped the pipe into a shiny leather pouch. Then he leaned back in his chair. "No, I don't think so, Art. You see, I'm running on the Republican ticket."

In the past twenty-four hours I had heard some shocking things, but this news was the most unbelievable. "Republican? You're kidding!"

"I'm afraid it's true."

"But why? What happened to the Young Democrats?"

He flicked a gold lighter and lit the pipe. "Art, you know my family has always been Republican. That business back in school was a hundred years ago. It was my little fling with liberalism. We all go through it." He puffed a few times on the pipe. Then he pointed the pipe at me and smiled. "And you know what they say about politics making strange bedfellows. The opportunity right now is with the Republican Party. What better reason could there be?"

It didn't sound like Tom. The entire idea of seeing him and sharing my problem had elated me, but now I was sinking again. "Well, maybe you won't be a Kennedy," I said in a cracking voice. I looked at the pipe. "But Abe Lincoln isn't so bad either. Good luck!"

"Thanks, Art." He tilted his left wrist and snuck a quick

look at his watch. Then he sat erect in his chair and laid his hands on the desk. "Well, I know you didn't come all the way to New Jersey to discuss politics. What can I do for you?"

I'll be goddamned! This whole thing isn't going right. This isn't Tom. I hadn't seen him in almost six years and he was already dismissing me. *No more friendly talk, Art. You're here to use me, so why don't you get on with it?* In a way he was right, so I let his comment pass without incident and proceeded with what was now a familiar story: Dinner with Wickers . . . terrible plane crash . . . strange reaction . . . horrible discovery . . . really upset . . . wish we could do something.

"Jee-zuz, Art. It's hard to believe. It must really have been a shock for you—just seeing him that night and all that." He was silent for a few seconds and I assumed he was thinking about Wickers. But then in a most incredible change of pace he said, "When are you and Carol coming in to the city?"

"What?" I gasped.

"Don't you guys have some kind of convention in New York?"

"I don't understand what you're saying, Tom."

"A trade show. Don't you and Carol come to . . ."

"Yes, I know damn well about the trade show. What I don't understand is how you just wrote off Charles Wickers."

"Wrote him off? Now I don't understand!"

"I just told you that a good friend and seventeen others were blown into tiny pieces and you ask me when we're coming to New York. Seems to me you might have more concern than that, or does this go along with your switching parties?"

"Jee-zuz, Art! What the hell do you want me to do about it? I feel bad about Wickers, but what can I do? Besides, I haven't seen him in over fourteen years."

He had said the magic words and I began screaming, "Will you tell me what difference that makes? Goddamn it! A friend is dead. Can't you say something besides that fourteen-year shit?"

"What the hell is the matter with you?" Tom said.

"You betrayed the Democrats and Wickers. How about the others? Did you betray Mitch too?" Until now Tom had remained cool, but when I mentioned Mitch's name, he flinched. It was almost imperceptible, but I picked it up instantly. It had never occurred to me in all of those years, at least not consciously. But now the realization ripped through me. "You're the bastard who tipped them off!" I screamed. "You called the Save-a-Penny! You put them onto Mitch! You goddamn son-of-a-bitch!" I dived across the desk and flew at his throat. His pipe and most of his papers fell to the floor. We scuffled for only a few seconds before he managed to pry my hands loose. And after I wasted several ineffectual shots at his shoulders, he caught me with a hard punch. My nose exploded in a red shower and I fell backward into my chair.

"Jee-zuz, Art! Are you out of your mind? What the hell got into you? That plane crash was too much for you." He dabbed my face with a cold wet towel he had quickly gotten from his private washroom. He had waited a little too long to deny my accusation, and when he finally did, it was only a token. "I really don't know what you were talking about before . . . You know, that incident was the best thing that ever happened to Mitch. Ask him. Even he'll tell you that. It shocked him out of his rotten ways. It turned his life around. I really think it was a big break for him."

Now I wondered if the great mediator had also tipped off Pidal. Maybe he blew the whistle on Al Carter. Anything was possible. But I was no longer concerned with the past. It didn't matter anymore. Tom had been doing his act a long time now—fucking his friends, both dead and alive, and playing shitty games—far more insidious than any conceived by the brothers of Delta Pi Beta.

My long silence must have implied forgiveness, or at the least some understanding. Actually my only feeling was revulsion. I had already written Tom out of my act, and there was no further need to berate him.

"Seriously, Art. If you're planning a trip to New York, we'd love to see you. You and Carol could spend the day here or we'd drive into the city and meet you."

"Sure, Tom," I said calmly and lifted myself out of the chair.

"Hey, guy!" Tom said. "Let's forget everything that happened today."

I ignored his outstretched hand. "Sure, Tom." I turned toward the door.

When I was in the hallway, he stuck his head out the door and called after me. "Art, if you think about it, how about sending me Wickers's address? I'd like to send something to the family."

Without turning around, I said, "Sure, Tom."

"Have a nice day, Mr. Arthur!" said the perky receptionist as I passed her desk.

I just couldn't resist. I turned and exposed the other side of my face. My right eye was swollen shut. Blood was again pouring profusely from my right nostril. It collected at the corner of my mouth and fell in large drops onto my yellow ski jacket. I smiled at her. "And you have a nice day too, miss!"

36

●●●

When I reached the car, I was crying. I had come to New Jersey to share something with a friend. I had tried to extract some feeling. But my mission had failed. I had put my faith in Tom and discovered what I had really known all along. What troubled me most as I guided the Mercedes onto Interstate 80 was that I was probably no better than Tom. If I hadn't had dinner with Charles Wickers, it would be business as usual for me too. Sure, I'd make a few token calls. But give me a day or two to tell the story to anyone who would listen, and then I'd forget about it. I should have been sad, but I wasn't. And that's what saddened me. And that's why I cried during the ten-minute ride to the Pennsylvania border.

I cried at the Delaware Water Gap Bridge even as I paid my quarter to an attendant who appeared to be genuinely fascinated by a bloody, sobbing man driving a Mercedes. And I continued to wallow in it for the thirty-mile trip through the Pocono Mountains. But as I neared the Atherton exit, a curious thing happened—I stopped crying.

I thought of the outrageous scene I had created in Tom's office, and I felt okay about it. When I reached Market Street, I was laughing out loud. When the car was finally parked in my garage, I looked at myself in the rear-view mirror. The blood had caked on my face, and along with the swollen black eye, I now had a fat lip—and I was elated.

I staggered into the bedroom. Carol laid her book down beside her on the bed and leaned over to the night table to turn down the stereo. She looked at my bloody face without flinching. "Hi," she said.

I closed the door behind me and fell backward against it. "Feelings," I said, "That's what it is."

"Do you know who you sound like?"

I shook my head.

She smiled. "You just did a Wickers."

"I did?—You know, you're right. I do him from time to time, don't I?" I walked to the foot of the bed. "I—uhhhh," and I pointed to my face.

"Yes, I know all about it. Tom called a little while ago. He told me what happened."

"Yeah, I'll bet he did. Did the bastard tell you how he turned Mitch in at the supermarket?"

"Is that why you tried to strangle him?"

"One of the many reasons."

"Tom really felt bad about it."

"That's funny. I don't. I feel pretty damn good about it. It's the best thing that ever happened to me."

"Were those the feelings you were talking about?"

I sat down on the bed. "No! Fact is, it's just the opposite. I have no feelings. I'm just as insensitive as Tom. I don't care about Charles Wickers! I don't give a shit about anyone. Then—now—anytime. I just pulled off Interstate 80. From the car I could see the spot where the plane went down. It looks like it took out half the goddamn mountain. And what do you think your dearly beloved husband was doing at that point of the trip?"

"What?"

"Laughing his fool head off. Just sailing down the old Interstate, giggling up a storm. On the side of the road they still haven't picked up all of the pieces of his close friend, but that's quite all right. Arthur's having a ball. How come? Because he just got the shit kicked out of him by another friend who screwed still another friend. Now isn't that the funniest goddamn story you ever heard?" I broke into a fit of hysterical laughter.

"I love you," Carol said. "Do you know that? I love you in spite of all your crazy merde."

I pulled a tissue from the box and dried my eyes. "I'm glad you love me, but I didn't catch that last word."

"Merde?"

I nodded.

"That's French for mierda. How can you say you have no feelings? You're the most sensitive person I ever met."

"And you, madam, are the craziest! You're a monomaniac. Do you know that? Just once I would like you to agree with me when I tell you my faults."

"Faults? Who said you don't have faults? You have plenty of them. But you also have feelings. Only they've been buried deep inside. They didn't surface too often. You never let them out. I cry a lot more than you."

"I've noticed."

"My feelings are right up at the surface. For me, it comes out easily. My belief is that you cared a lot for Charles Wickers. Your hangup was getting it to the surface and communicating it. And it's not only with Wickers. It's the major problem of your life."

The revelation began to take shape. I was Rip Van Winkle, asleep for fourteen years, ever since the night I rolled up my interviews into a ball and dropped it into the basket. No—that's not quite it. I'd been asleep even longer. Except for my memorable weekend with Carol, my stay at Keystone was spent in a dreamlike state. Floating—always floating—never really digging into anything. Never knowing. Never questioning. Holding back. It was the plane that finally woke me up. Jesus! Wickers was to me as Aunt Gert was to Mr. Zuckerman!

"My college career never really ended."

She smiled and said, "You just did a Wickers again."

"There was no cutoff between Arthur the student and Arthur the businessman. The two careers just flowed together. The only difference is that I've added stomach pains and headaches to my repertoire. And, as you know, I still sleep a great deal."

"It's really ironic! If I asked our friends who they thought was the most sensitive person in our group, who do you think would be the unanimous choice?"

I didn't answer. It sounded too familiar. It was still difficult for me to accept a compliment. Things hadn't changed much since Keystone. I was still charting a course on that tenuous middle ground, terrified of being a fool, but equally afraid of success. "I want to tell you something, my friend. Through all of these bullshit years, I've loved you. I don't care what showed on the surface. I always loved you. Do you know that?"

We sat on the edge of the bed, clinging to each other. "Yes," she said, "I know."

"There's something else I must tell you," I said.

"Aren't those the most terrifying words in the English language?" she asked.

"They don't scare me anymore. I'm going to change! Notice I didn't say 'try to change'—I said 'change.' Instant menopause!"

"I believe you, Art. I think you've already had your catharsis."

"Catharsis?" I shrieked and clutched my heart. "Oh my God, no! Who will call my mother? Who will break this dreadful news to her?"

"Art," she said, putting her hands on my shoulders, "I have a feeling you will."

I understood and nodded. Then I shot a quick look at the clock on the night table. I leaped off the bed and raced toward the bathroom, stripping off my bloody shirt en route. "It's so goddamn late! I must shower and get to work!" I called back to Carol, who remained on the bed.

And she was still sitting there when I reappeared, naked, a minute later. I stood at the foot of the bed and stared at her. She stared back. Finally I said, "I'm not going to work today."

"It certainly looks that way!"

"I'm driving to Philadelphia. I'm going to visit his family."

"Is that what you feel you should do?"

"No, it's more significant than that. It's what I want to do."

She smiled the kindest, gentlest smile since Señora Paz smiled at me in the office of the Spanish Department. Then she said, "Would you like some company?"

"Yes, I'd like that very much!" I sat down on the bed and we held each other for a long time. She broke for air first and said, "When do you think we should leave?"

"There's no real hurry—maybe in an hour or two. In the meantime, why don't you slip into something more comfortable?" And after she did, we resumed what we had started some fourteen years ago.